Upon This Bank and Shoal

A Novel

by

Alexander Raju

CCB Publishing
British Columbia, Canada

Upon This Bank and Shoal: A Novel

Copyright ©2008 by Alexander Raju
ISBN-13   978-0-9810246-5-3
First Edition

Library and Archives Canada Cataloguing in Publication

Raju, Alexander, 1952-
Upon this bank and shoal: a novel / written by Alexander Raju.
ISBN 978-0-9810246-5-3
I. Title.
PR9499.4.R35U66 2008   823'.92   C2008-906362-7

Cover image, *Satan Watching the Caresses of Adam and Eve* by British artist William Blake (1757-1827), is in the public domain.

Publisher: CCB Publishing
             British Columbia, Canada
             www.ccbpublishing.com

To my dearest wife Jessy, whom I fondly called 'J'
due to my irrational prejudice towards double syllables,
who tolerated me all these years and looked after
the well-being of my family, even in my absence.

Other works by Alexander Raju

Candles on the Altar (1985)

Ripples and Pebbles (1989)

Many Faces of Adam (1991)

The Haunted Man (1997)

The Psycho-Social Interface in British Fiction (2000)

Sprouts of Indignation (2003)

Magic Chasm (2007)

The Sobbing Guitar and Other Stories (2007)

But here, upon this bank and shoal of time,
We would jump the life to come.

*-- **William Shakespeare** (**Macbeth** I : vii : 6-7)*

PART I

"**I**n the beginning..." Confusion!

"In the end..." Again confusion! Confusion worse confounded!!

Adam, you are doomed! It's your fate. History confused you to the core. All these generations confused you about the beginning and about the end. It was all their fancy. And now, it's your turn...

Be reasonable. For the Creator breathed reason into your nostrils, the breath of life. The fire of immortality now burns in you. And you are eternal like your Creator. And, Adam, you are the perfect creation.

Generations will follow generations, and the flame of fire breathed into you will be transferred from one to another. Aeons will follow aeons, one era after another. Old ages will give way to the new ones. And so, there is no beginning for you or any end...

When you feel that it's all going to end, remember that it's only the beginning of the travail. The travail for the next... Experiencing the pangs of birth, you think that it is the sign of death; and seeing the pangs of death, you think that it is the sign of birth. How funny!

And the truth is that one dies and becomes manure for another. No end but only a sort of pause... a pause before the beginning. And that's the mysterious moment before every birth and every death.

So let me try to begin at the beginning. But where is that exact starting point? It is vague, quite obscure. Then, shall I begin from vagueness? Yes! Now it is very easy. Once it is clear that vagueness is the beginning, I must begin like this:

'In the beginning was the word...'

But before that... before that... and that...?

Quite an obscure beginning. But after some time everything becomes clear. First obscurity, then perspicuity. Through repetition, history becomes disinteresting, or rather; recurrence of events makes it obnoxious. And the cause is understandable.

History... it begins from obscurity, moves through obscurity and ends in obscurity. Standing in between an obscure past and an obscure future, let me try to clarify the present. It is a Herculean task. Nevertheless, it must be done. And the only person capable of scribbling down a history that begins from obscurity and ends in obscurity is 'I' and only 'I'. Yes, 'I' alone can do it, for, 'I am that I am'.

The only truth clear to me is the sole truth 'I'. There is history for 'I' the truth; and without history, there is existence neither for truth nor for me. As truth is as clear as truth itself, it has existence. And, therefore, the truth that is clear is 'I' and only 'I'.

And before me, or rather beyond 'I', there is the history, of a few generations. There is the generation of my father and mother and also that of my grandfather and grandmother. Yes, history begins just at that point.

And what is there beyond these few generations? That is quite insignificant, for an obscure truth is always insignificant. Perhaps there were generations of great grandfathers and grandmothers. But who cares? Nevertheless, 'in the beginning was the Word, and the Word was with God'... and the Word was Power, and the Power was Truth and the Truth was Beauty and the Beauty was God! Therefore, the only significant thing is word that dominates everything else. And the power of the word. 'The same was in the beginning with God', as the Book says.

Then... it was first the aeon of sound and power. The word was Nature and Nature was omnipotent. Therefore, it was an Age of Omnipotence. Every object moveable or immoveable appareled in celestial power. Power encountered power and word encountered word. And the word echoed everywhere, from all directions of the universe. It reverberated again and again till the whole universe, with all its galaxies and nebulae, drowned into a sort of divine tremor. From that tremor shapes were born!

'God said let it be and they were there'. Fishes, birds and animals. 'The word was made flesh', as the Book says. Oh, what a wonderful beginning.

Then all the created things began their struggle for existence. They fought each other; embraced each other and rolled on into one another. They copulated and amalgamated. Their power melted down into weakness. Like drops of sweat dripping down their foreheads! Their potency turned into impotency. From impotency Fear took birth. And thus began the Age of Fear. This sense of fear in due course showed light to all creations and led them to indifference.

Power slowly crept into the indifference of the earth through sound. And the Earth became passionate. The passionate dust transformed into Man. And Man, thus, became a synonym for passion and inertness and, above all, for sound. And also for dust, of course.

It is a mistake if one thinks that the history of the first generation ends as and when Man is evolved from Man. No! Never will it end. For the Age of Fear has just begun and fear has been dancing, keeping its hood raised over the head of man.

The emotion of fear crept all over the earth. The ever-turning wheel of a myriad of passionate faces... And the face of desire stood changeless. From there, it was a non-stop march towards the accomplishment of each and every desire, to the real source of satisfaction.

Was it an escape from the sense of inertia to the activation of the five senses? Or was it a flight from the world of grave responsibilities of light to the world of free pleasures of darkness?

Perhaps, the beginning can be made a bit simpler. God created Man. Is it not quite simple? Subject, verb and object, as the nursery teacher used to say. 'Man is made of dust and unto dust he will return'. A philosophical evidence to prove the reasoning behind the simplicity of Man's creation.

Quite simple, as the Scripture presented it. God takes dust and mixes it with water. He makes a sort of dough and gives shape to a wonderful creature called man. Just like children who make breads by pressing clay into coconut shells. Then He breathes into its nostrils and the clay-creature gets life.

Well... this story is taken for granted as it is God who created man. He called him Adam which means made from dust. God found him lonely, and so, one day, while Adam lay asleep, God counted his rib bones and realized that there were fifteen, an odd number. Odd numbers are ominous, and so, he took out one rib bone and created Eve. He forgot to count the rib bones of Eve, and they remain still an odd number. Perhaps, He was giving unknowingly an upper hand to Eve over Adam, or the mould in which both Adam and Eve were created had the same odd number of rib bones.

Adam and Eve lived in the Garden of Eden. One day they ate the forbidden fruit and realized the significance of the difference in the shapes of their bodies. God made Man and Woman as two different creatures but they, with the newly acquired knowledge of unity, experimented with themselves and tried to become one. God became angry and ousted them out from the Garden of Eden. Angels, with the swords of lightning, guarded the gates of Eden, preventing them from re-entering it.

Man proposes; God disposes! Whenever man tries to unite themselves, for reasons he can justify, God becomes too jealous and He gives them the cruelest punishment. Remember the example of Babel. He confused their language, so that they would never be united. Well, leave the digression...

The Man and the Woman went out into the world in search of a new Garden of Eden. Only Adam knew the covenant between God and himself and so he could not hate God who sent him out of Eden just for eating a fruit. The fruit of a tree, which was planted deliberately by God to tempt him! How simple it all was. But then...

There began the plight of Adam who represented the first generation. His long and tedious journey... his eternal search for a second Garden of Eden. For once the gates of Paradise were closed behind him forever...

Ah Paradise! Dear Paradise!

It is still clear in the mind, like the enchanting fragrance of a delightful flower, like the cool ripples of a small sweet dream and like the eternal lilt and tone of a heart touching song. It was an unforgettable glorious experience, a bliss that could be enjoyed only by a sound mind. A delightful phenomenon ready only for those who have sipped the honey of Virtuousness.

Ah Paradise! Dear Paradise!

For a moment... let the eyes that were tired of seeing this world, be closed. Let the waves of the troubled mind be pacified. Let the music of peace gradually enter into the worried heart. Let the mind become placid. Let all the five senses attain indifference and tranquility as the terrible darkness of fear and despair move away and away...

........dhammmmmm............Aaaaa............dammmmmmm........

The consciousness of 'I' melted and dissolved into nothingness. The expurgated ties with place, time and action, fly away into the far off horizon. The body, the mind and the spirit become one in a mysterious unity. Somewhere is lost the weight of the body and of the mind. The spirit that gained the transcendental power thirsts for something... something unique.

Aaaaa............dammmmm...........Aaaaa...............dammm...........

The thin ripples of the 'Adam Sound' strain into the spirit. For a moment, the mind absorbs itself into the delight of the 'Adam Sound', making the spirit and the sound one... the only one.

Adam........Adam..............Adam..........

The divine sound that comes up moment after moment. And in the 'Adam Sound' that echoes from every direction, the planet Earth transforms into Paradise. An immortal harmony evolves out of the lilt of the flood water and of the tone of the tempest. And while standing in the delight of that eternal; intoxication of happiness, the portals of Paradise slowly open.

Adam........Adam..............Adam..........

Again that pleasure giving, supernatural, divine sound! It spontaneously reverberates in the rustling of the thick, emerald leaves, in the murmuring of the crystalline streams and in the chirping of the colorful birds. And it dissolves gradually into the enchanting fragrance of gorgeous flowers and into the tempting taste of the mesmeric fruits.

Adam........Eve..............Adam..........Eve........

The sound that changes itself into a synonym of perfection. It disintegrates into the rapture of the birds that fly and sing in the sky and of the beasts that hop and play on the land and of the fish that swim and dance in the water. The sound of innocence. The voice of sufficiency. The voice of delight. The sound of bliss. The eternal voice of Nature. The sound that gives way to shape. The ever-beautiful sound that acts behind every creation.

............dam........Aaaa............dammm............Aaaa..................

And God created Man in his own image. Prudence which is the true reflection of God controlled him. He lived between virtue and evil with the freedom of choice, with the liberty to accept whatever he liked and to reject whatever he hated. What a wonderful life for Adam and Eve.

Eden. Ah, Eden.

The Garden of Eden that marked the boundary between freedom and bondage. Eden, the symbol of man's instinct for discretion. Eden that paves the way for the right selection. Eden that declares the bitter result of the wrong selection. And there stands Man in an idiotic stupor. To be tempted easily by anyone or anything.

Poor Adam. Poor Eve. Alas.

The man who forgets all obligations in his crazy race for novel delights. The man who stands paralyzed in utter helplessness when desire, the venomous snake, deliberately creeps into his peaceful and satisfied mind, arousing chaos and confusion there. The pitiable man, who being trapped in the magic vortex of temptations, loses even the innocence of his body and mind.

Ah Paradise! Dear Paradise!

What an encouraging memory. But... but now... alas. Darkness crawling into the world of light, weaves the co-web of despair. The darkness of sin that dances with its raised, spread-hood in the innermost cellars of the mind. The horrible darkness that raises the shackles of fear somewhere inside the head.

Poor Adam. What a horrible experience. Leave such thoughts aside.

It is taken for granted that Adam was my forefather. He might be the greatest or the enlightened one of that age, according to the Mutation Theory. Perhaps he was the chief of a much progressed human clan of that age. That is why the Scripture says, 'When God created Man, He created them as MAN and WOMAN, and on the day of creation, blessed them and gave them the name ADAM'. Isn't there a hint of selection in all creations, physical or spiritual or both? Well, leave it aside. For theology cannot cheat me so well. Let me think about Adam, my forefather.

He was a happy man and it was natural that he lived in Paradise. But curiosity killed the cat and he lost that Paradise.

His partner, Eve, my grandmother, guided him and showed him the way to a new Paradise. But he was so nostalgic that he could not find happiness in any other paradise. So he continued his search for good. I cannot blame my forefather who always kept in his mind the memory of a lost paradise, for anybody in such a situation would feel desperate and dejected.

Alas. My poor forefather...

While walking forward, thorns and thistles, brambles and briars wait ahead to receive. The feet tumble among sharp chisel-like flakes of stones and among hard orbicular rocks. The dark hands of the frightening woods beck and call. For a moment stands in stupor, seeing the new heaven and the new earth face to face... being tangled in the gossamer of ignorance.

Darkness, eternal dense darkness, awaits. While running helter-skelter for a speck of light, the scorpions that emit deadly venom raise their tails. While wandering here and there for a drop of water to quench thirst, the devil's children dance with their hooded-heads.

The vast earth spreads far and wide like some eternal sorrow. And in the brain echoes the curse of the Creator. Earn your daily bread from the earth throughout the span of your life. And in the sweat of thy face shalt thou eat bread. He who is taken from the dust shall return to dust. Until then, the herbs of the field will be the food.

In the sharp extremity of sin, the limbs feel tired; unrelieved by food spiced with the salty sweat that drips from the toiling forehead. And the earth being cursed by the sin of man, struggles under the feet.

The curse that tightens around the neck every moment like a Gordian knot! The head is bent with the heavy burden of sin, with the weight of the bundle of sin-stained clothes. The tired body yearns for a break, for a moment's rest. The paralyzed mind thirsts for Eden's ecstasy of happiness. Eyes, set in the pits of the skull, are fixed on the darkness of wave-beats in the sea of eternity.

While looking back...

Agony is doubled while looking back at those paths which were covered one by one. The sweet memories of those happy days in Eden give coolness to the heart. The greenery and verdure of the Garden that gave delight to the eyes. The magical fragrance of a variety of fruits and colorful flowers that throbbed in the breeze. The streamlets that thrilled and excited each granule of sand and every pinch of soil of Eden. And the golden fish which swam and played in those streamlets and brooks, making bubbles and ripples.

Everywhere there were herds of animals that ran and played in the excitement of innocence. With all these sights, sounds and experiences, it was a magical world of love, peace and satisfaction. And there, how far away was that feeling of fear?

But the entrance to that place is closed. Are those gates closed for ever? Oh no!

There... there grows the tree with wide-spreading branches bearing the fruit that cures all sins. Oh no... please don't close the way to the Tree of Life!

There... white-robed cherubs stand as guards. The blaze on their faces dazzles eyes. In their hands there are the double-edged swords that bring lightning.

Farewell, memories. Dreams, that have already been seen and forgotten, are quite irritating. Wait for new dreams. A dream to establish a new Eden here on this earth. With new dreams the journey will become less tedious and less difficult.

But is there any remedy for those things which happened due to mere foolishness? What happened to that branch from the Tree of Life that has fallen away from the grip of the hand in a moment of ecstasy? Does it mean that the hope to rebuild an Eden on Earth is coming to an end? Oh no!

Can't I recreate a Garden of Eden? But what can I do when memories of that lost paradise consistently haunt and gnaw away at the mind, when eternal agony exhausts the heart and eternal fear exhausts the body?

What's needed today is to face all opposing situations courageously. There is no meaning in looking back. Let the mistakes of the past prepare the path for correction. Let past failures faced along the way show the correct path. Hurry forward. Move only on the straight road. March forward… and only forward.

Oh, my great forefather. What forced him to move forward? Was it helplessness? Was it fear? Was it desire or ambition? Was it courage?

Poor forefather. I can understand his pitiable situation. Was it foolishness to taste evil just to discern virtue? In that attempt, Paradise might have slipped away from him! When he extended his hands toward the forbidden fruits, didn't he hear behind him the slap-bang of the shutting doors to the Tree of Life? Didn't he notice the flames flashing behind him from the ever-turning double-edged swords?

Yet my poor grandfather consoled himself by immersing in the sweet memories of that lost paradise. He, without knowing the right way, groped in the horrific darkness of ignorance. While caressing the rays of hope left in him after all those days of the ordeal, his heart chanted:

Asato ma sat gamaya,
Tamaso ma jyothir gamaya,
Mrithyor ma amrutam gamaya…

From untruth to truth; from darkness to light and from

mortality to immortality... and Adam, my grandfather, began his long journey. Of course, he had Eve with him, accompanying him through all the hazards.

And they walked and walked... the earth shuddered under their firm steps.

They felt the blaze and glare of the double-edged sword gradually fading away, while sitting under the cool shade of the banyan tree, quite exhausted after a journey that covered thousands and thousands of miles. Having hopes and shattered hopes as their only belongings, they tried to gain satisfaction in the intoxication of mutual touching and caressing. Being perplexed by the novel experience of an unknown ecstasy, Man breathed a long sigh in the ears of his mate, 'Eve... '

Then being bathed in the hot sweat drops that oozed from the hairy chest of the partner, another human creature was semi-consciously moaning in the ecstasy of exhaustion, 'Adam... Adam... '

On the zenith of passion, tasting the sweetness of voice, and feeling the delight and joy of sound, they forgot even the significance of sound and voice. When power blended with power, and sound with sounds, with all the additions, subtractions, divisions and multiplications of power and sound, their voice became inopportune. Realizing and recognizing each other in that inopportune voice, they found depth and breadth of meaning in their murmurs, moans and sighs.

Ah... the revelation of the power of the Word!

They dived into the depth of divine sensuousness. As they realized the blending of power and the ecstasy of inertia, the branch from the Tree of Life loosened itself from the grip of their hands and fell down onto the fertile soil with a divine force.

As they were sleeping thoroughly exhausted in that feeling of divine inertia, they did not know that the branch from the

Tree of Life which they sacredly carried all through their wearisome journey grew tender roots and fresh sprouts. In their eagerness to repeat history, they tried to leave everything in the fathomless depth of oblivion.

But for how long? Can they forget everything? No! Never! They continued their search, perhaps an eternal search for truth and happiness. Here ends the history of the first generation and begins that of the second one. A long journey towards me. Can I record the annals of that journey intelligibly? If it is clear, I can. But if it is obscure...

It is really a difficult job to write history. Once you start writing, it will become easy and flowing. But the beginning is very important. It must be capable of catching the attention of the reader. But what about the beginning of my story?

See here... what a monotonous and grave beginning for an autobiography! Why should one be so serious while writing a biography or an autobiography of a human being? Do you think that our life is so important that the beginning of one's story should be so vague and dull? Don't you remember that life is a comedy for those who think and a tragedy for those who feel?

Well... it is taken for granted that the prologue to the story of man is common to all and so one cannot make it too concise or too precise. But as you begin from obscurity, do take up a light vein so that you will not be too emotional to miss apt words. Well, now start... once again from the beginning.

History is continuum. It is indivisible. And so, neither does it end by the first generation nor complete by the next generation. It flows on day in and day out, spontaneously and vigorously. No break at all, no exhaustion even. The folds of satisfaction and disappointments towards light... towards the rays of light that come straining through the cleft in the closed door.

And there begins the history of the previous generation. Needless to say that it is the history of another grandfather and grandmother from whom I was begotten. For science says that the roots of the truth called 'I' has grown, extended and tangled somewhere into the groin of my father and the womb of my mother.

There too, I fully agree that it was sociologists, and not historians, who said that fatherhood is a belief and motherhood is a fact. But then, society has not so degraded itself by separating human relationships as sexual and non-sexual.

Then, all relationships were merely one, the holy sexual relationship. There was no discrimination like father, mother, brother or sister, and that is what we understand from the Holy Book. Then, the only race was Man-woman, the only religion was Sex, the only ritual was Copulation and the only god was Food. Here, I leave it to future generations to find further explanations regarding this aspect of human life.

Then, the parents were proud in bringing up their children just as boys and girls, or later as men and women. They taught their children the early lessons of existence. The childishness of turning the pages of that eternal truth delighted them. In a world of despair and dejection, those innocent creatures lived happily, sharing simple Joys and tears. Men and women copulated and, being drowned in that orgasmic ecstasy, they gained further strength for the continuation of their search.

Again, I do not ignore the fences erected by present day society against sexual relationships. How many helpless human creatures were misguided towards inertia, despair and, even to untimely deaths just because of these taboos? What I clearly state here is about a generation which was unconditionally licensed by God the creator to carry out copulation among brothers and sisters, not withstanding the fact that the partners belonged to the same parents! Well, let's forget such nonsense.

Halleluiah to the first generation that hid the branch from the Tree of Life in their body and the secret of creation in their mind, when they were pushed out of the Garden of Eden, and later, handed them over to the new generations. And praise to the hurriedness of the second generation that brought into proper practice a fact delivered in the midst of confusion, amazement and embarrassment.

In that hurriedness, without knowing that I would be created, a man and a woman, instinctively ate the fruits of Eden, tasted the fragrance and slipped into a divine ecstasy. Glory to them!

Here I, Adam, or Adam Junior, call me whatever you like, forget the names of the grandfather and grandmother. Or even the names of my father and mother. Well, that's immaterial for is it not a historical truth that the father is a man and the mother is a woman? And who can question a truth? Perhaps only a Pontius Pilate could ask the question, 'What is Truth?'

Again I, Adam, return to that man and woman of the first generation. Both of them together had two sons, Cain and Abel. They were the First Brothers, and one day, they went to offer sacrifice to their God. And Cain the Farmer, the elder one, sacrificed his younger brother Abel, the Shepherd. And praise be to the name of God.

Let me, by the way, point out that the poet's saying, 'Quarrels are many in this world due to gold and woman' is sheer nonsense... for there are a lot of other reasons too!

And the murdered or the dead Abel became the first martyr and, later, was declared a saint. Well, I do not exactly remember the reference number of that encyclical pastoral letter.

And the murderer, or the living Cain, first became the ruler of the land and later, the father of the nation. Well, I regret to say more, as the scribbling on the copper plate is highly illegible due to too much oxidization.

And what is left out? Just man and woman! They worked hard and enjoyed much. They ate the harvest of the earth with the salt of their foreheads. In the blending of their forces, a new Garden of Eden was created which smiled in the abundance of flowers and fruits. On the wet bank of the crystalline stream, the branch from the Tree of Life spread its roots and grew strong. In the over-brimming water of the riverlet, golden fish played crazily. They swam forward, swinging and beating their tails, moved ahead with an uncontrollable force that could split even a planet.

And let me recall that the present time is notable for the fish that bask or wither or dry under the scorching sun, lying on those graves that dream of rejuvenation, resurrection or metamorphosis, in vain.

But then... it was the spring season, the season for the seeds to wake up from their long sleep. The time for germination. On a full moon night, the man and the woman, lying under the umbrella of a banyan tree, twirled themselves into one like the crooked roots of that tree, and knew nothing of the biological changes that occurred to them. They were sleeping under the frenzy exhaustion, with the blessedness of the divine inertia, enjoying the aroma of each other's sweat and leaving everything else to the depth of oblivion except a faint memory of that divine orgasm.

Yes! Banyans and peepuls gave man enlightenment even from time immemorial. Does it mean that the story of the fish under the shade of the banyan tree and the history of the previous generation end here? No! Not yet! My journey towards light, rather my expedition in search of light, is yet to be commenced.

Wait patiently! Eggs too wait days and nights patiently to

receive their suitable fish. Many an egg awaits the magic touch of the neela-koduveli, the wonderful magic-herb, in order to be hatched. Is the common pheasant that brings that magical herb to hatch its rotten eggs only a superstition?

No! If it were a superstition, I would not have been born... my birth and search for truth would have become a part of poetic fancy. In fact, I myself was that common pheasant. I myself was that light movement of life in the egg. I am that I am.

Somewhere among the unseen branches of a Banyan Tree which was as tall as to touch the canopy of the sky and was spread to the edges of all the eight directions of the horizon, placing dried twigs one after another, I made my nest. My eggs pulsating with hopes, took rest on the softness created by my own feathers over the hardness of those twigs. I was brooding over them expecting the moment in which my dreams that consist of my own flesh, blood and marrow, came out with a cry of victory, breaking their hard shells.

I waited and waited unaware of the birth and decay of aeons, without hearing the hissing of the ever-turning Wheel of Time, uncared of the gaps in between the past, the present and the future, as if I were in the booze of a long sleep, or in the utter befuddlement of an obscure trance... I waited.

Ages of waiting made me myopic and my heart moved up and down in the ebb and flow of bitter thoughts. The sobs and sighs that strained out of the unbroken hard-shells beat in my ears perpetually. And as I woke up from my deep trance with a shudder, the germination of the divine prudence spurred me on and on.

As my long wings raised me higher and higher, I flew forward cautiously and meticulously observing every point of the vast earth. I wandered about every nook and corner of the world in search of that magic herb which was powerful enough to break the hard shells of my unhatched eggs. Irrespective of land or water, concentrating my whole attention on my single aim, I roamed and roamed over lands and waters, over hills and plains, without caring even about the changes of seasons. As I was passing deep seas and heaven-touched mountains, woods and valleys, lakes and deserts, I did not know even about myself.

As I was moving away into the depth of eternal vacuity, the blue koduveli watched me teasingly and laughed at me. And then, the sudden discovery of those blue koduvelies, growing with the abundance of flowers, in the real darkness of the bottomless well gave me a new life of hope.

As I was descending down the stone-steps of the well, my wavering feet sought refuge at the sliding mud-walls of the well. My heart was burning at the sadistic nature of the blue koduveli that went down deeper and deeper as my fingers were about to touch it.

And as my eggs were resting with throbbing hopes on the softness created by my own feathers on the hardness of twigs somewhere among the unknown branches of a banyan tree that was tall enough to touch the sky and wide enough to cover all the eight directions of the horizon, as wavelets and ripples at my feet were awakened in the black water of the well, by the hot tears that fell drop by drop from my myopic eyes, and as my heavy breathing and hot sighs stirred the solid darkness around me, I anxiously waited, being immersed in the remembrance of my eggs that rested in the expectation of an early hatching, somewhere among the unseen branches of the Great Banyan Tree.

Waiting for the moment in which that blossoming blue koduveli ascended from the real darkness of the bottomless well... I was waiting.

Adam, you're doomed! Your plight is that of the common

pheasant. Your fate is that of its eggs.

How hard is the plight of the common pheasant that tries to fetch the blue koduveli to hatch its eggs? And how cruel is the man who steals the eggs when the bird has gone in search of its food, and returns them to the nest secretly after boiling them, in his greed to get the blue koduveli?

Is it merely a superstition of the village folks that only a common pheasant can find the herb from some deep, unused wells? Later, when the boiled eggs are hatched, and the bird-ling fly away, the greedy man would carefully take the tattered nest and put it in the flowing water so that the blue koduveli would float against the water current and move upwards while the rest of the nest flows downwards.

In his efforts to fulfill his vaulting ambitions, man is ready to do all kinds of foolishness, and this too is, perhaps, one among them. But think of the play of luck in human life. And luck comes only to those who try. Or leave aside the man and the mother-bird. What about the bird-ling that breaks the hard shell and comes through the keyhole into the daylight with the thrilling aspirations of a new life?

And inside the shell of the egg... what a horrible experience it was!

That room was too small like an urn or quite blank like a newly constructed tomb. For many long years the idea of 'I' was throbbing in it.

It is confusing that the room was existing there even before the idea of 'I' began to palpitate in it. But the consoling fact was that, then, no other idea or even a similar thought that was there existed.

And what was the state even before that? Then there was not even that room. Or even if there was one, it was only a part of the 'null and void' Nature, a mere part of that eternal vacuity. But that time was far beyond the age of Motion or

Mutation, and so I must leave it aside.

As the idea of 'I' began to throb in that room, its vacuity began to undergo color-changes. At times, it was the color of the 'red-blood'. Later, in the lengthening of moments, changes came to that stagnant color and at last, it turned into the color of the 'black blood'.

Then suddenly, on an unexpected moment, the color of the 'black blood' disappeared and the room became colorless. Again, the voyage began from there to the gradual returning of the color of the 'red blood'. And the Wheel of Time was turning consecutively. And the idea of 'I' alone throbbed consistently with all its indefiniteness, in that formerly 'null and void' room.

Was it that the room always remained changeless, as it was at the beginning? No! It was also throbbing together with the cataleptic idea of 'I'. And the whole room puffed up and shrank alternatively, like the pulsing of the heart or like the movement of the lungs.

Was that room completely void as it was at the beginning? No! At times the sudden appearance of a planet from eternity made a mark in that vacuity and after staying there for a while, it disappeared together with the color of the 'black blood'. And this phenomenon continued for ages.

And suddenly one day, the Age of Motion gave way to the Age of Flood, for it was the need of that room to gain a general shape and a definite structure for the idea of 'I'.

On that day, the color of the room was light red, a milestone on the voyage from color-less-ness to the color of the 'black blood'! And a new planet coming from eternity was searching for its own orbit, lingering in the room for a while.

And then occurred that cataclysm! In the force of a flood, it was made clear for the first time that the room had a keyhole. The room shook in the powerful spray of the new flood water that came in through the keyhole. In the vitality of the flood water, millions of golden fish rushed and moved in a frenzy of desire. They beat their tails and energetically swam everywhere in the room with an uncontrollable and instinctive eagerness to break whatever they encountered on their way.

And those exhausted fish, one by one, came to a standstill and gradually disintegrated into the flood water. The disabled ones and the aimless ones gradually melted into the concentration of the flood water and disappeared without knowing the pleasure of existence.

And then, the strongest and the fittest sole survivor in the gang, rushed in its full power, broke the outer wall of the planet with its head making a vent pushed the idea of 'I' through the vent and closed the cleft forever with the tip of its tail.

Then a moment's tranquility. The Wheel of Time stood motionless. The head of the golden fish and the idea of 'I' together melted in the burning lava inside the planet, amalgamating all into one. A sort of indefiniteness remained stagnant in the room.

The force of the flood gradually deteriorated. The lid fell over the keyhole. An age of darkness crawled into the room and began to weave its gossamer.

And the color of the room remained unchanged. The age of darkness covered the planet like a thin layer. And inside the planet, without a sense of the passage of time or the change of seasons, in a sort of unconscious stage, the idea of 'I' was undergoing gradual evolution, acquiring shape, characters and emotions.

Then, it was a journey from that unconscious stage to a semi-conscious deep slumber. As I awakened with a shock from that sound sleep into the stage of consciousness, I, in utter confusion and embarrassment, stared for a moment into the curse of darkness that enveloped me.

Later, being tangled in the cobweb of darkness, I waddled here and there in the room. I was restless as I knew that it was time to begin my search. And if I delayed more to begin my long journey in search of light, I would not have even my own existence.

There was one thing which I always remembered, the power of the fish head that could even split a planet. That tradition and legacy, which made me conscious of the power of my own head, encouraged me.

And one day, in the force of my head, the keyhole together with the door slipped away. The long awaited future stood agape in front of me. Once again, in the force of another flood I slipped out. I dived out of the eternal darkness that divided the boundary of the room into the source of light that strained through the keyhole.

But, was that the real source of light? It was only my first step in my journey towards light! The search for the light is a continuous task. And I am fully conscious of what history taught me about the power of my head. Then why should I hesitate? March forward to light... towards more and more light.

How wonderful! Do you mean that you remember all these? How can you? It's all simply odd... Adam, you are a strange man.

Well, you said it. Miracles can happen at any time. I still feel that movement. I really feel that swinging motion... as if you are lying on a banyan-leaf. You move to and fro in accordance with the movement of the leaf... and the leaf is moving according to the ripples aroused in the water by the gentle breeze. You float as if lying on a lifebuoy in a pool of water... slightly moving sideways... moving to the tune of the warm water in the pool. You feel the safety and security of the womb... of your own mother's womb.

Or perhaps you were in the lap of your own mother, covered in a white cloth, coming from the hospital where you were born. And all of you were in a small boat... and the boat was moving sideways. And you were imagining that you were then in your mother's womb.

Your mother took you out of the boat and she walked, carrying you safely in her hands, towards her house. You opened your eyes and saw the clear blue sky. You breathed the fish-smell of the riverside. You heard the sound of the wind among the sugar-canes. You felt the warmth of your mother's full breasts. You tasted the sweetness of her first drop of milk.

Yes! I remember all. I, Adam Junior, keep everything in my memory... because I am a miracle child... the first born of a father and a mother. I am born to give birth and lead a new generation.

Then it was the childhood days. You were learning. You used all the senses... learning about you... about others... about the wonders of Nature... wonders of the universe.

Your birth, Adam, itself was a miracle. It seemed as if nature itself was waiting for such a birth.

Then... a strange star appeared somewhere in an unknown galaxy of the vast universe. I, Adam Junior, like my great grandfather Adam, also took birth, at the culmination of the age of darkness, in the birth-house or labor-room of a silent night, in order to be surprised at the eternal secrets disclosed time to time by Nature. Just think about me. Don't you know that I am your representative?

Poor grandfather Adam. He struggled hard, being tangled in the sticky cobweb of ignorance that tightened around him. The more he tried to escape from that vortex, the more he was absorbed into that gyration of puzzles. He stared at that Gordian knot of a life in bewilderment. When his fruitless efforts weakened every joint of his bones, Adam cried aloud, fixing his eyes in the vacuity.

Later, Adam watching the so-called omnipotent darkness fly away in fear, stood motionless and brooded over the vanity of power and the mutability of authority. He looked at the silver orb that radiated light to distinguish things around him, and knelt down in obeisance before it, in a rapture of joy, fear and adoration.

As the silver orb became red hot and its beams of light turned into darts of fire, Adam's blood transformed into sweat. In confusion confounded, first he stood aghast and then looked around him in a stupor. Then he took refuge under a banyan tree that stood with spreading branches as if to give him shade and protection from the hot rays of the fireball up in the sky.

And that stirred his mind and he thought how useful it would be if he could make a platform around the crown of the tree so that he could come there regularly to take rest.

Adam felt his throat dry as the divine curiosity led him to wonderful secrets of the sensuous universe. He consoled himself in the mesmeric effect of the water from the springs that cooled and refreshed his mind and body. He discovered the First Cause in the crystalline water that rippled in the cup of his palms.

When the silver orb burned out, Adam once again felt fear as Nature began to cover herself with the black blanket of darkness. A myriad of bright eyes from the heavens winked at him creating a magical world. When the yellow orb came up in the horizon, emitting light and coolness, pouring a sort of emotional frenzy into him; Adam, with reverence, kowtowed before it. He looked reverently at those black stones that helped him to make fire as it helped him to save his body from the stinging cold. He took them and consecrated them by placing them on a raised platform. He was frightened to the core when the wild fire roared towards him, turning every plant and every animal into ashes. And Adam began to offer flowers and worship all those forces of Nature that could not be tamed by his willpower.

Adam was boozed by the magical play of colors in Nature. He felt thrilled at the clearness of white, at the horror of black, at the excitement of red, at the charm of yellow and at the coolness of green. And in his helplessness, he accepted flowers, which disclosed the secrets of those colors either as objects to be worshipped or as objects to be used in worship.

Forgetting himself in Nature's genuine intoxication, Adam moved forward crossing many a new zone of beauty. As the memory of a myriad of objects piled up in his mind, they took the shape of passion, and broke the bund. Being shocked at the force of that flood of passion, and being trapped in between the difference of masculine and feminine beauties, Adam stood wonderstruck.

He felt as if he was in the whirlpool of a magnetic power, until he gave shape to those beauties on stones and wood, and knelt before them quite surprised at his own power of creation. The aesthetic sense that gathered, concentrated and swelled in his mind, led Adam through living passions to the magic of creativity. The sense of the highest power and the sense of the deepest powerlessness which he realized from the act of creativity as well as the realization of the sense of the most wonderful forgetfulness and the unexplainable sense of loss which for a moment he gained in between the former feelings, culminating into an altogether sense of the vacuity of satiety, compelled Adam to blindly worship the power of a creative union.

Adam began to worship everything that was out of reach for him, and all things that aroused fear and amazement in him. He gazed at all new scientific inventions, geographical discoveries and philosophic principles in awe. He underwent enlightenment while leaning against the ant hill erected by him under the shade of the banyan tree. Adam, who was incapable of depending solely on himself, continued his journey in search of new gods.

And I, Adam Junior, every time I resume my journey, worshipping at intervals each cosmic or natural secret, revealed to me, time to time, in the passage of time.

And that's the reason why I believed in a number of gods. First it was the Fish that lived only in the water. Then it was the Tortoise that lived both in the water and on the land. And then it was the pig that lived only on the land. Then it was Narasimha the half animal and the half man. Then it was the smallest man... the Dwarf of a man who was capable to grow into the biggest man. Then there was a train of great men who were experts in martial arts... who could use weapons like the Axe, the Plough and the Bow and Arrow. Then it was the man of emotion and intellect, the man of reason and intelligence. And then... and then...

A long list of incarnations and manifestations... of sons of god and prophets of god. God of Creation gave way to God of Nurturing. God of Destruction gave way to God of Protection. God of Terror gave way to God of Sympathy. God of Punishment became God of Reconciliation. God of Brain gave way to God of Heart. God of Violence gave way to God of Non-violence. God of Law gave way to God of Love. God of Physical Power gave way to God of Mental Power. God of Sacrifice gave way to God of Survival.

What a wonderful creation is man. God created man and the godliness in him made him a creator. But he could not become immortal like God. What a pity.

Can man become immortal? Was he immortal even in the Garden of Eden? Though Adam was created from mortal dust, he was immortal before his fall. Does it mean that dust is also immortal? It was the sin, and not the substance with which he was created, that brought mortality to him. So, there is hope for man to attain immortality.

Adam, how could you gain your immortality back? Only by pleasing God. How could you please God? Well, of course through sacrifices. Offer sacrifice to Him and his nostrils will be widened at the smell of your sacrifices. Sacrifice whatever you produce... your farm products... the best of your animals... even your own children who too are your products.

A long list of sacrifices and offerings. First it was human sacrifice. Of course, the victims were other fellow human beings. God was not pleased. Then your own first born child, to get immediate benefit. Abraham attempted it, but God could not tolerate man's foolishness to that extent. God sent an angel to prevent Abraham, and advised him to do animal sacrifice. But King Jiphtah was foolish enough to sacrifice his daughter.

Human sacrifice gave way to animal sacrifice. Animal sacrifice gave way to vegetable sacrifice... vegetables filled with a mixture of lime and turmeric powder in water. Vegetable sacrifice gave way to the sacrifice of fruits or flowers. Then the sacrifice of uncooked food... then, cooked food. Yet God is not pleased to give back man's immortality.

What should be next? All sacrifices overlapped each other. What about self-sacrifice? But man was not daring enough to do that. Adam, can you do it? Is one person's self-sacrifice enough for the redemption of all others? Then, find another person for you. If so, why not your Eve? Can man return to human sacrifice once again?

Death stood before man as the only invincible thing. Death became just another God. Fear of death haunted man. Death became the only truth before him. The curse on the head of Grandfather Cain followed him wherever he went. How sad was the fate of Cain, one of my forefathers.

'You'll become just like God!'

Those words were too tempting. The mysterious hissing sound that echoed in the ears of the first man of the Garden of Eden. The sin-stained sound that could trap any man in the magical web of excessive desires and vaulting ambitions.

The sound that reverberated in the Garden of Eden, strained and slipped out of it. And then it began to wave-beat eternally to enchant each generation that entered the arena of life, one after another.

That sound continued to echo spontaneously in and out of the Garden of Eden and then to spread towards the Land of Nodh in the east and from there to all the eight directions of the universe.

Forgetting himself in the intoxication of that sound, Adam was turning himself into a termite fly that lost its sense of discernment at the sight of fire.

Alas! Here, the fate of my forefather Cain is repeated in me and I am burning myself into flames. The unavoidable death and the fear of its unexpected occurrence.

Here the name Cain becomes a synonym for sin. Perhaps the best word for cruelty, betrayal and murder. It has become the name for the fear of death that haunts man for ever and ever.

Adam Junior, in you there is a Cain! In fact you yourself are a Cain! For it is quite natural that the parents who desired to become God-like by gaining the knowledge of good and evil, the quality of prudence and the ability of discernment and the great wisdom which was quite exclusive to God, begot an issue of their nature.

Owing to the result of their uncontrollable desires, they were thrown out of Eden. And what about the fate of their son? What a horrible punishment was he undergoing day in and day out!

God created man in his own image. Adam too produced children in his own image. The spontaneous urge for creation. The second step of the foolish man to become another God.

God is the creator, the protector and the destroyer. And man, who produced children and gathered food from the earth with the sweat of his forehead also proved to be creator, protector and destroyer, through Cain. The reflection of man's secret desire to become God! Yet another step of the foolish man towards immortality.

Well, Adam Junior, aren't you that foolish man?

Yes, I myself am Cain. I still remember.

On that black day...

My own brother Abel writhed and died at my feet. When he was hit on the head with a huge stone, warm blood splashed onto my face too...

The nauseating smell of human blood pierced into my nostrils. The sight of his utter helplessness stuck into my eyes like poisonous arrows. Seeing that horrific and grotesque sight, man shocked and trembled for the first time.

For a moment Cain stood there completely confused, as if breathing stopped forever. The whole body turned stone-cold. And the smell of death that hovered over him, followed man for generations to come.

The mind was troubled realizing the shocking truth that the life once taken from the body of a fellow man could not be given back by the person who took it. The body felt paralyzed without knowing how to withdraw the stone that had already slipped out of the hand.

The blood of Abel that spread all over the place was begging for mercy. And the sky and the earth were alternatively asking me: Where's thy brother?

Suddenly the beasts and the birds became silent, the plants

and the creepers turned to a standstill. Even at that moment when the whole of Nature was standing in utter horror and terror, was I not trying to justify myself by gathering courage and confidence?

Then it was a life and death race. A running away from the Creator and his creations. But the fact that one could not run away and hide from oneself forever stopped me on my way. Everywhere, even in the Land of Enodh, those frightening memories hunt me like hounds and haunt me like nightmares.

I will ever remain a synonym for man's wickedness, a symbol of the imbecile and credulous man. What was the passion that tempted me to judge my own blood? Was it jealousy? Or was it greed? Was it arrogance? Or was it mere short temper?

On that day, as I was unable to do any good, my face turned pale and ghastly. I did not care for the sin that was lying just at the door step, like a venomous snake. And I alone was always the goal and target of that poisonous serpent. And I could not crush its head nor could I chase him away or subjugate him.

And then, what a terrible consequence followed. The whole field turned damp with the blood of innocent Abel. Grains were marked with blood-stains. Even now I feel the disgusting taste of human blood as I eat the grains from the field.

Frightening days. Sleepless nights. Painful evenings and shocking mornings. Every moment fear crawls towards me like black scorpions.

As sleep turns my eyelids heavy, I feel as if somebody was raising a black stone over my head. And my intuition warns me that my head will be crushed into pieces at any moment.

Any time arrows that can pierce my chest may fly towards me from behind those verdant bowers and shady trees. I feel the long, lean and dry fingers of death approaching closer and closer to my neck, to strangle me.

The wailing that penetrated my ears, when my brother's life separated from his body, still echoes around me. Like the roaring or howling of some monster, it paralyses even the marrow of my bones.

I feel as if the identification mark that God gave me to protect my life from those who would kill me, fading away gradually. Perhaps those who fail to see or to recognize that mark will kill me. Perhaps the wild animals out of their brutish instinct will break my head. I also may lay somewhere dead, like my brother at my feet, with broken skull, shattered brain and fully drenched in blood.

Of course, God promised that he would do seven times to the person who would kill me. But what's in it? Though God could do seven times or even seventy times to the person who would kill me, still the matter of my death would remain a fact. What is there if after my death something worse happens to the murderer?

When untimely death follows me like a shadow, how can I repose? How can I walk among those fruit-bearing trees? How can I sleep on those green pastures? Where can I hide myself?

Even the rising sun cannot wipe away the darkness of fear from my heart. Its hot rays pierce my body like venomous darts. My flesh is cracked and charred in the hot noon-wind that blows incessantly. My whole body is burned, and melted, as if even the cold water of the brook cannot cool it down. Even my voice fails to come out of my dry throat.

When the sun sets, the moon and the stars appear on the canopy of the sky to laugh at me. In the moon light, long shadows of trees like the angels of death, try to catch me. And my mind trembles in the ear-breaking noise that sneaks through darkness.

All the objects in nature shake their heads and raise their

voice to frighten me. Abel's blood spreads even onto the saffron flowers. The wailings of a brother reverberate in the horizon and the odor of his blood hangs over in the atmosphere. And the voice of God echoes and re-echoes...

'You'll be a wanderer on this earth... '

Yes, Adam Junior, it's your fate! Wander on this earth till death makes her unexpected smite. If the fate of one of my forefathers is this, why am I born? Just to die like any other animal? If death is the end of all, why should we toil and struggle, as the poet asks?

Adam, it's your fate! Death is inevitable. And it is unpredictable. At any moment death may come to you. Then all your dreams are shattered... all your hopes are crumbled. All these days you have been making castles in the air. Such palaces of playing cards will fall down at the lightest wisp of a breeze.

Adam's body trembled. He felt difficulty in breathing. Why should I die? Why is death inevitable and unpredictable? What is the meaning of death?

Unanswered questions disturbed his heart. The fire of inquiry still burned within him. He always wished to die for the quest of knowledge. And his sole aim was to reach immortality.

Adam Junior, it's your turn. Try and acquire what you want. First get knowledge... then reach excellence. Adam Junior felt the spirit of Nachiketas in his heart of hearts, as he began to ponder over the secret of death.

Adam, you were the Nachiketas. You had to face the god of death. Keep your questions ready with you.

He wandered here and there like a tramp, carrying the heavy burden of many an unknown and obscure curse that piled upon his head. He was strangled by the unbreakable duties and ambiguous obligations imposed upon him by ancestry. He felt suffocation at the secret of death which was as vague as the secret of birth. He yearned to know its mystery as death is the one and the only truth in human life.

Various images of death performed the cosmic dance of wrath around him. In his heart, fear, the reflection of the god of death, raised its hood. He looked around in the utter vagueness of grief.

He was shocked, hearing the echoing and re-echoing of the chant, whispered carelessly by his previous generations: I must be offered to the god of death... hmmm... I must be offered to the god of death?

He looked fearfully at the figures that approached him to take away his life. Then tried to run away and escape from that long shadow which lay down at his feet. He felt completely exhausted of his energy. His face turned pale and ghastly as he approached the vague laws of birth and death. Those naked truths of fate, which were ignored from time to time in order to be questioned by the past, disfigured his face and made it ugly and ghastly.

Yet he ran far, far away until he felt that the long fingers of the Banyan tree would get hold of him and trap him forever. He kicked away on the sea shore the sand that tangled on the toes of his feet. He struggled hard at the smell of death that blew strongly around him like a tornado.

His heart desired to move away from the octopus-grip of time, and to take rest at a far away spot on the other side of the calm and quiet sea. He could only stand and stare at the indifferent face of the sea that consistently raised shackles and fetters to bind him.

In his hurriedness to escape, he cried aloud, "I must be given to the god of death... hmmm... I must be given to the god of death... Ha! Ha! Ha!"

He laughed aloud like a madman. And the sea received the

waves of his laughter. And as the sea raised huge waves, he stood there impatiently for that glorious fraction of a minute, waiting for that unknown moment in which the god of death came to take him away.

Among the confusion of the roaring waves, the laughs of the crooked old man of the sea fell on his ears. He stared at the frightening figure of the monster that slowly rose up from the darkness of the waters. He stood immovably, as the bison with sparkling eyes and curved horns gradually approached him. And on its back, carrying a roll of rope was that frightful rider, looking for his next prey.

As the bison reached him, it seemed as if its sense of smell recognized the prey. The rider took out a scroll of old lambskin, with a sneer on his lips. He unrolled the sheet and began to read aloud, "Mr. Adam M.A., Ph.D., LL.B?" He looked up at him and raised his eyebrows in query.

As he nodded, meaning 'yes', the rope in the rider's hand uncurled. Staring at the rope that came towards his neck, he demanded or perhaps rather begged: "Wait a moment, please! Give answers to my three questions first!"

The rider laughed aloud devilishly and murmured something in disbelief. Then he snorted, "Alright! Come on!"

The questioner's heart trembled, as the rider laughed at the childishness of the first two questions which were answered very easily. His body began to shiver like that of a malaria patient. He felt sweat streaming along his face, as he looked at the placid face of the rider who demanded the last question as quickly as possible.

For him nothing was there to think about the third and the last question. To put an end to that mystery that time to time many generations were fondling with awe, as well as to quench his own thirst for knowledge which he considered greater than his own life, he asked the rider aloud: "What is the secret of death?"

The rider was shocked! The bison was frightened and snorted. The uncurled rope rolled back to the rider's hand. The bison and its rider began to turn back to the darkness of the waters. Looking at the back of the rider and the bison, he repeated the question. Then he laughed aloud and in a roaring voice, again demanded: "Tell me... tell me... tell me the answer... "

The frightened bison and the devilish rider moved away silently into the waves that rose higher and higher up into the darkness of the water. He too was following them, repeating his unanswerable question... his last question.

Adam! Come back, come back! Your question will never be answered. Of course, it seems answerable. But every answer you get is obscure. The next question hides in every answer given to you.

Philosophers wait with ready made answers for all your questions. Theologians take every serious question very lightly and give answers as if the rabbit they caught has three horns. But they all know themselves the final hollowness of their answers. However, that fact should not prevent a Nachiketas from his eternal enquiry. He must try, till his last breath, at least to quench the thirst of his knowledge. People like Nachiketas brought meanings to human life. Otherwise human life would have been a mere waste.

Adam, beware of this!

Once man becomes old, such unanswered questions will trouble him much. Then, man will try to satisfy himself with whatever meaningless answers or foolish explanations he has with him. He dies and people will say, "Oh, what a peaceful death." Shit!

All these days you have been living without a real life. Yet, one day you die and your life ends meaninglessly. Therefore enjoy your life. 'Eat, drink and be merry, for tomorrow you may die', remember the Rubiyats of an eternal poet. Work hard on the land. Cultivate all kinds of fruits and vegetables. Keep all kinds of edible animals. Feel a settled life. This is your paradise. This is your Garden of Eden! Eat, drink and be merry. That's your pledge, and your predicament as well, Adam.

Relax, Adam Junior. Forget all your worries and fears. Why should you ponder over unavoidable matters? Be ready to face inevitable things in life.

The problem is that you don't have complete faith in God. Know yourself, Adam. Then know your Creator. God is the First Cause. God is the Power behind all creations. God is Almighty. God is omnipotent. God is eternal. God is omniscient. He knows everything. Everything happens according to His will. And nothing happens without His knowledge. So be relaxed.

Don't worry even if the whole world is in floods. Take rest on your armchair. Keep the cup, filled with wine, in your hand. Sip the wine, drop by drop, taking the maximum time. If you drink less, you can drink more. And relax, just like grandfather Noah.

Forty days and forty nights of heavy rain. The whole world drowned in the flood water. And you float in an ark, up above the whole world. Just like Brahma on a Banyan leaf. That's the benefit of confidence. That's the reward for faith in God. Relax on an armchair, sipping the best quality wine, lightly swinging in accordance with the movement of the ark.

All your sons and daughters and their families are around you. All the creatures of the world, animals and birds in male and female pairs, are under the safety of the ark. And all of them are happy. They all eat and drink. They all engage in merry making. No problems. No worries.

Nothing to do. Leave everything to God. Let him do whatever he likes. There's scarcity for drinking water. There's shortage of food items, both for men and beasts. And here and there, Noah, your ark leaks. Your wife complains; your children run in panic.

And Grandfather Noah laughs. Perhaps just like what the poet imagined. 'Ha! Ha! Ha! No problem! I don't care unless water leaks into my wine!'

Just imagine, Adam. Those carefree days of Noah. Put your entire burden on God. Let him manage everything for you. That's the best way of living.

But a day comes in which the rain stops and your ark lands on the top of a barren mountain. You and the members of your family, together with all the animals and birds, have to get out of the safety of the ark onto the reality of the barren land. All other creatures move away from you, seeking their own means of living. You feel lonely, quite burdened with the responsibility of a starving generation.

Till the soil and produce your food, your conscience murmurs. Floods cannot hinder the free movement of the fish. Remember the power of the fish-head? Eat your bread with the sweat of your forehead. Change this barren land into another Garden of Eden! Here's a new world under your feet.

We worked on the land. We ploughed the field, sowed the seed, watered it and gave manure to it. We reaped the fruits of our toil. And enjoyed ourselves.

Let there be music, and music was there. Let there be dancing, and dancing was there. We ate, we drank and we enjoyed life... from sunrise to sunset we worked hard. From sunset to sunrise we enjoyed our life... is there anything wrong in it?

Adam, you are blessed to do so. You make a vineyard. The vineyard gives you grapes. Cornucopia! You crush the grapes and make grape juice. You keep it for a few days and turn it into powerful wine. You drink it and enjoy life.

It is quite simple. You prepare a land for cultivation. The land gives you wheat. Cornucopia! The wheat gives you flour. With flour you make bread. You eat it and enjoy life. Adam, you are blessed to do so.

You call your wife and children. You invite your friends and neighbors. They all engage in eating, drinking and merry-making. Human life becomes quite wonderful. A life of sufficiency. A life having no concern over tomorrow. A life free from worries and pains.

Once again the gates to the Garden of Eden are opened. Paradise is recreated on earth. Adam, aren't you happy? All your efforts have turned successful. All your dreams are fulfilled. What else do you need?

You united all the people into one nation. You made them all happy. Heaven came down to them. Or they tried to reach heaven. They worked hard with one aim, one business and one purpose. The Tower of Babel grew higher and higher. The Tower of Unity. The Tower of Hard Work. The tower of Human Happiness.

But... one fine morning... everything turns upside down. A wind of jealousy blows, spreading confusion, fanaticism, nepotism and madness among the people.

Adam, life is like that... you work hard and make everything fruitful... but at the last moment misfortune plays a trick. There seems to be a thousand miles between the cup and the lip... bear it. Believe that everything is mere coincidence.

Adam, you are the chief architect of the Tower of Babel. It is no more the tower of your plan and scheme. It is now a Tower of Diversity. A Tower of Laziness... a Tower of Misery and Confusion.

Run, Adam! Run to the plains of Shinar. Prevent them

from destroying your dreams. Stop those foolish human beings.
The city throbbed like the heartbeats of the Shinar plains.
The beautiful Babel Tower stood silhouetted against the blue
sky.

Every moment changes were occurring in Shinar. The
Shinar plain which had been full of thorny bushes and pointed
rocks changed into a wonderful city within no time. And its
tower was rising up and up, higher and higher, as if it would
touch the heavens by the next day.

Standing on the terrace of his mansion, the Chief Architect
of the tower watched the progress of the construction work. His
long cherished dreams were coming true. His hopes were
flowering in the form of a huge tower.

The hard-earned knowledge of architecture was taking
shape on the plains of Shinar. The sum total of many years'
thoughts and calculations, a well-planned city and a heaven-
touching tower.

Looking at the tower that was growing up into the heavens,
the Chief Architect drew heavenly inspirations.

Dawn was just breaking at the eastern horizon. The golden
rays of the rising sun reflected from the smooth stones of the
half-built tower.

The dark green leaves of the olive trees which beautified
the city showered dewdrops. The wind, heavy with the
fragrance of the frankincense trees, caressed the city. The
sweet smell from the flowery vineyards and pomegranate
gardens lay stagnant in the atmosphere. The song of the
skylarks from their nests among the cedar trees and the voice
of the cuckoos from their resting green bowers echoed in the
plains of Shinar.

Shinar. A place of permanent peace and happiness. Shinar.
The synonym for dedication and hard work. Shinar was a
symbol of human fancy and imagination. Shinar was the call

for unity. Shinar was the source of all inspirations and provocations. Shinar helped in realizing the long cherished dreams. Shinar gave shape and beauty to human feelings. Ah, Shinar.

The Chief Architect was observing from the terrace of his palace the construction work of the city and the tower. As the supervisor of the whole work, his heart was beating fast with pride. With uncontrollable emotions, he stared at the fulfillment of his life's mission. Joy and satisfaction waved in the sea of his heart. Tears of happiness concentrated in his eyes. New dreams and ideas danced in his brain.

There in the city... cheerful laborers started their work. The city and its entire construction works drowned in the voice of those busy and vigorous honeybees.

The cries of the workers, who prepared lime-mortar, by mixing lime, sand and clay, stamping the mass in the rhythm of a folk song, rose up. The voice of the masons who cut and smoothed to shape the red-stone bricks echoed everywhere.

The black smoke that came up from the kilns where mud-bricks were tempered slowly went higher and higher, gradually melted in the air and then vanished into the heavens.

The Chief Architect stood on the terrace of his palace, staring at the column of black smoke that rose up from the brick kilns. Those pillars of smoke had no fixed shapes, he thought. But all his dreams, one by one, had been taking shape in the plains of Shinar. Those pillars of smoke would hang over in the atmosphere and would disappear into thin air. But the city and its huge tower will exist forever. Aeons will pass. But they will remain eternally, as the grace of Shinar. A smile of confidence blossomed on the lips of the chief architect.

When the Chief Architect saw more and more thick columns of fire rising up from the kilns, at first he was surprised. He wondered: 'What? Does it mean that the whole brick kilns caught fire?'

Soon, wailings and howlings, cries and roars, began to rise up from the plains of Shinar. People were running helter-skelter in panic.

What's happening? For a minute the Chief Architect stood in a complete stupor.

Then a sort of mutiny was breaking out in the Shinar plains. The roars and cries of the laborers echoed everywhere. Trees and plants swung to and fro in the heavy storm. Thunder and lightning terrified and shook Shinar. Flames of fire were rising here and there and licked the walls of the city.

The Babel fort cracked from side to side. Clefts and crevices appeared here and there in the walls of the tower. The Babel Tower was crumbling down, stone after stone. The Shinar streets open agape their mouths wide as if to swallow its pedestrians. The gates and towers of the city were swinging in a frightful manner, as if in a massive earthquake.

The Chief Architect cried aloud, beating his right and left hands alternatively on his chest. He ran towards the street, without knowing what was happening there. He ran here and there like a madman, asking questions to the labourers and checking the work sites.

The frightened labourers were leaving the city in small restless groups and noisy gangs. He tried to stop them and ask them the reasons for their exodus. But he could not understand their replies. They also stared at him as if they could not recognize his words.

'What do these people say? I can't make any sense out of it! Did they forget their tongue? Or did I forget their tongue? Am I going crazy?' The Chief Architect ran along the streets like a mad dog.

He took a whip and flogged the labourers who tried to take out the basement stones. He kicked at those who loosened the brick work. They threw stones at him and chased him away.

Staring into the burned down kilns, he sighed. Beating on his chest he lamented at his inability in understanding their language. He ran around the fallen tower, crying and sobbing bitterly.

All the people of Shinar left the city and went to the hills. Shinar, being drowned in a frightening silence, looked like a burial ground. Grief lay stagnant in the atmosphere.

And the sorrowful cries and painful lamentations of the Chief Architect echoed and re-echoed among the stones of the crumbled city and the fallen tower.

Everything is destroyed... nothing of your towers of hopes remains, not even a stone on another stone. The efforts of a long period... the outcome of the toils of a great generation... all lay scattered.

Adam, there's something wrong with theology. Here's a God who destroys a generation of definite aims. They were about to touch the zenith... but then... Adam, how can you escape from the cruel smites of fate?

No use in running helter-skelter. What's the use in pulling at your hair and tearing of your clothes? You did not commit any crime. You tried to create a heaven on earth. You toiled day in and day out.

Yes, Adam is destined to eat his bread with the salt of his sweat. And bread leads to clothes, and clothes to shelter and shelter to everything else.

He worked round the clock. In the place of sweat it was now blood. He plodded and plodded on. What he earned, he kept it precious. He expected a better tomorrow... a day in which he can put an end to his toiling. He saved for a good day. He accumulated the gains of his hard work for a better future.

Well, he enjoyed life. There was music. There was dancing.

He tasted the sensuous pleasures of life. He loved everything beautiful. Human life became charming and enjoyable. Life became meaningful. Till the wind of jealousy blew.

Soon, fate takes up the reins. Thunder and lightning. Fire and sulphur fall from the heavens. And the earnings of your blood and sweat become food for the fire. Adam, here you have no choice. Just submit yourself to fate. Here you are compelled to admit that whatever you do is a sin and you are nothing but a mere sinner.

And then you run away from the place where you felt settled. You are not allowed even to look back at your earnings... the outcome of your labor. And suppose you turn back, you turn yourself into a salt pillar. Your pathetic plight becomes exactly the tragic fate of Lot's wife.

Man is a salt-pillar! Yes, just a pillar of salt! A salt-pillar that melts and vanishes into naught by the culmination of Time.

Aeons take birth and decay. Ages burn to ashes. But, oh Man, only your existence is unchangeable and eternal.

And when you shift yourself into 'I'.

There's the howling of the blood-thirsty jackals. There are the bell-beats of the flesh-hungry vultures. And they are the only sounds of truth that continuously echo in my ears.

And behind me Sodom and Gomorrah burn down to ashes. The wealth that I earned through toiling day and night. The fame that I gained through the sacrifice of my blood and sweat, my flesh and marrow. And for what? Just I looked back upon them and that's all! The biggest sin that I ever had committed. And I have to undergo the punishment for that sin through out the course of my life.

And I grope for something in the darkness of ignorance as if I were in a sort of strange somnambulism. And as I breathe the stench of the decaying era that storms in like a mad woman.

The wrath of Nature shakes me head to foot. Thunder and lightning shock my very being. Winds and rains arouse tremors in my heart. The light and blaze and the snow and fog exhaust my body.

And every moment, I am melting and melting down. The dead-sea raises heavy waves at my feet. And the never-ending sobs of my soul dissolve into those waves. The eternal salinity dissolved in the drops of my blood, sweat and tears arouse ripples in the dead-sea.

Ahead of me, there's the unending vacuity. And what guides me is just the mirage of desire. And behind me, my Sodom and Gomorrah, everything, is burning and burning into mere ashes.

Yes, that's the fate of a salt-pillar... to be melted into nothingness. Some day, you have to face it, Adam. That's inevitable.

Adam, leave everything. Leave your wife, your children, your relatives, your animals and all your belongings. It's all mere repetition of history. If you were daring enough to leave the Garden of Eden, why not this Sodom and Gomorrah? You have that courage to face adverse situations. You have that power of creativity. You have the ability to create everything out of nothing.

Hey, bird Phoenix! Can you fly up from the ash of your own pyre? Can you? Can you?

You are blessed to grow into a great people. You have to spread yourself all over the earth like the stars in the heaven, like the sand on the seashore. Go forward with whatever you have. You have enemies around you. But all your enemies will fall before your determination and tolerance. Don't feel desperate. Don't be dejected. Be optimistic. At least you have your hat to throw at your enemy. Or you can cry aloud, and at your voice the whole forts of impediments will crumble down.

Adam, you are not alone! There are many others like you. We have nothing to lose but our chains. Come on my people. For we stand on the threshold of victory.

In between them and us...

There stands a big wall between them and us. We live on this side of the wall and them on the other.

And we...

We have reached up to this place, breaking the yoke of slavery and shaking away the iron shackles of bondage. Yes! Here, at last, on this border of the Promised Land, we have arrived passing mountains and deserts, crossing thick forests and wide rivers. Though we are very tired after the long journey, the fact that we are approaching our destination consoles us.

We are weak, we are destitute. We are too behind them in number and power, in wealth and health. We, who live in the old and tattered tents, eat our ordinary food from our broken vessels, though it is insufficient even to silence our hunger. We have with us not even sufficient food or clothing, yet what guides us is the clear awareness of our aims, and what stirs our enthusiasm is the consciousness of our rights.

Behind us, a black age of bondage has come to an end. And now it is time for us to breathe the fresh air of freedom. But for us, who have freed ourselves from slavery, true freedom is still a dream. For, those things which are promised for us are enjoyed only by them and not by us.

And they...

They, living in big mansions and ivory towers, eat delicious food from gold vessels and silver utensils. They drink and dance, eat and enjoy. They drink life to the dregs in their intoxication of wealth and luxury. They find delight in arrogance and in acts of appalling atrocity. And their laughter echoes from all directions.

They are far ahead of us in everything. Nobody can defeat them in number and power or in wealth and health. They do not have even the slightest idea that what they enjoy is just what was promised for us. They enjoy their life with their rights devoid of their obligations.

And there is this big wall in between them and us. A heaven touching stone wall which nobody can destroy. The wall separates the rich from the poor. The wall that stands in between the rulers and the ruled. The wall that divides the happiest from the most desperate. The stone wall that separates the powerful ones from the weaklings.

On this side of the wall we, who live in tents and on the other side they who live in palaces. On one side, we the weaponless and on the other the well-equipped stalwarts. Here we suffocate ourselves in the climax of helplessness. Our hearts shiver with pain and tremble with fear. And where is that Canaan, the land where milk and honey flow, promised for us? Oh, where?

It is high time that this stone wall that stands high in front of us should be crushed. We cannot wait so long. We have been exhausted by laziness and fear of failure. We have to unite in full optimism to fight against the cruelty of fate. If we wake up, even the strongest enemy will throw his gloves down.

But all our attempts fail miserably. Our battles cause much loss of life and property. Yet remember, we have the Ark of the Covenant with us. We'll carry it on our shoulders wherever we go. We will walk around this wall of Jericho with cries of victory and shouts of joy.

Our slogans and jeers of victory will arouse a tremor in the atmosphere. We will raise our fists and hit in the air with a renewed enthusiasm. We will walk around this wall blowing our horns and beating our drums. As we walk systematically, in well-disciplined manner our voice will break these black stones of the wall. It will loosen the stones from their joints. And the big wall will crumble down, its stones will fall one after another and be scattered, leaving not even a stone on another stone.

And thus we will regain all our rights. We will occupy the Promised Land. Then we will experience true freedom.

Come, brothers! It's time! Let's go forward with firm steps. Our steps should not tumble on obstacles. Let's be systematic. Let's march forward... forward.

There are obstacles and impediments on your way, Adam. Life is not so simple, as you know, Adam. When you overcome one obstacle, another one comes up. Life is a desert and you have to cross that desert. There will not be any drop of water with you. The oasis you see at a distance turns to be mere mirage. You waddle in the hot sand. You drag and pull your legs to the top of the sand dunes in the expectation of seeing a spring in the desert.

At last, when you find a pond of water, what rapture! You think that your life once again acquired some meaning. You feel as if you conquered the whole world. You rush towards the pond and take the cool water in your palms and raise it to your lips.

And then... all of a sudden, you realize that the water is not good for drinking... it tastes bitter. That's your fate, Adam. You are like one amongst those poor people who came from Misra, the Gift of the Nile.

Yes, I am coming from Misra, the Land of the Nile.

There...

What I breathed was the stench of hard slavery. What fell on my burning bruises and throbbing sores were the flogs of power. The red-hot iron-pikes of black-faced edicts pierced my ears.

And I was wasting all my youthful energy there, in the

decay of aeons.

My blood was oozing out. Each drop of my blood solidified in itself and turned into blocks and tiles. Pyramids were erected on my back bone, the pyramids built with my own bones.

On my neck, there was the heavy yoke that increased its weight moment after moment. And the gold capped rulers who drew out even my last drop of blood did not care to give me even water to quench my thirst. I drank my own tears; I swallowed my pain.

Bubbles and foam filled up in my mouth. On my head, there was the burden of bondage. House flies swarmed onto my wounds. They licked the puss off my sores.

The kiln was burning in the eyes of the rulers. I was burning in the flames of those kilns. Whips tangled in the joints of my bones. And my bread was withering in the hot winds that rose up from the Nile.

My sunken eyes scaled the canopy of heaven. Around me the legendary hornbills which could drink water only when the rain fell, cackled aloud. My charred lips trembled, my throat chocked with meaningless words, my dried tongue tumbled on weak sounds and my wrinkled muscles yearned to vibrate.

And then... the pyramids quaked at my voice. Inside them, the dead bodies of the rotten ages turned pale and ghastly. They were transformed into mummies for the use of the future scholars. And I shook away my yoke.

I walked... walked on with firm steps. In my brain there was the column of cloud and in my heart there was the column of fire. I walked on and on.

And I am going to Canaan... the Promised Land.

There...

For me the honeybees let their honey flow for me; the cows fill their udders with milk. Olive trees spread their cool shades for me; and on their branches, birds roost and shower songs for me. Fig fruits look for baskets and lyres for fingers.

Around me, the cedars exhale fragrance and the oaks discharge cool shades. Esop plants ready to purify me and herbs to heal my wounds. Syth oil for my head and fragrants for my body. And to caress me the cool breeze from the Jordan. For my hand the silver scepter and for my head the golden crown.

And I walked on... walked on with firm steps. There is the flame of hope in my eyes; there is the smile of freedom on my lips. There is the cloud-column of faith in my brain and the fire-column of solace in my heart. I walked on and on.

But now... I am wandering on the banks of Marrah. Here...

Above my head, the frightening shadows of the palm trees that grow on the bitter-water of Marrah. Around me, the irritating wind that carries the vapor from the bitter-water of Marrah. And at my feet, the black waves of bitterness beat incessantly.

I am thirsty. Around me, Horn-bills, the legendary birds of unquenchable thirst, cackle in agony. My heart yearns for an odd drop of water. I wander, I feel completely exhausted.

Around me, only the vacant deserts. My paths are wiped away by the storms. And what beckons me from the endlessness of life is just the wavy mirage of an oasis.

I am waiting. There is the column of cloud in my brain; and there is the column of fire in my heart. I am waiting... waiting and waiting for that auspicious day in which the bitter-tasting water of the Marrah is changed into sweet.

Raise your staff, Adam, and beat the water of Marrah. Think of your forefather Moses. Abracadabra! Let the water change itself into honey... into sweet wine.

Adam, you are a fool! You always wait for the impossible. You wait for the moment in which the taste of bitterness is changed into the taste of sweetness. When human life in itself is bitter, how can you expect sweetness from its surroundings?

You wait for miracles to happen. You expect the arrival of a miracle merchant. You are not getting any sort of help from anybody. Because all others are just like you. They too expect a savior in their utter helplessness.

The hope of the arrival of a savior is a consoling matter. Even in the midst of despair, when all your efforts turn futile, when all your hard work changes into piles of dust and ash, when your dreams shatter down having no stone upon another stone, this expectation consoles you. It encourages you.

Adam, let's all wait for the savior. A miracle merchant, who can change water into wine, stones into bread, snakes into fish and scorpions into eggs. Let's all wait.

Yes, we all are waiting...

We wait and wait for that great day of the wonderful star's appearance to mark the birth of a new heaven and a new earth.

As the dreams given for us and the wisdom gained by us twined into a unique oneness, we are waiting with our frankincense, our gold and our myrrh, the outcome of our toiling and the products of our blood and sweat.

Our eyes, looking towards the fulfillment of the words of prophets that survived the test of time, have become myopic. As they scale the skies that spread from horizon to horizon, our necks have swollen with pain. Why, oh why don't you appear, dear wonder-star?

On the basis of our acquired knowledge, we make calculations and analyze the zodiac. In accordance with our statistics and laws based on certain vague evidence and symptoms, the time is over for the birth of a savior. Are the calculations of the highly intelligent turning into mere miscalculations?

We don't know how long we should continue our waiting. Why do you test us, oh you great star-to-be-risen up in the sky as a sign of redemption? Why don't you realize the truth that the more you delay your appearance, the deeper we slip and fall into the pit of despair?

Our individuality is withered in the intensity of waiting. Yet we wait individually on these mountains, in these planes and in these deserts, for the appearance of the wonder-star.

I wait on this mountain top. And as these peaceful, delightful mountains wait together with me...

Silver clouds pass these mountains, caressing their snow-capped peaks. A gentle breeze decorates these flowered woods with the ornaments of rapture. And the chill wind that blows from the snow-mounts sings an eerie song in the valleys.

Hills are appareled in green gowns to greet the savior. Cedars and frankincense trees spread fragrance. The sweet smell of the wild flowers has filled the whole atmosphere.

But...

Is there no use for my waiting? Did my calculations go wrong? Why should the rising of the wonder-star in the horizon as a sign of salvation be delayed?

My body trembles in the frozen winds that come from the mountains. My tangled beard too has turned frozen and has been looking like dried twigs. And my eyes, looking for the rising of the wonder-star, have exhausted of their powers.

My hut, facing all the rains and the snow, has fallen down and become useless. And the frankincense which I have been keeping in the casket, in order to be offered to the savior, is spoiled by fungus.

Yet...

Still my eyes scale the heavens for the wonder-star. My heart yearns for the sight of the savior's face. And outside my hut my camel scratches among the stones with its legs in utter restlessness.

Oh dear wonder-star! Why do you delay yourself to rise

up?

I wait on this fertile land. As this peaceful and magnificent field waits together with me...

A cool breeze passes, caressing the healthy growing wheat plants. Black clouds stare at those fields lying ready for harvest. Crystalline streams flow giggling and jingling. Birds fly away in the tune and rhythm of the west wind. And Nature feels thrilled in their chirping and chattering.

Fields are appareled in their golden gowns to greet the savior. Trees and plants stand with their heads bowed with the heaviness of fruits. And the delicious fragrances of various fruits linger everywhere in the atmosphere.

But...

Does my long waiting turn fruitless? Does my calculation go wrong? Why does the rising of the star in the horizon as a sign of the salvation delay so much?

My body sweats in the humid wind. Each long hair on my chin has turned into decayed stalks of hay. My eyes, waiting for the rise of the wonder-star, have lost their brightness.

Suffering all the tempests and rains, my house has been in a dilapidated condition. The gold which I have been keeping all these days in the box in order to be offered to the savior, has spoilt by oxidization and corrosion.

Yet...

My eyes still scale the heavens for the rising of the wonder-star. My mind longs to have a vision of that savior's face. And outside the house, my camel scratches in the mud with its legs, in complete helplessness.

And why, my dearest wonder-star, why do you delay yourself to rise up?

I am waiting in this desert. As these glorious and peaceful sands wait together with me.

Fire-hot wind, sweeping over the desert, blows towards its

unknown destination. Red clouds have begun to roost on the palm trees. The granules of sand, flying up in the power of storm, whistle continuously. And the cacti restlessly wait listening to that music of the winds.

The desert is appareled in the silvery gown in order to greet the savior. Bunches of date-fruits shower honey. And the oases accumulate coolness.

But...

Does my waiting have no use at all? Did my calculation go wrong somewhere? Why does the wonder-star still delay to rise up as a sign of salvation?

In these blistering winds my body appears to be dried and scarred. My long beard has lost its softness and become as dry as palm-fiber. And the light in my eyes that waited for the rise of the wonder-star had dimmed.

My tent, undergoing the tortures of heavy fog and severe sunlight has rotted into an unsuitable abode. The myrrh which I have been keeping in a vase in order to be offered to the savior has rotten with fungus in the passage of time.

Yet...

Still my eyes roam in the horizon looking for that wonder-star. My heart yearns for the sight of the savior's face. Outside the tent, my camel scratches in the sand in utter restlessness. Oh, my darling wonder-star! Why do you still delay to rise up?

We are all waiting...

We wait consistently for that great day on which that wonder-star will rise, marking the birth of a new heaven and a new earth.

But...

What fragrance is there for our frankincense when we all drown into the depth of despair? What value is for our gold when all our castles in the air crumble down, one after another? What quality is there for our myrrh when we wander in the mirage of dreams?

Things that must happen will happen in the ripeness of time. Then, what significance is there for our wisdom? Wisdom only suggests the way while it is the fate that leads to the end. When the mind and the body try to hop up towards the accomplishment of desires, wisdom compels to wait patiently.

These mountains and these fields and these deserts strangle us day after day. We feel exhausted of our frankincense and of our gold and of our myrrh. And our camels continuously scratch among the stones, in the mud and in the sands in utter helplessness.

Yet...

We have to wait. The faith aroused in us by wisdom, gives us the strength to wait. And we are waiting...

We continue our waiting for the rise of that wonder-star at the ripeness of time as a sign of salvation.

Endless waiting. That's my fate. And my fate is the fate of all human beings. We wait and wait but without any use. We wait for a savior, a promised one. Perhaps we wait for a savior who will never take birth.

In the course of our waiting, we are paralyzed top to bottom. We are bed-ridden. And so we must get a savior to lift us up from our present plight. But the pity is that we don't see even a small sign to mark his arrival. But still we wait, as for us there is no other option.

Adam, you have patience to wait. You have tolerance to suffer. But remember this... all these years you have been thinking about you and you alone. How selfish you have been. You have been thinking that your birth is a mission. You forgot that everybody's birth is a mission at large, big or small. You expect only individual salvation. What about others, Adam? What about a sort of mass salvation?

Adam, you have no existence as an individual. You are part

of the society and your existence is marked only in the presence of others. Look around you. Feel yourself as one among them. The success of human life depends on the fullness of ones personality... this fullness of personality depends solely on your co-existence amongst others. Victory comes when you are involved actively and sincerely.

Don't be an introvert, Adam. The individual and the society is not a dichotomy. They are complementary. The significance of 'Vyashti' evolves from the harmony of 'Samashti'. You have been thinking only about your birth, childhood and youth. You passed those stages in perfect harmony with Nature. You obeyed your parents and they loved you. You were inquisitive during your childhood and tried to acquire as much knowledge as possible.

You strictly followed the Law of Brahmacharya, the celibacy. Its strict practice in adolescence will help you to have a healthy and lengthier sexual life in the years to come. Now you move towards another stage in your life. Now, Adam... it's time for you to have a better understanding of human life. All these years you did not care about the lighter side of human life. You forgot that life is full of tears for those who feel and full of laughter for those who think.

Therefore be relaxed. Be optimistic and be happy. Try to pick up the granules of happiness lying scattered on your wearisome way which often others used to overlook, and gather them so that you will be blessed at the end of your journey.

Yes, Adam Junior, break the chrysalis and come out! You have been living like a worm, a caterpillar. Now, Adam, break the cocoon shell and come out like a butterfly. Here's the vast world spread before you. It's yours, Adam, it's all yours!

PART II

It's all just like another birth...

Once again with the force of a flood, I slipped out of the darkness of loneliness into the dazzling light of the crowd. Breaking the chrysalis of indigenous individuality, I stepped into a world of variety and diversity.

Perhaps, it's all the game of Nature! You feel the monotony of childhood and yearn for something more to add to your life. You thirst for novel experiences; your body urges you to move forward. Then...

The pupa hesitates and holds for a moment. Then the cocoon breaks... the butterfly comes out shaking away its inertia of a long age. There's a stupor for a few seconds... then comes a sort of realization or enlightenment, and suddenly you drop down and down and become a part of the crowd... like a drop of water amalgamating into the vast ocean. It's really a second birth... from the solitude of the mother's womb into the crowd of the world. There is no more individual identity. You understand that your entity cannot be separated from society's existence.

Like a rain-drop on the surface of the stagnant water in a pool, you stand for a split-moment in utter amazement. Soon you merge with the whole mass of water in the pool. For a second you think that you are something in the crowd! Suddenly you realize that you are nothing in this world. You are only a cog in a large machine. Nobody will notice your disappearance for a few days, or for many days, or for many weeks, or for months or forever.

Soon you begin to love this world. Your body becomes firm. Your mind acquires stability. Your five senses turn highly active. You begin to feel strange sensations. Your life gains a sort of real meaning. And your whole being realizes that wonderful truth... the inevitability of completeness.

You drop away the old skin of childhood. You are now passing through adolescence. Nobody is here to save or help you. You alone are responsible for your existence. You perish, if you are incapable of facing the realities of life. For only the fittest will survive here.

Now, think about the power of your head... the fish-head with which you broke the shell of the planet. Be courageous... be adventurous... be confident of your talents. Now, it's your turn... now or never!

Adam, all these years you waited for a savior. You and the people like you patiently waited. And what was the result? Of course saviors are in abundance, but every savior needs at least one follower! They came with fixed purpose but left us with incomplete missions.

So... you yourself are the savior here! You can do miracles! Think about the blessings of thrills. The divine sensation your mortal body gives. Can't you feel that heavenly thrill in every genuine movement or activity of your body?

When you blink your eyes... when you crack your knuckles... when you touch your lips with your own tongue... when you inhale fresh air... when you yawn... sneeze... cough... belch... fart! When you relieve yourself... by urinating... defecating... ejaculating... sweating! All give you thrills! The realization of its divine pleasure solely depends on your sensibility... that's all!

No more you are surprised at the strangeness of sounds and sights. Every sensation gives you divine pleasure. But Adam, be cautious! Think of history. Think of your inevitable fate. Don't forget yourself. Beware of the unexpected vortex. Once you are in, even God cannot save you! You will suffer the consequence. Then, there's no meaning in weeping and wailing afterwards. There's no meaning in blaming others or cursing yourself. Let your prudence lead you on... towards the real light of immortality.

Adam, you are pushed into the crowd. Don't look back! No more escape for you! It is the force of gravitation, the wonderful power that helps the co-existence of everything in this universe. The great force that promotes the mutual survival of every being. So be a part of it... learn from them. Their experience is your own experience. Bravo, Adam, or Adam Junior! Call yourself whatever you like.

Crowd! Crowd! Heavy crowd!

Rush and stampede! The milling throng of crazy human creatures. The multitude of human worms moving frantically in their efforts to survive. The teeming millions running helter-skelter and struggle amongst themselves each and every moment for their unique survival.

Every second private cars and taxi cabs fly along the roads like bullets. Every minute trucks, vans and buses roar along the streets. Every five minutes, electric trams and trains shake their tracks with their hooting and honks. And every fifteen minutes, airplanes fly in and fly out, creating an unbearable tremor in the air.

Heavy gatherings! Routs, rabbles and mobs! The infinite swarms of human beings. The ceaseless flow of vehicles. Rush and crush! Pushing and pulling! Hell of a heavy traffic jam!

Plazas and malls overflow with people. Taxi stands, bus stations and railway platforms are thickly packed with masses. Human beings like houseflies swarm over buses, trams and trains. They clutch to their sides and stick onto their tops. People milling in and out of shops, jostling each other.

No space to stand before the restaurants. No place to sit in the hotels. No rooms to stay in at the lodges. No place in the hospitals for the ailing patients to lie down. Even no space in temples, churches and mosques to stand and pray!

What a rush of human crowds! A generation which physically and mentally hastens for nothing. Gangs busy without business. Meetings and assemblies are summoned with no serious purpose. Crowding just for the sake of crowding.

And in the midst of these heavy crowds, I walked with short steps, lazing around the city, without any haste at all. I moved along the streets, keeping my hands in the pants-pockets as if looking for something at their bottoms. In fact, one of my hands was resting on the handkerchief in the left pocket and the other on the smallest coin in the right one.

Seeing a familiar person approaching me from the opposite side, I greeted him as in the usual manner: 'Hullo friend! How do you do?'

He whispered some inaudible words in reply and walked past me as if in a hurry. And I too resumed my slow pacing.

Suddenly, hearing a screech and a shriek, I turned back. Someone was rolling under a car, spreading hot blood around him. As I stood in a stupor, pedestrians hastily walked away, commenting with sympathy: 'Alas! What a smart youngman!

It's all fate! Just fate!'

A policeman, who rushed to the spot, waved his baton and cried: 'Move away! What the hell are you staring at? There's an accident! Well... ! What's in it for sight-seeing? It's a city and such things happen! Ay, Mister! Didn't I tell you to move away?'

I have to resume my tramping.

A middle aged woman with high heeled shoes, who was walking just ahead of me, stepped on a banana peel, slipped and fell down with a loud thump! The humanitarian instinct provoked me to extend my hands to help that mother of a woman to stand on her legs. She gripped on to my extended hand, stood up with difficulty, and then turned against me with a snarl and slapped my cheek! Pretending indignation, she cried aloud: 'You rascal! Excellent way you discovered to get hold of the hands of young ladies from good families! Hmm... and never will you come with such dirty tricks! Didn't you hear, you scoundrel?'

I stood quite embarrassed and looked sheepish. What reply should I give her? When she walked stomping away, making earthquakes with the heaviness of her buttocks, what else could I do but simply smile, looking at the dung of the stray temple-ox stuck onto her bottom?

Somebody familiar to me, patted on my shoulder and said, with a sinister smile: 'Dear Brother-in-law. It's a city, and that I agree too. But don't go for such dirty tricks during daylight!'

He walked away before I could reply. Caressing my swollen cheek, I too, slowly moved away.

A cigarette butt, thrown down through the window from the second floor of a building, made a hole in my shirt and burned my body! While I was caressing the burned part, the sharp corner of the iron box, carried by a head-loader hit against my head. While I was rubbing my head with unbearable pain, I heard that laborer say aloud: 'Well! Iron boxes will hit on the heads of people like you! Why can't you walk and watch the road? Oh, it'll be like that! That's the problem with all young men of your age! While walking, their eyes are on the girls who move on the other side of the road!'

Rubbing the swollen part of my head, I resumed my walk.

The betel juice, spat by a fat man who hurriedly walked away, shaking the folds of his fleshy belly, fell on my clothes. Not even a drop of his blood-colored spittle was wasted on the ground, but drew modern art paintings on my garments! Making sure that nobody was watching, I took my handkerchief and rubbed some of that artwork off my clothing.

I tried to walk away unnoticed, from that crazy swarm of human insects. Soon, a beautiful woman deliberately brushed the tip of her spear-like breast against me and walked past! Her new bridegroom, who was following her just behind, discovered the incident, turned to me and shouted: 'What the hell! You damn idiot! Don't you have eyes on your face?'

He was trying to show his mettle in front of his young wife. His wife, who knew the fact, pulled at his wrist and as they walked away, I heard her say to him, 'Don't be angry, darling. If he had no eyes, how could he select the most beautiful woman to touch?'

The new bridegroom nodded his head and said: 'Ah! Yes! Really! Why should we blame him? Anyone who meets you will naturally brush his body against you!'

As the couple walked away, laughing aloud, I too moved on with a pale face.

A cyclist who came by the wrong side of the road solved the brakeless-ness of his vehicle by hitting it against me. As I looked at him with severe pain, he roared, shaking the horns of his moustache: 'What's the matter? Should we, the poor laborers, go to prison on murder charges, just because you, the neatly dressed gentlemen have no sense of hearing?'

After uttering a few more obscene words, he cycled away. And I resumed my walk.

Yes, in the city, victory is for those who speak first. If I had showered vituperations at him immediately when the cycle had hit me, he would have begged for my pardon. Here, waiting for words, is equivalent to confessing one's crimes!

Here, everybody runs crazily for some reason or the other. Nobody wastes even a second. In fact, they run here and there without any real business at all. But it is consoling that everybody does his work as neatly as possible, within the short period of time available to them.

And the intense rush is increasing moment after moment. Everywhere there are notice boards: Q-Please! There are long queues in the bus-stands and in the railway stations. Very long queues in the hospitals and in the cinema houses. Wherever you look, there is a queue... queue... and queue!

Still there is no decrease in the rush. All through the twenty-four hours of the day, the rush and crowds continue.

Crowd! Crowd! Heavy crowds!

Rush! Rush! Intense rush!

And feeling quite lonely in the midst of these crowds... being uncared of by these crowds... with seldom haste... I walked on and on.

Still you feel lonely. How funny it is. How can you be alone in this heavy crowd? Adam, be clever! You can be as innocent as a dove. But you must be as intelligent as a snake. Then only can you survive. This world is for snakes!

Be ready to face realities. Apply all your senses. Adjust them to your surroundings. Try to be familiar with the crowd. Absorb yourself into the features of the crowd. Try to enjoy the sight. Try to enjoy the touch. Try to enjoy the taste. Try to enjoy the sound. And try to enjoy the smell.

Adam it's your fate! Pass your days inhaling the bad smells emitting from the gutters of the world... of human life.

Stench! Odor! Bad smells everywhere! How horrible is the bondage of the sense of smell?

No! One can't bear this stench any more. One should escape from this hell of smells as early as possible.

The piercing odor of the sweat of human creatures that lie jammed in the cellar-like-rooms. The stench that comes out of the mouths of those who sleep like wooden logs and snore away the heaviness of their day's labor. The nauseating smell of their exhaled breaths hangs about the room.

The broken walls emit the odor of old plaster, and the roof stained by beer and cigarette smoke emits the stench of nicotine.

The alkaline-smell from the droppings of crows is piercing the nose. It's already morning. Endless steam is rising up from the 'morning products' left on the roadsides by the street urchins. The stench of the street-cleaners who move away with their stinking buckets and brooms. The rotten smell spread by the municipality trucks that ply hurriedly along the streets.

Oh! Yes! Today is the day for rest! This means one has to stay chained to this stench for the whole day. Wearing the dress that smelt detergent, chlorine and ultramarine, I came out of the room and walked along the street.

With a spade, a sweeper of the city was taking out all the decayed waste-foods and decomposed garbage from the municipality zinc-tank kept by the side of the road. He caught the leg of a dead dog's decomposed carcass and hurled it into the garbage van. The laborer was so indifferent to the smell of the carcass that I asked him anxiously: 'How could you bear this fetid odor?'

He raised his head and looked at me. I stared at him as he began to laugh aloud. There was an unhealed sore on his nose.

Worms were struggling out of his nostrils! And slowly I walked away.

What? Do the premises of the holy Hindu temple of the city emit the smell of human feces? Surprising! It's all the work of some goblins or urchin-demons! Yes, hurry up! Wash your bottoms in the holy water of the temple-pond! Chant the Vedas! Repeat the mantras! Tamso ma jyothir gamaya... Durgandho ma sugandh gamaya... Oh, God! Lead us from darkness to light; from stench to fragrance!

There is a strong desire to repeat the chant a bit more loudly. But there was the horrible odor of sweat that comes from those who stand around. The stench that comes from the mouths of my temple-folks. And the smell of burning camphor and incense-sticks dilutes and melts into nothingness. And I quietly slipped away.

The richest man of the city or the so-called pillar of society was approaching, keeping his nose closed with his fingers. He murmured aloud and expressed his disgust at the concerned government officials who did not care to sprinkle perfumes all over the city with the help of helicopters. He barked: 'Oh! How could you bear this stench?'

I raised my head and looked at his face and I couldn't help but laugh aloud. He stared at me in confusion. There were sores from diabetes on his fingers with which he pressed his nose. Puss was oozing out of those stinking sores and houseflies laid their eggs on those unhealed wounds! I walked away slowly.

What? Do the walls of the holy Christian church of the city emit the smell of human urine? Miracle! If it is not the work of Satan, what else is this? And the courtyard of the church smells of raw-flesh and white-meat! Priests and laymen! Pray aloud! 'Our Father Who art in heaven...'

'Hallowed be thy city! Thy fragrances come! Thy perfume

will be spread on earth as it is in heaven! Give us this day our daily scent! Help us to bear our stench as we bear the stench of our neighbors! Deliver us from stench. For thine is the city, the stench and the fragrance, for ever and ever, Amen!'

There is the strong desire to pray a bit more loudly. But the odor of sweat coming from those who stand nearby is unbearable. How nasty is the smell that comes from the mouths of these poor believers. The fragrance of the frankincense-smoke seems to be dissolved in other bad smells. I walked away.

Here comes a member of the so-called intelligentsia of the city, quite unaware of the horrible waves of stench that beat in the atmosphere. Watching his indifference I began to laugh aloud. He raised his head and stared at me. I asked him: 'How could you bear this stench?'

Now it was his turn! He laughed louder than I and extended his hand towards me. In his palm I saw a small tablet. I took it from his hand with great reverence and wonder.

As he walked away, arrogantly and carelessly, I looked around timidly and quickly swallowed the tablet, with all the sanctity of taking the Holy Communion. Two minutes passed and I began to jump up and down like a child in uncontrollable happiness.

At last, I have lost my sense of smell for ever. What an experience! How happy and cheerful I am. I am freed from the shackles of all bad smells. A moment of thrill and pleasure! No more am I a slave to the odors of the world. No more does the stench of the city benumb my body, life and spirit.

Holding my head high I walked along the crowded streets of the city.

That much is good! Adam, life is wonderful! You know how to learn things! Go on, Adam! It's your time.

But Adam, do you think that you won the race and received

the crown? Do you think that you bagged the final emancipation for which you desired so long?

It is very easy to find solutions to all your problems... especially once you are in the city. The solutions may be a bit cruel or just temporary. But who cares much for tomorrow? Tranquilizers may help you to forget everything. Tablets may help you to relieve you of all the smells. But for how long? Can you escape so easily, so carelessly like that? You move from one smell to another, from one place to another and from one crowd to another. And you are quite helpless while facing similar other situations.

Are you tired of the crowd, Adam? Be busy! Engage yourself in some or other activity so that you won't think much about adverse circumstances. Once you are so busily engaged, everything will be alright. You won't get time to escape. Of course, unless you are incapable of performing your duties.

The instinctive inertia haunts you. You think only about yourself. About your drawbacks, inconveniences and illnesses. Adam, don't give too much importance to your own interests or disgusts. Relax for a while, if necessary, and regain the societal way.

There was a time when life was so busy that it seemed the so-called twenty-four hours of the day was insufficient. At times, it was necessary to escape from that busy schedule, forgetting all about the busyness imposed by oneself in the expectation of making life a bit more successful. But one would be too late in realizing the fact that both busy and non-busy life were one and the same, and everything was part of that great 'vanity' as suggested by Solomon the Wise.

When doctors advise complete bed rest one is naturally forced to change his busy routine and to accept an inactive way of life. After a few days of such an ascetic life one would feel disgust towards the busy life which one had been undergoing, and would love to become a hermit or a wanderer. You might go to the mountain ranges or to the deserts or to the sea shore. But memories of the previous world would haunt and one cannot escape completely from them or most probably one would be tempted and, fallen victim to the worldly man's lot! No man can escape from temptations, even if he is Adam himself.

Go to the beach, Adam. Converse with the waves, the only true and faithful friends you would, perhaps, get here in this world.

And he reached the beach just to pass time. Sitting on the white sugar-like sand, he unbuttoned the neck of his guru-kurta and felt the coolness of the salty sea-breeze. The distant wailings of the seagulls dissolved in the roar of the waves. Crabs were building their hideouts in the wet sand. Exhausted waves dragged themselves to the shore and licked away the footprints of children, the footprints deliberately left by the children to tease Mother Sea. The footprints that were clearly etched on the black sand and illuminated by the rays of the setting sun.

'Time-pass peanuts… Brother, Sir! Time-pass peanuts… '

From the wooden tray that was hung on the neck, the chena-mungbali boy measured out some fried ground-nuts into a paper cone, and after sprinkling some lemon juice and masala-powder onto it, extended it towards each idler.

'No! Don't want your bloody time-pass!'

He turned his face away from the boy in utter disgust. And the boy, a bit surprised, moved towards the next person.

'Get lost! With your nuts!' Crushing a handful of white sand of the beach in uncontrollable indignation, he whispered harshly and threw it away onto the face of the laughing sea.

People come to the beach, either individually or in groups, to pass time. They pass time smoking and laughing aloud. If only time passed... whatsoever the way. If only one could find some means to pass time.

'Come and buy, brothers! Here's time-pass cashew nut!'

Munching a few cashew nuts, as if he could not resist the temptation, the old man was howling.

In order to pass time, some of the idlers buy cashew nuts or peanuts. Many of them prefer groundnuts to cashew nuts as the former helps better to pass time. Take each ground nut very slowly, break the shell, keep the hard shells away, remove the brown rind, enjoy the beauty of the white nut, chew each nut for ten minutes, appreciating the taste fully and then swallow the pulp. One peanut helps one to pass at least fifteen minutes. Hours are taken to munch a few peanuts in a thin paper cone. One has to pass time, whatsoever.

'Hey, Sir! Just for time-pass!' A toothless old woman is extending a half-burned, tender maize-cone. From the charred, hanging lips of the hag, betel juice is dripping down. She too, realizing her customer's mood, moved away without wasting her valuable time.

Sunset is at the threshold. The red face of the evening has turned burnt-ember and black. Many of the idlers are preparing to leave the beach.

A child of eight or ten years, with round and protruded eyes and running nose, a blob of sputum hanging on his upper lip, approaches. With one hand he prevents his button-less knickers from slipping down and with the other shows that secret signal. A circle formed with the forefinger touching on the thumb, the 'popular' secret sign of the red street. With much hesitation, he asked in a lowered voice, 'Do you want, brother Sir? Just for time-pass... '

'Shit!' Spitting in disgust, he stands up and walks away to a deserted part of the beach. The round-eyed pimp-urchin moves away looking for the next person. Still anybody can hear the howling of the vendor boy: 'Buy and eat, brothers, Sirs! Time pass peanuts! Just for time-pass... '

Alas, Adam Junior! You wasted a day! In your age, how could one realize the real length of a day? Such evenings are wasted forever. But with every human being, there is a period in which he finds no means to pass time. There is also a period in which he finds time quite insufficient. And life goes on like that, hearing the cries and seeing the signs of those who help others to pass time or those who hate to pass time.

Such evenings are not wasted, at times. One can utilize them by employing the power of imagination. Adam, what about you? Evenings with the setting sun burning like an ember at the western horizon where the sun touches the sea... and the fire of the sun spreads on the sea and fast approaches the beach full of idlers, or people too restless to pass time.

No! The sunset is not yet over! Sitting on the beach, you relax yourself by watching the setting sun. Once you forget everything, a sense of relief comes to you. Your eyes are fixed somewhere in the vacuity of the universe; you see nothing but only feel everything.

Waves, the thirsty lips of the sea, suck at the shore. Anklets of silver-foam are placed at the feet of the bride-earth. The beach is fresh with white, sugar like sand. And the sea appears to be telling thousands of stories to the people gathered on the beach.

The people who are different in every way. They belong to different age groups. They are of different races, colors, nationalities, languages and religions. They vary in their dress, professions and profiles. They differ in their caliber; some are educated, others illiterate, some are rich, others poor; some are fools, others wise; some are cowards, others valiant.

And the crowd thickens on the beach every moment. A noisy world of passions expressed on one side; a silent world of feelings suppressed, on the other.

Giggling and laughing; hissing and sobbing. Flirting, caressing, kissing, embracing and slapping each other to express their emotions. Tears of happiness and tears of sorrow. Relationships are tightened or loosened. People greet, talk, smile and sigh. And the smell of the beach? Is it the fragrance of fresh love? Or is it the odor of rotten sex?

The charred lips of the sky yearn for the wet lips of the sea. The sea, like a bride, kisses the sky only to make her face blush in delicacy. Clouds, like the bride's maids-in-waiting, carry the rustling gown that trails behind. Waves rise up like the heartbeats of newly wedded couples.

The roaring waves, the giggling wavelets and the smiling ripples of the sea. The land and the sea play hide and seek. Bubbles disappear like aborted fetuses. The Mother Sea kisses on the tear stained cheeks of the bank. The horizon raises the silk curtain for the bride and the bridegroom. Heartbeats, pulses and waves! The seaweed, like the locks of the bride, is tossed in the gentle breeze. The face of the sea turns ruddy in the even tide. And the dancing of the maids; of the clouds in the sky and the foams in the sea.

The breeze, like a thief, is trying to steal the charm of the evening. Evening has started her embroidery work with her cold needle. The rare joy that one gets only during dawn or dusk spreads everywhere.

The smell of the beach! The saline wind carries the smell of nicotine and cheap perfumes. The horrid smell of voluptuous men and wayward women. The smell of dried fish and decomposed crabs. To forget the fever and fret of life they come to this beach. Here they forget themselves in the acrid stench of life.

Black clouds cover the face of the eastern horizon. Like the wild elephants, they move away in herds trumpeting. But on the western horizon, glittering clouds still play with colors. The clouds are ready to bid farewell to their master. The sun burning in passion hurries to go to sleep with his bride. Like the last flame of a dying lamp, the sun blazes.

All eyes are fixed on the setting sun. All breathing stops! For a moment the sun rests his face on the heaving breasts of the sea. The sun and the sea sigh for a while and their sighs spread like gentle breezes. The tired sun looks deep into the eyes of the sea. The sea falls into the arms of the sun, as if quite exhausted from waiting so long.

For a moment, the sun disappears and the sea burns like the sun. Water gets the fire from the burning sun. Water dances in the fire and the waves carry the fire to the shore. The water level rises up and huge waves of fire beat the shore. Tongues of fire begin to lick the beach.

People run in utter confusion and panic! Gone are the differences of race, class, nationality, language and religion. All engage only in the single action of escape, escaping from the inevitable doom!

The fire creeps up and up to the strand. The white sand on the beach turns red and yellow, into solid fire, into the lava of some erupted volcano. The whirls of fire consume everything. Only the fittest will survive!

Time passed... the wheel of time rolled on and on... soon everything becomes calm and quiet. The fragrance of a cool breeze begins to blow. The breath of a lovely flower. The smile of some lovely angels. The rays of a new sun of love and peace. The song of an unknown fairy spreads everywhere.

Everything happened all of a sudden! The whole world underwent a change! The birth of a new heaven and a new earth. Does it mark a return to the old Garden of Eden? Or is it merely a reverie? A mere dream that ought to be realized?

Suddenly everything turns calm and peaceful. The voice of

peace resounds. The rays of happiness come into my thoughtful mind. The pensive mood gives way to cheerfulness. All evils are burnt to ashes. The entirety of wickedness has vanished. And now virtue wakes up with a new life. A world of good and virtuous people. A new lamp is lit and the world is filled with its light! A new flag of universal love and peace is hoisted and it flutters from the flag-post!

A gentle breeze begins to blow, carrying the smell of sandal woods. From the heavens, the waves of a new song usher in. It is the voice of love; it is the voice of peace. And I am immersed in the beauty of that thrilling moment.

There is coolness in my heart. Everything seems alright. Nothing to worry about. The beach is deserted. People have gone back with full relief. Many have to resume their duty. The world will go on like this for ever. One cannot escape so easily like that.

Adam, how cruel you are! You want immediate solutions to everything. Don't be so self-assertive! Don't think that the world should go according to your wishes. Variety is the keyword for this world's existence. You can't change it.

Don't be in a hurry! Don't be excited! Everything will turn out alright with the passage of time. You still try to escape from the reality of this world. Something troubles you! What is it, Adam?

You are so impatient, so restless. You move like a madman. You feel incapable of facing this world of tragic realities. Every day you face tragic scenes. Every newspaper brings you heartbreaking tidings. Oh Adam! A man with a heart cannot live here. Or your heart should turn into stone. Be a normal human being. Or others will throw stones at you; treat you as if you are mad. Who is there to hear the cries of your heart? 'Oh, I'm not mad; I'm not mad... '

Please do not think of me as a madman or as a fool when I

search here and there for a heart of stone for mutual exchange. Believe me, I continue my search because I am fully conscious of my difficulty to exist among the members of my own species with an ordinary heart that feels and even, at times, thinks.

You may say that the heart is only a blood pumping component in the highly complicated machinery of an animal body. But for a man of intellect and emotion the case is quite different. To such a human being the heart stands for the very existence of the so-called human species. Once a man loses his heart, his capacity to think and feel, he is no more a man but only a member of the various other species of the vast animal kingdom.

Whether or not human life is a tale told by an idiot, I think the above description of the human heart will be a prologue to it. Many a time I wish my heart was turned into a stone or is substituted by a stony heart, so that I could live without thinking and feeling. Please do not blame me for I always find difficulty in surviving the heavy blows of the inevitable fate that befall my life.

For instance, the unexpected death of a dear relative, especially in his or her prime, numbs my heart. It throbs again only to become silent once more at the death of another relative. I usually recite the poem 'Death be not proud', but the truth that such dear relatives vanish forever brings me back to the reality that death always leaves a permanent gap in human life. If my heart turns to stone, a piece of granite, I, with such a hard and solid heart, will never feel any such vacuum.

I have no more tears to shed, for my eyes have turned pebbles seeing many horrible sights with the passage of time. Now-a-days, I am not even hearing any tragic news as my ears have turned into stone-plates. Nor these days, do I feel the smell of death. My five senses are more or less dead like stones. And my heart still throbs like a sixth sense of which, these days, I am worried about.

The newspapers daily arrive with hundreds and thousands of stories of rapes and murders, suicides and genocides. The radio announces news of international deaths and the television projects scenes of national deaths. One cannot walk even a pace without seeing or hearing such hair-raising and heart-numbing incidents. Here, I wish my heart was turned to stone or was replaced by a stony one.

Happy are those who live in our midst like statues of bronze and marble for they look but never see and they hear but never listen. While I stand before such statues, I beg them like a madman to lend me their hearts for a transplant but always they deny as they wish to continue their existence among the human species whose hearts still beat.

I think that all of us lost forever that ancient spirit of mutual respect and tolerance that existed amongst us for the survival of our own species. Instead, we have accepted the barbarian spirit of the cannibals. Man is a rational animal, says Ethics. If so, are these rapes and murders, these suicides and genocides, the signs of that rationalism? If the answer is affirmative, bravo! Double cheers to my co-existing members of the human species! Do carry on your rational activities! But let me first transplant my heart. And so, when I continue my search for a heart of stone, please do not call me a madman or a fool.

What a pity! Oh, Adam! How long can you go on in search of a heart of stone? Only fools and madmen expect that their hearts can be transplanted with stones. Therefore, try to adjust with this world.

Accept the fact that you once adjusted with the realities of life. There, at the Garden of Eden, you took a firm decision. You ate the forbidden fruit and walked out of the garden, holding the hand of your Eve! Of course, you lost the brightness of your eyes, then. That's why you fail to see facts as they come to you suddenly. But, remember, a day will come, when you can hail that lost brightness of your eyes.

Gone are the days when human beings watched this wonderful universe, especially this beautiful earth, with their shining eyes. Look into the eyes of the people around you, irrespective of their age, sex and creed. If you are one with sensibility and intelligence, you can see despair and pain stagnant in those eyes, and this truth will definitely move your conscience. Yes, somewhere in the evolution of the human species, we have lost the hopeful and happy eyes of our First Parents, Adam and Eve.

If children's eyes lose their brightness, it is evident that they are suffering from some illness. If the eyes of the aged lose their shine, it may be because of their long, weary life and of decrepitude. But when we see youth without a shine in their eyes, the causes, whether individual or social, may be fatal.

It is a pity that our eyes which are supposed to be the twinkling stars of our body, are no longer shining. Of course, they look but do not see and they watch but do not understand. They fail to absorb the rays of pleasure from nature; they fail to radiate the waves of rapture from the heart.

No longer do they serve our body as the pinpoints of light. They don't serve now as the mirrors of our hearts! Dark clouds move over them and a shade of gloom covers them. Look into their depths, and there, you can see only the stains of despair, grief and agony. Oh, what has happened to them? Where has their majestic glittering and glorious sparkling gone? Can the light give way to darkness?

Many a time, I thought about my eyes which God created from dust with His own hands. Like a true artist, God might have poured his soul into the eyes of his masterpiece. Those two pairs of eyes belonged to my ancestors, Adam and Eve might have been the most shining and powerful of all the eyes that ever looked at this marvelous earth. But, they too had lost their light when their possessors had been driven out of the Garden of Eden. Adam's eyes lost their shining due to the loss of Paradise and Eve's due to the Original Sin. And therefore, they and their successive generations could only regain the brightness of their eyes as and when they regain that lost Paradise.

Then various religions with different creeds and dogmas came forward as the God-anointed protectors of the shining eyes. Like the wayward quacks, they offered instant cures for the people who had lost the brightness of their eyes. In the midst of the tragic realities of life, they preached a life after death, full of happiness and satiety. They tried to keep up the spirit of the downtrodden masses by pointing out that suffering is ennobling. But, in the prolonged course of misery, the poor believers gained nothing save the darkness below their gloomy eyes!

When the people became dubious of a life after death, and when they began to think of Paradise as a castle in the air, they completely lost whatever was left as brightness in their eyes. In a desperate attempt to save their eyes from utter darkness, sages and philosophers pointed out that ambition was the real cause of suffering in the world and one must be free from the clutches of vaulting ambitions. But, in fact, without ambitions human beings would not be any better than all other species of creatures on this planet.

According to the Buddha, Desire is the root cause of all human misery and, unfortunately, to man, his desires and wants are unlimited. The more his wants, the more his misery, and his chance to lose the brightness of his eyes. The poor, the unemployed and the married who find it difficult to make ends meet or who live by the skin of their teeth, cannot be blamed for their despair and dissatisfaction. It is funny that all human beings try to hide their genuine sorrows, dejections and disappointments under an artificial appearance. Our smiles and laughs are mere masks which serve as hideouts for the true reflection of our hearts. But, nevertheless, one's eyes cannot pull the wool over the eyes of others!

It's true that we worry over each and every issue whether it is serious or silly. See what a poet says: 'Our parents are worried when their daughter-in-law forgets to fetch their bed-coffee, and they are worried more when their own daughter brings it.' So, it may be assumed that 'we pine for what is not' and that is the real cause of our despair which leads to the loss of the brightness of our eyes. What if the crow worries over its feathers and the leopard over its spots? But, if you cut your coat according to your cloth, your eyes shall begin to shine once again.

Haven't you read the poem captioned: 'Why worry?' It can be read like a nursery rhyme: 'There are only two things to worry about, either you are well or you are sick / if you are well, then there is nothing to worry about; but if you are sick, there are only two things to worry about, either you will get well or you will die / If you get well, then there is nothing to worry about; but if you die, there are only two things to worry about, either you will go to heaven or to hell / If you go to heaven, then there is nothing to worry about; but if you go to hell, you'll be so damn busy shaking hands with friends that you won't have time to worry.'

Therefore, Adam, the only solution to regain happiness and, thereby, the brightness of your eyes is to labor hard, realizing the truth that every dog has his day. Do your duty and don't flirt with the fruits of it, says the Bhagavad-Gita. If a person has many things to do, he will not have time to worry about himself. Oh, for the life of a Ulysses rather than that of a Tithonus! Giant oaks live for ages in the darkness of despair but the short-lived willow-plants spread the light of happiness.

Adam, you still live in a fool's paradise. You are lazy and you wait for miracles. You laze away your days, like a madman. You wait for the impossible to happen and ignore the possible that works out. The myth that those things you wish at the time of a shooting star will be realized carries away your talents. What excuse is there when you waste away your days waiting for the meteor?

Please do not think that I am a pickpocket plumped to cheat you or a madman who attacks you in his fits of insanity, when I bump into you while walking along the road with the typical absent-mindedness of a professor.

I admit, of course, that it is a fault with me that I always walk looking up at the sky, my eyes scanning each and every pin-point in the far and wide firmament. In fact, many a time I tried to look down at the road as well as at the passing pedestrians but I simply could not help looking up.

Fortunately almost all the persons against whom I had bumped were polite enough to sympathize with my eccentricity. I express my deep gratitude towards them because their lack of manners would have resulted in the loss, at least a few, of my teeth.

However I cannot forget the profiles of a few persons who timidly snarled and hurled profane or rather obscene phrases at my face during such encounters. Some of them asked me question-word questions like, 'What the hell are you dreaming about?' and some others asked auxiliary questions like, 'Do you keep your eyes in your ass?' and 'Can't you look ahead and walk?' I stupidly blinked at them and ignored their interrogations like the Wiseman of Gotham.

Except for a few such collisions, I have not invited the

wrath of the fairer sex. At one time, I innocently bumped into one wheat-complexioned lass who looked at me, afterwards, with a wry face and spat on the road as if she was spitting on my face. At another time, I remember that an ugly looking girl and I knocked together, and she said nothing but smiled invitingly as if she had diagnosed my problem or rather, if you think so, my disease. But my problem simply is that everybody doubts my sincerity and misunderstands the purity of my purpose.

Do you think that I am some kind of a maniac who always looks from horizon to horizon during his lonely evening walks? I do not think that a person who looks up at the starry-heavens for the flash of a meteor needs to be treated by the alienists! In my case, I eagerly watch the sky just for the light of a shooting star which, I hope, will change my luck for good.

All these problems began when the secret was disclosed to me that whatever one wished for, when a meteor burnt down, would be fulfilled. In a mysterious tone they said to me that they too tried to wish something special while the burning meteoric stone showered silver rays. They did not get the opportunity, they said with an air of sadness, for at the nick of the moment they used to forget their heart's desire.

At first I did not care for their mysterious theory and ignored it as a mere superstition. But as years passed, I found my efforts and hard work turned futile and meaningless to achieve even a little part of my vaulting ambitions. Then miraculously, one fine morning, I remembered the value of that great secret and instantly decided to try my luck with it. Well! Circumstances make man superstitious!

Thus began my idiosyncrasy and I continue the practice of scaling the heavens for the falling stars as I move along the road under the spell of that optimistic obsession.

At the beginning stage of my dreamy walks, my ambitions

were quiet fantastic or rather weird. Sometimes I wished to become the emperor of the world within the blink of an eye and, at other times, to become an omnipotent wizard who could solve all the problems of the world with a single snap of his fingers or wave of his magic wand.

Later I realized the foolishness of such desires and my wishes turned to be more practical. So I simply began to wish for an average job with a reasonable income with which I could win the daily bread for my family. Unfortunately, even this very modest ambition seemed to be out of my reach.

It does not mean that I am not seeing meteors flashing through the atmosphere. Many a time I saw them burning down just above my very nose. But at that nick of a moment, I enjoyed that rare natural phenomenon with a full heart that I forgot all my eager desires. Then, I stood wonder-struck, looking dazedly at the meteor which made a dazzling silvery streak in the blue canopy of heaven. I have then the mental condition of Kuchela who forgot all his personal problems at the very sight of his old friend, the King of Dwaraka.

I continue my search for that heaven sent moment of the aerolite. One day, I am sure I will be able to wish something very important at that flash of the meteor-lightning. And so, if I bump into someone, do pardon me then and there, without much snarls and curses because, to be sure, I am only a humble well-wisher of the world at large.

Adam, you are very clever in making funny excuses! You bump into others and, then, regret your foolishness. How long can you be a dreamer? You wait for miracles and when miracles happen, it will be too late. Be practical, Adam.

You think too much about your importance. Everything was at hand there in that paradise. You are a spoilt child. Spoiled by easy gaining... spoiled by the ready-made things... spoiled by the all-helping hand of God Almighty. Keep the truths about human life with you, Adam.

We are all mere travelers and we travel with no clear knowledge about our destination. We meet companions in the buses, boats, planes and trains. We think that others too are just like us. But Adam, this world is not for belated travelers like you! We are travelers cursed for a long journey. Remember, what happened to you in the train.

I began my journey on some cursed moments. Once you commenced a journey, you had to continue it until you reached your destination. It meant that you couldn't return to your starting point.

It might be because nobody was expecting your returning. And the fearlessness, warmth and security of that place from where you began your journey would remain a dream for you. It might be the comfort of your mother's womb. However, the memory of that lost paradise would continue to give you courage throughout your journey.

I waited at the station together with others who too were fated to travel like me. We, the travelers, who lost their sense of hearing in the heavy noise of the trains that arrived and departed, stood in utter silence, staring at each other. Of course, there was a glittering of hope in our anxious eyes, as we sat there, our hands gripping on our burdens. And the railway tracks lay stretched to an unknown destination, without touching each other, like our own non-similar ways of life.

And we, who were quite helpless before our fate, couldn't stay at that camp for ever. Suddenly there was a quick movement amongst us, as the train came towards us, coughing and spitting like an aged destitute, and stopped in front of us, panting incessantly. In fact, the loud noise it made while approaching the station poured a sort of vitality into our exhausted bodies.

We ran here and there like wolves chasing their prey. In a

moment's selfishness, we forgot ourselves and competed for each one's survival. While rushing and jostling with each other's bag to get a seat for the long journey, where was that so-called prick of conscience? Who cared for the fellow travelers with whom you were waiting all that time? Where was the philosophy of a wider world of sacrifice and tolerance, where human life was only a journey?

In such a journey, limited was the number of passengers fortunate enough to get reserved seats. They were born with golden spoons in their mouths, and their journey would be just a pleasurable time-pass for them. Though unlucky we were in getting reserved seats, we had to travel! And once we decided to begin our journey, we couldn't turn back till the culmination of it.

And some how we, the unreserved passengers feeling equality in our misery, struggled into that cellar of a compartment and clutched to the wooden seats covered with coal-powder, ash and dust. Of course, we tried to ignore the fetid smell of our sweat in the smoke of cigars. We looked at each other aimlessly like those birds that finally roosted on a tree after long hours of a fight.

Some of us were caressing those bruises and wounds of our body, hiding and keeping together in shame the torn parts of our loin clothes. For the battle had come to an end for the time being.

The old vehicle began to move, concentrating all its strength, breathing heavily and wheezing, coughing and spitting, like a tuberculosis-patient. We the travelers clutched to our temporary seats like the old man of the sea, trying to find lilt and tone in the ear-breaking noise of the train.

No one cared for those trees and woods, rocks and farmlands, roads and brooks, which hurried backward, at the forward movement of our train. Our hearts wished that if a gush of cold wind had entered through the ventilator of the train, it would have reduced at least the unbearable stench in the compartment.

Of course, we were not jealous of the convenience enjoyed by those travelers who got seat-reservations. From childhood onwards we had been taught that jealousy was a sin and death was the reward for sin, and if we curse those lucky persons, it would cause our death. So, we tried to keep away our boredom by enjoying the helplessness and misery of those vendors who came into the compartment with tea or peanuts. Some of us were nodding our gloomy faces, remembering the tear-stained faces of our dear relatives whom we had left behind.

In fact, our faces looked ugly due to our unnecessary, unreasonable and unknown fear about our journey. Of course, the sweet memory of the place we left and the sad thoughts about the place of our destination doubled the ugliness of our faces. Our minds had already begun the sincere efforts to break open the outer shells of silence, in order to forget the insecurity and inconvenience of our intolerable journey.

As hours passed, our instinctive animal tendencies began to find expressions. We began to look at each other, make faces with insincere smiles and engage in useless talks. We contested each other in acting as if we were familiar for years. We soon became friends, with a sort of intimacy seen among the sheep, waiting for their turn in front of the slaughterhouse. We told lies in the most believable manner about the place we left, about the place we go and about our occupations and missions. We even introduced ourselves by telling our surnames, instead of our actual names. For we had, by then, no individuality, except that we were all mere travelers.

I was sitting like a stranger amongst those soldiers who were going to the capital city. I was not a soldier nor was I traveling to the capital city! How different was my journey from that of theirs? I had to get down somewhere in the midway. I had to get down from this train, catch another one and continue my journey. But until then, I had to sit here in this narrow compartment, tolerating the useless conversation and hollow laughing of those soldiers. Though I tried to give their color to my feathers, I found it very difficult or even impossible to do so.

The cellar of that train was really a small world. Nobody bothered or grieved at the suffering of the train. It was in the outside world that minutes, hours and days crawled like a snail. Time stood paralyzed in this cellar. The travelers had to think only whether the train reached the place where they had to alight.

Well, in order to kill time or keep away boredom, some subject should be found. For if every traveler brought out the animal in him that would be sufficient. And it was not difficult for the male community in the compartment to stir up the brutes in them. A male community that cared only for preying and mating!

A crowd of animals! The animals that raised their noses only to feel whether there was any smell of woman in the air that came through the windows of the train. What the animals needed first were food and water. Many a time they got them in the train. What they needed then was the smell of woman... the smell of woman that could give the animals in them a long exhausted sleep!

As the train stopped at a station, I stretched out my neck through the window and realized that I should get out at the train's next stop. Some of my fellow travelers, with their baggage, managed to jump out of the train and they melted in the dazzling light of the platform. New travelers, who too had no seat-reservations, struggled through the crowd and entered into the darkness of our cellar of a compartment. As the train moved, I stood up from my seat, pressed my numbed bottom and walked through the corridor to the dark little toilet room.

In the urgent call of nature, I ignored the nauseating stench and disgusting sight of the particles of feces and drops of urine laid spread all over the toilet, of course, scattered by the jerking of the train. When I returned to my wooden seat, I felt an odor in the compartment which I couldn't recognize at first. It was an odor familiar to my fellow-travelers; it appeared so from their reactions. Soon, watching their bloomed faces, I recognized that it was the smell of woman. A real enlightenment in the compartment of a train!

A woman was standing in the narrow space between the two rows of seats and was changing her clothes, as if she were in her dressing room! And the travelers' eyes were enjoying the beauty of her body, as she carelessly packed her clothes in the box kept on the upper berth. She deliberately took more time in packing, knowing that the eyes of the travelers were feeding on the curves of her body. She powdered her face and sprayed some cheep perfume on her armpits, breasts and waist. The soldiers were describing her private parts in a language unknown to her, and were acquiring a sort of vicarious sexual satisfaction through their eyes. She must be cursing herself for entering into a compartment of soldiers who spent money neither for food nor for sexual pleasure, during their free travel.

It was evident that she used to earn her daily bread by hosting different types of travelers! And it seemed that, finally, she had decided to enjoy the fun. As she approached the seat, the soldiers contested each other to give her some space to sit. Of course, they pretended to give her space, but as she attempted to sit, they quickly moved so that they could receive her on their laps. Each time, they laughed aloud and the game continued, giving a lot of fun to other travelers. It seemed that she too enjoyed the game, as she felt the hardness of their laps on her buttocks. Finally, pretending innocence, she clutched the thighs of two soldiers, pushed those sideways and managed to sit on that wooden plank of a seat.

The two soldiers who blessed to sit on both sides of the woman, put their hands over her shoulder in a friendly manner, enquired about her family pretending sympathy and, in accordance with the movement of the train, caressed her breasts innocently. They expressed their surprise at the beauty of her dress and pressed the private parts of her body, as if testing the texture of her clothes. They praised the sweetness of the perfume she used, by inhaling the smell and, indirectly, rubbing their nose against her armpits. Of course, she acted better than they, and replied their questions with appropriate lies.

Soon it seemed that she felt quite bored of the naughtiness of the soldiers. All the time I, who never experienced the pleasure of brutality, was sitting there indifferently. For I was neither a soldier nor was my destination the capital city. But I was shocked when she said that she too was getting off at the next station. For I too had to get off at the same station.

Of course, the soldiers requested her to continue her journey up to the capital city. In fact, they wanted to enjoy the fun and, thereby, keep away the monotony of their travel. I heard her telling them that she was getting off at the next station, that she had managed to travel without ticket up till then and she didn't know what would happen in the next train. Of course, it was an indirect request to get some money. The soldiers expressed their sympathy at her sad situation but introduced me to her, as another part of their joke. They told her that I also was going to the same city and she could help me as I was new there. I wished to declare that it was my second journey to the city and I needed no help from anyone. I noticed her looking at me with some hope of a good customer!

I sat there helplessly, looking through the window of the train, into the darkness outside.

The train that dived through the darkness slowly came to a stop into the thick darkness. As I was looking for my bag, of course, deliberately taking more time to avoid her, she took her box, jumped onto the platform and waited for me. While getting down from the train, she helped me to bring my bag to the platform, and reminded me to be careful as it was all darkness on the platform. She told me that the train to our city would come on the other platform after only an hour, and until then we could rest on one of the cement benches there.

She walked too close to me, or rather stuck to me like the bag on my shoulder, as if she was afraid that I would run away from her. As I was groping in the darkness, she guided me towards a cement bench. Behind us, the train to the capital city slowly moved away and I heard my fellow travelers, stretching their necks through the ventilators, cry aloud: 'Congratulations, comrades! Best wishes!'

What a cold evening! The chill wind blew benumbing even the bones… as if a needle was pierced into your very marrow. The feet lost their sensation though they were kept tight in the leather shoes. What a horrible cold! The muscles on the body tightened unintentionally. Lips shivered; teeth gnawed. It would be better to sit somewhere and curl yourself into a bundle.

In the train, I didn't feel that much cold. The doors and the windows of the compartment were tightly closed. The hot bodies of the travelers who sat so jammed conveyed some comfort. Even the fire and smoke from the smokers' lips gave some heat. And moreover, there was the fire of sex burning in the stories, anecdotes, songs and jokes of the soldiers!

But in the thick darkness of the platform, a fire and its heat were only a dream. I tried to believe that it was really the station from where I had to get another train to my city. As electricity had gone, the whole platform was in a deep sleep. The sound of someone's snoring or the hushed voice of a man and a woman who were trying through their amorous acts to keep away the attack of cold, at times, strained towards me through the darkness. The sound of the train that deserted us on that platform, went further and further away, reducing it to some murmur, reaching us from a far distance, amalgamating with the whistling of the cold wind.

If only I could get a cup of hot tea. But the train that brought us to this place during the small hours might be the last one of the day, and the tea-vendors would have entered into their own deep sleep. In the darkness of the dump-yard, the train to our city might be hidden away from cold, having her sound sleep too.

Our train, as if from a nightmare of an early morning, suddenly woke up with a shriek. Together with it, the tea-vendors too. One could only count and keep the moments that were spent in that cold darkness of the platform.

There appeared a light at the extreme end of the platform. Somebody might be warming himself by burning some newspapers or an ankitty, a tin-drum for burning charcoal. By sitting around it, a few passengers might be smoking their hookah, filled with tobacco. From their mouths, together with the smoke, curses on the coldest winter and chants of prayers for a warmer summer, would be coming out. Should I not move towards that place? Would I not, a stranger, get a seat near that ankitty?

'Ah, what a cold!' A hot breath from my side seat. The figure of a woman traveler, whom I ignored for a few moments, was sitting next to me. What? Hadn't she left? I had forgotten that a woman was sitting very close to me all that time.

91

When other fellow travelers were with me, she was only a 'joke' for us. But, then, I was alone with her, and that's dangerous! I should avoid her by fair or foul means. She was also coming to the city. The city that awaits with open doors for every destitute. And if I got down with such a woman at that railway station... ?

'It's too cold, isn't it?' she murmured, expecting an answer from me. I wished to hum in agreement with her. But sound didn't come out due to the extreme cold. Spontaneously, I could only nod my head. Could she notice my nodding in that blind man's night?

'Luckily there are no bedbugs or cockroaches on this cement bench!' She talked as if in a soliloquy. 'No attack from mosquitoes even! They all would've perished in such a cold! If we were here in the summer, we couldn't even sit on this bench. Then the number of mosquitoes, cockroaches, bedbugs and houseflies would increase by millions! And also the number of passengers!'

She laughed as if she was telling some jokes. I felt as if her laughter conveyed a sort of warmth into me. She would be laughing like some beautiful actresses in the films; I wondered. Could this woman even laugh so innocently? I could not see her face in the darkness. I tried to remember that face of hers that I had seen in the compartment of the train.

A face that was beautified with face powder, lipstick and mascara. Her real face might be different! But I could guess her face even in that darkness. The face of that woman who talked in a soft and childish voice and laughed with a jingling sound. And there was no possibility that the owner of such an attractive voice to be an ugly woman. Moreover, my heart was not so hard and cruel to imagine in that way.

'See! Cold will creep up from this cement bench and numb the whole body. My hands have already turned like wooden logs! Look!' She placed her palm on my cheek and caressed. I felt her hot palm! Perhaps, I felt so because my cheeks were colder?

Moving her palm on my ear and neck, she whispered: 'Your ears have turned like ice-cubes, how sad!' I wished her hand to be kept a few more minutes on my face. I raised my hand, placed my palm over her palm, and pressed to my cheek. As if tickled by my touch, she pretended to pull away her hand, and laughed like soft jingling of bells. I felt her hot breath touch my neck.

She touched my chin and, with the authority of an intimate friend, said: 'Please, do stand up for a second! You'll be paralyzed if you sit on this bare cement bench. My woolen shawl is in this box, and how can I find it in this darkness? For the time being, I shall spread one end of my sari on the bench. Please, stand up.' She held on to my shoulders and made me stand up. She took one end of her sari, with which she was protecting her head from the cold, and spread it on the cement bench.

'Come and sit here!' She caught my hands and lovingly compelled me to sit. In her presence, was I changing into a mechanic doll? Could a woman speak and behave in such a soft manner?

I didn't feel any tension while sitting in that darkness, with a strange woman. My mind was that of a small child who yearned to stick to its mother's breasts. Or did my five senses turn inactive due to extreme cold?

My lips were trembling with cold, and I asked her softly: 'Aren't you feeling cold?'

She moved closer to me and, placing her face on my chest, said: 'Oh, that's nothing! Here's enough heat! You're so warm here!' Her lips moved on my chest and I felt tickled.

Suddenly, the same old fear gripped me, perhaps, too

irrational in such a situation! I placed my hands over her shoulders and tried to push her away. Even in the extreme cold, I felt sweaty. For a moment, I experienced a strange sensation and sat there motionless. As if somebody had thrown a blanket to protect us from the cold, a sheet of mist unrolled towards us. I tightly shut my eyes.

What was really happening to me? Some fundamental change had come to me. Once I was too shy even to look at girls. I felt a sort of shivering when girls touched my body unintentionally. I felt even a sort of dizziness, if their eyes locked with mine unexpectedly. Many girls, who desired my company, left me disappointed. Some of them, who offered their love to me, became later my enemies at my rejection. Why did I maintain such a meaningless self-assertiveness? Some of them requested that I just to go with them to the cinema house, or shopping. Then I cleverly avoided them, pretending to be busy with my studies. Why did I lack that courage which all my friends had? As I sat on the cold cement bench of that dark platform, was I not getting relieved from that tormenting unnecessary fear?

Cold disappeared from me like a fast train. The more I tried to push her away, the more she clung on to my body. If only she were suitable as my life partner! I was always afraid of pre-marital sex; for I wanted to make sure, rather a selfish intention, that the woman who shared my body should be my own rib bone. And the woman with me there was only a street harlot. The germs of venereal diseases might be there on her body, seeking their new prey. If so, a relationship with her would end my future in darkness! Yes! I must escape from her by all means, and hide away somewhere else!

Suddenly, from the darkness of our back-platform, a hooting of a train broke the silence... like the trumpeting of an elephant that woke up from its sleep experiencing a nightmare.

With a shock, I pushed her away from me. She angrily looked at my face and murmured some curses. I jumped up from the cement bench, took my bag and said: 'That's the train for us!'

She silently pulled the end of her sari and covered her head with it. For a moment, she covered her face with her hands and began to sob. Incapable of understanding why she cried, I placed my hand on her shoulder and said consolingly: 'Don't worry! Come! Let's board the train!'

She took my hand, kissed it and said: 'Look! For the last two days, I've been starving. I'm so star-crossed that I couldn't make even a single rupee! What shall I do now?'

She looked at my face helplessly. I saw the whole poverty and misery of the human race dammed in her eyes. If only I had some money to help that poor woman! Could she believe if I said that I had no money, except a few coins to reach my city? Could she find a new person with money, at that time of the day? My mind murmured: 'You're lucky, my dear lady! For you have at least your body to sell! What about me?'

She stood up, took her box and walked towards the train. I followed her with a guilty conscience. In the darkness, somehow we found the door and entered the compartment. I placed my bag on the upper berth and also helped her to place her box.

'They put on the light only half an hour before the train starts!' She said in a hopeful and convincing tone. She opened her box and took out a red woolen shawl. She spread it on the wooden seat and asked me to sit on it. Even in that utter darkness, I saw in her eyes hope and despair glitter, one after another.

I went out of the compartment quickly and walked towards the vendor. I bought two samosas and a tea in a clay-cup, came back and gave them to her, extending my hands through the ventilator. I sat on the single seat, a bit away from her, watching her eat and drink.

Suddenly, the light turned on and she hurriedly pulled the sari over her face! The train moved, from the darkness into the dawn of a new day. Soon the compartment filled with passengers.

After an hour, our train would reach the city where she would get off the train and melt into the milling crowd of the city, leaving only a vague memory in my mind.

The railway track! It started from the eternity and ended in the eternity. The beginning and the end remained unknown to the travelers.

Somewhere in the womb, the trains of the future struggled for their first breath and somewhere in the coffin, the trains, of the past rotted till the last stink.

Eons passed, hearing the whistles, seeing the fire and smelling the smoke of the passing trains. Many people entered the train and exited it at their stations. Yet, the arrival and departure of each train remained unknown to everybody.

When I entered my train and sat on my seat, none of you were there. Though there were four seats, all of them were vacant, and I sat there alone, dreaming the glorious sights which I will come across on my journey.

Somewhere the train stopped, some of my fellow travelers stepped off the train and disappeared forever, and some others entered the train, including you.

When the train moved, you came suddenly into my apartment of the compartment and sat on the seat, just opposite to mine.

We looked at each other with surprise; we talked casually and laughed heartily. I wished to invite you to the seat lying vacant near my seat; instead, you invited me to sit near your seat and to enjoy with each other the beautiful sights during the course of our journey.

I hesitated and thought for a while, but before I came to a decision, a person came from the other apartment of our compartment and sat near your side, unexpectedly. Then, for a moment, we exchanged our bewildered looks helplessly.

The train was moving and both of you looked at each other, talked causally and laughed heartily. You became happier when you found that both of you were going to the same destination.

You did not know my destination, and that made me laugh, and perhaps, you might have wished for a new companion to occupy the vacant seat near my side where I kept my literature.

And, when I understood that my presence there would annoy both of you, I stood up and went into another apartment where nobody was present and sat there, keeping my literature as my refreshing companion till the arrival of my station where I had to step down and disappear forever, leaving behind my companion in the train to refresh both of you and other fellow travelers.

Yes, Adam, you don't know what awaits you at the other end of the road! For your path peters out deep into the wilderness! That's the greatness of human life. At any time, anything will happen. Have patience and wait patiently.

This is the city where you have to find your life. Here everyone seeks and finds their own means of survival. Seek and you will find. Knock, and the door will be opened. Of course, you may not be able to adjust with the surroundings. That's your bad luck... your misfortune.

These misfortunes are not new for you. Think of the unexpected smites of fate. Remember history. Every time fate strikes at you and you are crumbled to dust and ashes! Again you work hard; you struggle and fly up like a phoenix bird, only to fall into another pyre. It's the fate of all human beings!

Sometimes you miss your chances. Perhaps your opportunities are snatched away by less competent persons. You have the right to get a particular chance. But those who have lesser needs, those who are not even eligible, get away with your share. You remain in utter helplessness like the paralyzed man at the pool of Bethesda.

Adam, haven't you been waiting by the side of the miracle pond?

Today the Bethesda Pond is really quiet.

Those ripples that kiss its banks and those water plants that toss their heads enjoying the dampness of its sides are all silent, today.

If only this long wait has come to an end on this day. Perhaps the meditation of many a year may come to its culmination today.

Yes! It's time for the waters of the Bethesda Pool to stir up! In this long span of human life, shall a person not get a moment of luck? At least, a single chance to become optimistic?

The eyes that longed to see the waters move have turned myopic. The ears that yearned to hear the movement of the waters have turned deaf. Yet today is the day of happiness, a day of hopes accomplished.

All eyes stare into the blue water of the Bethesda. All hearts palpitate around the Bethesda Pool. All legs desire to get the first touch of the moving water of the Bethesda. All brains thirst for the coolness of the Bethesda.

Yes! The helpless human creatures that compete with each other for their luck! For luck is only for the most selfish one who touches the water first when the waters move. He will be cured.

But as I lay completely paralytic, I feel a sort of indifference. And all the hopes and desires that I have been cherishing for ages also lay paralyzed just like my body.

My body and my mind are stinking alike! And I know that the sinned body and the desperate mind make life devoid of its meaning!

My body has become charred and broken here and there and a nasty odor comes out of those wounds. Flies lay their eggs in the puss that oozes out of those rotten wounds. And worms make their home there, forming bubbles playfully in the life-blood of my heart.

Whatever I have with me is decayed and ruined in itself. And the parasites take benefit from my own decay. The roots of the parasite plants go into the depth of my mind and suck whatever abilities are left there. And in my utter helplessness, I stare at those exploiters who conduct the cosmic dance of destruction.

My cote is decayed suffering all the wind and the rain, all the mist and the sun-light. Its legs have gone down deep into the muddy ground. Even the worn out blanket has stuck to my body. What a terrible change that time brings even to lifeless objects!

As I was born in impurity, am I supposed to grow up in impurity and to die in impurity? And the waters of the Bethesda must move to make me pure and to give me a new life.

The crowd increases on the banks of the Bethesda. My mind compels me to infiltrate through that crowd. But my weak body hesitates even to make a slight movement.

There, the movement of the waters begins. I can feel the stirring up of the water. The blue water turns upside down, making it red with the subsided slime. The long awaited, invaluable time has come at last.

The wavelets of the Bethesda beat against the banks of the pool. The water plants that grow on its banks also move up and down in the force of the water current.

But nobody is there to raise me up and lead me towards the water. My muscles are tightened. My bones dissembled of their joints, lay broken. Is there any time left for these men who run helter-skelter in order to achieve their selfish motives?

Yet still my heart throbs with desires and hopes! My soul consistently chants to me, 'to live... to live... ' But my self, who drowns every minute into the depth of despair, is destined to live my life lamenting and lamenting all throughout.

How better it is if the water of the Bethesda turns into a flood and covers my head? But for the indifferent Bethesda are not flood and drought the same and the one?

Some lucky man has jumped into the disturbed waters of the Bethesda and got cured of his illness. Be consoled, oh heart, for what fate offers you is only the endless pain.

My chances are stolen away from me, one by one. But it is natural. For life is just an endless waiting for chances. When one opportunity is missed, wait for the next. And push away the days, immersing in the memory of those opportunities lost forever.

But this endless waiting exhausts even my soul. How long could I continue my life in such a situation? A life that is prolonged in the mirage of hope! No, it is impossible for me to live like this. I am totally broken and scattered to the core!

The qualification to jump into the Bethesda Pool is the same for them and for me. Perhaps I have a better claim. But matters go on here as if the might is right. Does it mean that even miracles are denied to the poor destitute?

My cote, my blanket and my self will be decayed into naught on these banks of the Bethesda. For no one is here to push me into the pool when its water moves.

Somewhere from a far distance I hear the master asking, 'Do you want to get well?"

'Indeed! I do!' My heart whispers. Otherwise why should I

postpone my death?

'Arise, and take your bed and walk!'

Whose voice is that? Whose is that great, heavy sound that strains towards me with the cool breeze that blows from a far away place? Is it the voice of the master? Or is it merely the echo of my sincere hope?

But the master's voice is far, far away. It will take ages for that voice to come to me bit by bit. How long should I have to wait for such a lucky moment that usually comes rarely and unexpectedly? Where injustice and the supremacy of the might prevail as unopposed facts, am I supposed to live again in that mere dream-world of consolation?

Say, Bethesda! For whom your waters stir up? When there is the movement in your waters, the persons who get into you are lesser qualified than me. And the voice of the master which can raise me up is far, and far away.

Oh, dearest Bethesda! Tell me, for whom your waters move and stir up?

How long could you wait for a master or a savior? Years of waiting paralyze your whole being. Then one day you will turn lifeless like a statue. Your talents will go rotten and you will become a mere waste for the world. Your relatives will think of you as a foolish human being... just a dreamer... an impractical nincompoop! The whole world will laugh at you... and will, rather worse, sympathize at your fate!

Nobody is going to help you. Nobody is coming to guide you to the cool waters of Bethesda. You will be the last person to get natural justice. So, Adam, listen to that voice! Arise, take up your bed and walk! You can't continue to stay here. Take only the very essential things with you. Move from one place to another. See for yourself the contradictions of human life. Go to the city and see how people like you barter their talents and earn their daily bread. Adam, this world is so vast and wide... it's time to begin your real search.

Adam, all these years you believed in the success of the barter system. You thought that there is justice in the exchange of goods. Your sweat, blood or brain can be exchanged for food, clothing or shelter. You never thought of the exchange of human flesh. Come to the city and see how clever human beings are.

One can understand if a woman exchanges her flesh for food. It may be to fetch food or fruits for her Adam and his children. But in the case of man, this type of an exchange becomes strange and unnatural. Here both men and women exchange their faithfulness with utmost infidelity, without any scruples. The very instincts which make them human beings are exchanged for subhuman reasons, with inhuman manners.

Here, these people are all quite busy. They are engaged in buying and selling. Exchanging whatever they have for whatever they need. In their excessive enthusiasm to survive, they forget history. They forget not only all about their past but also about their future. They are ready to ignore the scope of their future, just for the sake of surviving in the present.

Adam, don't you remember that look of indifference in the eyes of Eve when you passed the gates of Eden? Yes, the sense of practicability was highly active in Eve! There was firm determination to face any adverse situation. When women found that their sweat, blood and brain have no market, it is quite natural that they might have tried to sell their flesh, their genital organs and even their sexual feelings.

And in the passage of time they lost their sense of touch and other similar delicate sensations. Their bodies lost their sensibility. Their hearts lost their sensitiveness. They themselves turned into statues... into statues of cold stone... into statues of hard wood.

Adam, go and see them! Touch them! Find for yourself

how far human beings can degrade themselves! Is there left any sense of feelings in them? At least a little warmth of that divine breath?

Don't be frightened by this new face of Eve. Don't forget that she knows how to exploit your weakness. Adam, while you are a dreamer, your Eve is a pragmatist. She knows how to argue logically, even when she drowns into the depth of death.

It's the fate of your generation, Adam Junior. There's a Cain living in you! Go and see for yourself what happens in the red-streets where Eves set traps and snares for Adams, Cains and Abels.

There are four-storeyed buildings on both the sides of the street, perhaps the most undeveloped part of this great metropolitan city. Those who walk along the road look at each other in suspicion. When some familiar face is seen, in order to avoid an encounter they either turn back to walk away or cover their face with handkerchiefs as if to wipe away their sweat or bend down as if to dust off the shoes like the Englishmen.

Suppose they happen to meet face to face by chance or accident, the victory will be for the person who asks first: 'What a surprise! Might have been at the family house, eh? Am I right? Well! Your luck and best time! What else! Er.....!'

While the friend's face turns pale with shame, the former moves away hurriedly without waiting even to hear the other one's reply.

It is for the first time in life that you walk along this street. Many a time you wished to roam along this part of the city and that's natural, but always that serpent named fear, to be precise, fear of venereal diseases and even HIV/AIDS; and not mere morality or instinctive withdrawal from committing sins, was dancing in your heart with its fully spread hood. Was it just fear that prevented you? Or was it the picture of a small house and the starving figures of human beings who lived in it that always haunted your mind?

In front of the ground floor of the building complex on both the sides of the road, women stand in rows. Girls, who became women before their age, and hags who pretend to be too young for their age, stand there displaying their artificial beauty. Their frocks move up and down in the wind that carries the odor of cheap scents and face powders. Or are they deliberately raising their frocks to attract the pedestrians?

The wrinkles on their faces, hidden cleverly under a coating of lipstick and colored face-powder, become quite visible when they smile. Their teeth and tongue, reddened by chewing betel leaf and betel nut, arouse lust in the minds of the spectators. The middle-aged women, biting their lips to redden them, throw their eyes on the passers-by. Of course, they are the senior elephants who give training to the amateurs. The young girls stand there exhibiting their overflowing breasts that grew more than usual for their age. Their eyes, stagnant with despair and sorrow, extend even towards those old men who waddle along the road.

An exhibition of passionless pieces of flesh! Just like the flesh that hung in front of the slaughter-houses. Human bodies and their muscles that move like machines. Women who lost their sense of touch, who suffered the fate of dead bodies, of mere statues... in the show cases.

'Walk only along the middle of the road! If you move to the sides of the road, women may get hold of you! Many of them are beckoning but don't look at that side! If you look to one side, the women on the other side will begin to shower vituperations!'

'Don't be mesmerized by the moonlight of their smiles! There is terrible darkness hiding behind it! In the milk of their smiles, there is cobra-poison! In the folds of their colorful clothing, black serpents wait for their preys! In their flowery-ponds, there swim and play the thread-snakes that suck blood-drops from the male- groins!'

Like the warning of God given to you in the Garden of Eden, the voice of friends echo and re-echo in your ears. Adam, don't be tempted!

Something soft falls on one's head. The hand goes up automatically in search of the fallen object. The fingers touch a small reddish rose flower tangled in one's hair. A flower smeared with attar.

Who could have thrown the flower so exactly on your head? You look up to see that expert. She stands there on the veranda of the first floor. You are astonished at the magnetic beauty of her smile. She beckons you and you only notice the magical power of her right palm, her plump fingers with long, well-cut, polished nails.

Like an innocent child, she makes gestures to give back that red flower which you keep in between the forefinger and thumb of your right hand. The flower emits the sweet smell of attar. And she stands there extending her hand for the flower, the flower that carries the smell of her body.

What about going up to the second storey of that building to hand over the flower to her? Nothing more than that. Just handing over the flower. To give that flower, wrapped in a twenty-rupee currency note and to place it in her beautiful hand as an appreciation of her accuracy in throwing flowers exactly on the heads of passers-by. And then just return, murmuring 'congratulations' in her beautiful ears.

She will be surprised at my weird behavior. Here's a man who pays for nothing, she may think. She may also laugh secretly thinking that this fool doesn't know that she has been doing this for years. Whatever may happen, the final decision is to go. The unquenchable thirst for adventure. There is an urge from the depth of the heart to have a closer glance at her.

Yes! She still beckons with a nod. With a movement of her chin, she invites you, and her lips were murmuring: 'Come! Come! Be quick!'

When you reach the base of the steps that lead to the first floor, an experienced, fat woman holds you by the sleeves and says, with an ugly slang, in her mother tongue: 'Come brother! Come and spend a few minutes in my room!'

She might have mistaken you as a person from that part of the land to which she belonged. I freed my shirt from her grip and climbed up the steps, cursing her disgustfully: 'Brother! Shit! Your bloody brother!'

It seems she heard your words. She spits out the betel juice to a farthest spot and you hear her speaking in a strange language: 'Phoo! You beggar! I won't lose anything even if I miss you! I'll get men with bigger... '

Before you hear the rest, you reach the first floor of the building. Adam, how glad you are. About the epiphany of the Babel Tower. The miracle of different languages. Adam, you are blessed with them!

A variety of sights and views. The sculptural beauty of Khajarahoo temples is in live exhibition in each room. There is only one difference, there they are rocks and stones, but here they are real, living flesh and blood. Their hearts beat and pulse like ours. And their eyes, that forgot innocence, look at the preys desirously. Yes, Adam, they are statues with flesh, blood and marrow! Human beings with hearts of stone.

While walking along the verandah of the second storey towards the girl who threw the flower at you, other girls pass you brushing their breasts deliberately and expressing their regrets with attractive smiles.

The flower smeared with attar is now drenched in sweat. And at a distance the owner of the flower waits with a smile to receive.

'Hullo, dear!'

Hearing an unexpected addressing in your own language, you turn your head spontaneously. There stands a beautiful girl fully covered in a pure, white saree. Her natural beauty, her charming smile and the nobility that reflected from her eyes - all work like a magnet. Her eyes appear longer with those black thin lines that sadness drew under them. She has spread her long hair as if to dry it in the sunlight after a bath. A jasmine garland is tucked on her long black hair.

She asked like an innocent child: 'Can't you come to me today, dear?'

When you look up towards the girl who is waiting for you at the other end of the verandah, she says apologetically: 'Oh, sorry! There may be persons where you make regular visits! Alright! Go on, my dear!'

You hesitate to look at her face once again. How can you say to her that you are a new comer there and you are going to the other girl just to say a word of appreciation? You walk forward feeling your legs heavier.

The owner of the flower seems to be very happy. She leads you to her room perhaps to show others that you belong to her. You look back at the girl in the white saree. She still stands there like a smiling marble statue.

Entering the room, you appreciate the ability of the girl in throwing the flower exactly on your head. You take out your purse and give her a twenty rupee note. But she is so clever that she snatches away your purse and takes all the money out of it! Realizing that it is dangerous to quarrel with such girls in such places, you rush out of the room and move hurriedly to the street.

While returning you look here and there for a glance of that girl in the white saree. Some intoxicated, barbarous maniac may be crushing her soft body within the grip of his strong and hard palms. As you step down heaving a long and heavy sigh, you hear again that sweet voice: 'You're going back, aren't you, dear?'

I can't help looking at her face where an innocent smile always lingered. She gives you her jasmine garland with a sort of love and affection in her eyes. She must have that natural urge to fall in friendship with a person who speaks her language. As you kiss the garland she gave, she asks: 'Won't you come this way tomorrow, dear?'

You shudder and look blank at her for a moment. How can you say that you are only a stranger in that place and have come to that street quite accidentally? How can you say that you are only an observer who wants to get a first hand knowledge of that notorious place? She may be expecting some money as 'baksheesh'. Poor girl! She also must live, mustn't she? At least you should give her the price of that jasmine garland. You take out your purse and look into its folds. The other girl has taken even the smallest coin from your purse! Noticing the shock on your face, the girl asks you with a smile: 'Do you want some money for the bus fare, dear?'

At first you think that she is laughing at you. But you see her fingers search among the folds of her saree for some hidden coins, perhaps, the baksheesh offered by some kind hearted customer.

With a shameful face you return that garland to her and you notice a shock on her face. You know that she needs that garland for the next customer. You look into her eyes. They are filled with pain and sorrow.

She tells you in a painful tone, 'I know you hate me, dear! But do you hate these jasmine flowers just because it's given by me?'

She might have recognized from your bewildered behavior that you are an amateur in visiting such streets. You feel as if the sigh that comes from the depth of your heart stuck somewhere in the throat. Placing your heavy feet, one by one on the steps, you get down onto the street. You passionately kiss the jasmine garland. There's once again that rough voice of that fat woman with betel juice in her mouth: 'Come, brother! Come... '

You walk away with long strides. When you reach the extreme corner of that street, you cannot but turn your head back. There on the second storey you see her wiping away the tears with one end of her white saree. The next moment she turns into a new white ivory-statue, to remain forever in your heart of hearts.

Yes, Adam! This is instinct! Sometimes in life, you come across such encounters. Adam, learn to resist temptations! Remember the lesson you learned from Eden!

But oh! The fate of Eve. It's too cruel. Once a rib bone gains life; how it turns again into a lifeless bone. An ivory statue of a woman.

How painful is this transformation? Thousands of women and men live like marble statues... turning themselves into mere stones. How unfortunate is this metamorphosis? The pleasure and ecstasy given by sex is misused here. And the partners suffer the punishment for it.

Years of mechanical life turns their lives lifeless. Their bodies lost the blessings of sensuousness and their minds lost the blessings of sensitiveness. But these statues carry a great message... a message that contains the meaning of human life.

There you are, Adam! That's the secret of human life! Eve knew it before she came out from the Garden of Eden. That's why she was calm and quiet when God drove the couples out of paradise. The forbidden fruit gave her that mysterious knowledge. She knew the power of sex! The happiness given by sex equaled the happiness given by paradise.

Yes, Adam! Sex is the only natural force that makes life worth living. Sexual thrill is the life force that makes living meaningful and wonderful. There are men and women who live without experiencing real sexual thrill. For them the orgasmic ecstasy is only a mirage. But such a life is abnormal and unnatural. All other forces of nature are secondary to sex. Real power comes out of the real union of male and female sex.

That's why from time immemorial, men and women have been worshipping sexual organs; sometimes directly, other times indirectly, sometimes genuinely, other times symbolically. Women are phallus worshippers and men are the worshippers of vagina. And the male genital organ thrust into the female genital organ is the greatest symbol of divine power! This unity is the secret of creativity! This is the mystery behind the chants of 'Satyam, Shivam, Sundaram... '

The power of God appears before us in the form of male and female genital organs. The copulation becomes a divine action... a ritual in every sense. That's why we construct temples for such representations of God. We decorate the walls of our temples with a myriad of scenes related to sexual union.

But still there's the original sin of misusing the blessings of God. Once they began to misuse sex, they lost the divine happiness of sex. Then, men and women turned into statues. They all lost their real sensations. Then, they faced the punishment of venereal diseases. Yet that delicate human feeling struggles hard in their hearts to survive. But Adam, beware of God's wrath on those who misused the natural gifts.

Adam, it's time for you to continue your search... to the temples of sex and sexual relationships. There is divinity in sex. But the crazy human beings manipulated it. The heavenly sex becomes a garland in the hands of monkeys. But the promotion of sex, the suppression of sex, the practice of sex, the dreams of sex, the memories of sex, the hopes and imaginations of sex... all continue to make human life worth living.

People moved towards the temples in large numbers. Small and big groups of foreigners and of natives. Those temples were very famous... famous all over the world... famous for the erotic sculptures that decorated the walls. And all roads led to those temples of love and lust.

Foreigners came walking fast from the nearby aerodrome, their disheveled golden hair fluttering in the wind. They wore tattered half-pants, T-shirts and canvas-shoes, and carried heavy burdens on their backs.

Handsome boys and beautiful girls walked hand in hand creating an exotic air. Girls walked swinging their waists and exhibiting the play of their young rams through their light, transparent silk blouses. The eyes of the native spectators were pierced by the spearheads of their breasts. The cameras that hung from their shoulders slapped against their legs as they walked making their naked thighs look blood- stained.

Natives too with combed, black hair came walking fast from the nearby bus stand. The men wearing knee-touching kurtas under which their thighs were scarcely covered with a light dhoti, and women with a heavy burden of gold ornaments on their hands, legs, ears and nose moved hurriedly towards the temples.

With great curiosity and interest, the scantily clothed white people absorbed the natives who wore multi-colored dress and talked different languages, into their cameras. Different cultures met there. All the peoples rushed to those temples with one aim, one purpose and one business. To feel the mysterious experience of those temples of erotic art and architecture.

Many native youngsters roamed in and around the temples trying uselessly to imitate the foreign hippies. They wore bell-bottom pants as well as pied, spotted shirts and walked behind the half naked European girls, secretly enjoying the beauty of their naked parts. At times they begged in a dignified manner: 'Please, give me some charas or marijuana, will you?' Or at other times they stretched their heads quite indecently to get into the photographs taken by the foreigners.

As the native devotees entered the temples, they began to pray in a frenzied tone and to kneel down or prostrate before each and every sculpture. The more the sculptures are naked, the more the devotees became crazy in their manners of worshipping. They touched and caressed the private parts of the naked statues with their fingers and placed those fingers reverently on their lips.

The foreigners watched the sculptural beauty of the temple walls with amazement and stupor. Can human beings perform amorous arts in such a way? They wondered. 'If only you think of sex in a spiritual stream!' The reply comes from a true devotee.

They took the photographs of the statues made in various natural, unnatural, non-natural and supernatural sexual poses. Staring unbelievably at certain sexual postures, they exclaimed: 'How wonderful! Marvelous! Enchanting! A magical world of art and architecture!'

They stood wonderstruck, trying to find new words to describe that fabulous world of divine sex.

'Excuse me, Sir! Are you a native of this place?'

Hearing the voice of a foreigner, I turned back. Though the people of this place were not ready to accept me as a native, politically I was a citizen of that country and, so, I made a careless reply: 'Yah... '

A European, all red and blood with the heat of the summer sun was standing there with a helpless look. By his side stood an innocent looking girl, of course, quite sexy like other tourists of her age. She said in a pathetic tone: 'Friend, please do help us! We are really in need of a guide.'

It was true, for without the help of a guide, one could not notice or understand certain highly complicated stone carvings of sexual yoga.

From their appearance it was clear that they were not rich tourists, born with golden spoons in their mouths and conducted tours just for the sake of spending their money. I also understood that they did not know anything about those so-called guides who got into friendship with foreigners through whatever means and walked with them sharing their food and drinks and got 'free lifts' in their cars and, at least when they depart, asked them to give their cameras or radios as presents.

'Alright,' I said. I walked with them hiding the joy of getting something to do in that strange place. I enquired about them and replied to their enquiries. I had to tell them that I was not really a guide but tourists like them, except that I had learned something about these oriental sculptures. In fact, I had arrived there only that morning and my real understanding about those temples depended mainly on the words of the professional guides who moved with rich tourists, things I overheard while walking with them, of course, at a hearable distance, as if I did not know the guide's language.

They told me that they had heard about sculptural and architectural beauty of those temples and had come to get the delight of seeing them with their own eyes. The brother and sister had visited many other temples of this country but they were overwhelmed with the magic of the temples here. It was happy news for me as I also came there to feel the delight of watching those temples, but alone. And as I was walking with that white girl, our bodies touched or rubbed each other, of course while answering her questions in a very confidential tone and I did not feel the absence of a mate at all.

When I told her the history of those temples, that they had been constructed as a result of the timely decision taken by certain clever kings to give sexual stimulation to their subjects who were not interested in sex and reproduction due to the excessive influence of certain celibate religions, I noticed the bony face of my European girlfriend turn red.

When I pointed to a father and his daughter who prayed earnestly before an 'extremely sexy' statue, if not an obscene one, and said that they were praying to get the luck of a suitable marriage and of a boy-child for that girl, my white girlfriend smiled meaningfully, and blushed.

I noticed how she was inspired when she saw a sexagenarian press his palm against the pelvic depression of a nude woman's statue of about five and a half feet and kissed his fingers in the manner of a ritual and gained a sort of heavenly rapture. My fingers were crushed under her grip, when I said, 'See, it is a simple rite to regain sexual potency.'

I noticed a French couple who whispered to each other, standing in front of a sculpture which was the full-fledged expression of the fantasy of inimitable copulation. I saw his partner's face change colors, pale and red, with passion and desire or shame and delicacy. I guessed that they were discussing how they could implement such an unnatural sexual union in their practical life.

There was an exclusive statue of a maiden, tearing apart her pyjamas, in her ecstasy. A scorpion was crawling up her left thigh, and in her hand she held a letter, perhaps, from her lover. 'How grotesque!' she whispered.

'No!' I replied. 'It's quite simple! Snakes for Europeans and scorpions for Indians! A sting, a pain and a pleasure, and then, a relief! That's sexual relationship! And snakes and scorpions are one and the same!'

I pointed my finger towards certain taverns that stood at a

walkable distance and told her: 'Those men and women who visit these temples complete their worship by staying in the rooms of those taverns. There you will get the pictures of these sculptures and also their models in plaster of Paris.'

My girlfriend bit her lips and stared into my eyes. I raised my eyes towards her brother. His eyes were looking for his girlfriend whom he had met in the airplane. And I understood that he would never know that his girlfriend was completing her worship in some rooms of those inns!

'Oh, dear! Please wait! I shall come back within a moment!' He said in a hissing voice and walked away from us like an epileptic patient. His eyes were madly scaling the area for that girlfriend of his.

For a moment I looked into the eyes of my girlfriend. She closed her eyes, put her hands around my neck and forced a kiss on my lips. While the male birds wandered in search of their mates, she moved, holding my hand tightly in hers, towards a lonely room in the tavern... to complete the worship!

No, Adam! Don't misuse your sexual talents. The bedrooms of such taverns are the cellars of God's punishments. Respect sex, honor it! For sex is the most valuable blessing of God. Nobody can worship God without sex or ignoring sex. Sex is the natural call for finding meaning in human life. At the same time, in sex you forget that you are just mortal human beings.

Sex is a clear proof of our animal tendencies. We would like to become animals, at least, in our imagination. Remember the story of Shiva and Parvathy and of the birth of Ganapathy, the half man and half elephant? An elephant's sexual organ might have aroused the fancy of man. Doesn't the scripture speak of women who desired the genital organs of horses and donkeys? What about the vitality of the mongoose? What about the madness of the hot-cats? What about the amazing number of repeated matings of sparrows? What about the prolongation of dogs? Adam, no longer can you stay alone.

No more are your eyes dazzled by the frailties of adolescence. It's all mere vanity! Have a disciplined life! You can't ignore the gravity of your mission in life. Try for immortality; try to regain that lost paradise.

See the termite flies that come out of the anthill and fly up in the sky just for mating? Break the anthill and fly out in search of your partner. How long can you live in the darkness of the damp anthill? Fly up and find your lost rib bone. That too is a part of your mission.

It's high time that you should find your own rib bone. Start your search just for that. Somewhere lives your own part of the body. Climb the mountains. Walk along the plains… and sail through the sea. One day you can find her. You will find her… for she is part of your fate!

PART III

Again a birth?

You crept out of the ugly and disgusting slough. Now the so-called frailties of adolescence lay deserted on the treaded path. And the glittering snake has come out quite rejuvenated.

Once the old rags are soiled and stinking... one has to throw away them. They are beyond repairing or cleaning. They must be hidden away among the thick bushes... or must be buried deep in the soil.

Adam, don't be a slave to temptations! You have a mission in your life. Memories of the past can't help you. Memories of a lost paradise should not dishearten you. Depend fully on your fate. Fate is everything in human life. The predestined fate!

Don't be perplexed by impediments. Don't look behind. Look forward... and continue your search. Whether to find it or not depends on your fate... and of your fate, you don't know much about it. That's the secret of human life!

Here, realization comes at last. Many an experience teaches

man the purpose of life. He learns the significance of laws, the relevance of discipline in an undisciplined world. Natural instincts compel him to go wayward. He may lead a corrupted life until he feels that sex is a curse to him. Lucky are those who think of sex as a blessing. Sex creates enthusiasm in man to live, and gives an exclusive purpose for life.

But that doesn't mean that sex is everything. Disciplined sex makes life sweeter. Sex in itself is not the purpose of life. Unlike in animals, it adds spice to our ordinary human life. It helps man to attain the goal of his life, and the aim of human life is to achieve immortality.

Well, Adam, an abrupt ending for your undisciplined life is the need of the hour. A thorough understanding of the facts about human life has given you maturity. But you feel guilty about something. Your heart is heavy with some sin you committed or not in the past. You yearn for the effortless life of the Garden of Eden. But then you had a partner of your own with you... to share your worries, to console you, to advise you, to love you. Where's your Eve, Adam?

Perhaps it's another trick of Nature. You sleep quite innocently and peacefully, bereft of all responsibilities, enjoying the thrill of a noontime siesta. Your Creator stealthily approaches, and without your consent, takes away one of your rib bones to create an Eve. When you wake up, you feel a sense of loss and, there, begins your search for completeness. You feel you're incomplete; you feel something missing from you. An uncontrollable urge forces you to come out from a self-satisfied world.

'Go and look for her!' Your conscience whispers to you. You have no existence without her. It is true that she once gave you the forbidden fruit? But she also gave you a lot of other things. She tried to open another Garden of Eden for you. She gave you immortality in her own way. But you still live in the hope of regaining that old worn-out Garden of Eden. But she is here; ready to give you a new heaven and a new earth. Be practical, Adam! Be practical!

You can't ignore or desert your Eve. She is a part of your body... a part of your life... a part of your soul. For God made her with one of your rib bones. Look for her in every nook and corner of this world. Find her... and try together... to solve this puzzle of human life, the puzzle of your very birth.

It's all part of fate. You cannot escape from it. Try to find your Eve before it's too late. Knock, and the door will be opened. But luckier you are, if the door is opened spontaneously, without a knock. Yes, Adam, you are always lucky! Except that yours is always a belated luck.

Far, far away, beyond the borderline of the horizon, beyond the seven seas, there was that sin-stained, noisy world where I was born and brought up. And now on this isle, around which the waves danced, I was sitting, gathering the granules of memory from that disgusting world that lay subsided somewhere in the dark corners of my brain, and throwing them one by one into the white waters of the sea that wet my feet.

I heartily smiled, tasting and deliciously swallowing the delights of solitude of this new Eden. I laughed aloud when the canoe and the oar that brought me to this isle were crushed in the mighty waves, and went down into the depth of the sea. And I heard my voice echoing among the black rocks and boulders of the isle.

Now the breeze was consoling and comforting me. The greenery of the island intoxicated me. The sweet fragrance of various flowers and fruits invigorated me. The waves of eternal peace consistently beat around me. That isle seemed the rare meeting place of unexplainable delights and raptures. There... neither were there hopes or broken hopes nor were there wants and desires. Far away from those root causes of sorrow, this isle was a synonym for eternal satisfaction. Or so I thought for a while.

Suddenly I felt some natural force compelling me to turn my head to another side of the sea shore. I was amazed to see a female figure standing silhouetted against evening sky. She was completely naked, and was curiously watching those sea-crabs that made holes in the wet sand.

She was playing like an innocent child quite unaware of her nudity. She threw the white sand up against the wind and giggled at the cawing of the seagulls. She swam amongst the waves like a goldfish. She relaxed on the wet bank like a mermaid and played some strange games with them. Her long brown hair moved and fluttered in the saline wind, covering and revealing her naked virgin breasts.

She lisped with the seabirds and complained to the wavelets. She hopped up and down like a lamb, ran here and there and played as if she did not know anything about nakedness.

I felt a sort of divineness stir in me. An urge to become a part of her presence. To make her existence mine... and mine forever.

As that angelic beauty walked away from me, I could not resist my urge, and I called aloud to her, with an uncontrollable sense of inevitability: 'Eve... '

She turned her head quickly towards the place from where she heard the voice. It seemed as if she was expecting such a call for ages. For a moment, her face brightened and bloomed like the lotus flower at the sight of the morning sun. She hopped and jumped and ran towards me like a young doe.

She stared at me in utter bewilderment and surprise. Her wide eyes moved over me top to bottom and it seemed that she was expecting my arrival for a long time. She looked at me with her long eyes in which the pain of loneliness seemed stagnant. She did not notice my wild eyes that crept over her naked body, enjoying the perfection of feminine anatomy. She embraced me like a child who did not know anything about feminine delicacy or shyness. And then she, with the curiosity of a monkey, touched, checked, pulled and pushed at the clothes I was wearing.

Holding my right hand, she walked forward. In an indescribable excitement, she pulled me and brought me to the front of a cave, naturally formed and smoothed in the passage of time. I stood there wonderstruck, watching the lion cubs which hopped, jumped and played together with the lambs.

The sun was setting beyond the western sea. Darkness slowly crept onto the isle. Mist began to spread its blanket over the cave. And the chill wind, beginning its usual course, howled and whistled around us.

When she noticed that I was shivering in the cold wind, she ran into the interior part of the cave and brought some dried twigs and leaves and also a burning coal-ember. With them she made a fire for me. I warmed up my body, bearing the hunger that gnawed at me every moment.

She moved towards a tree with spreading branches and thickly growing leaves that stood in front of the cave. She pulled at one of the lowest branches and plucked a handful of fruits. Coming towards me, she extended her hands towards me, with an assiduous smile. In my excessive hunger, I greedily ate those delicious fruits.

I looked at her as if I was seeing her for the first time. The flames of the burning fire brightened her body. Her face glittered like the full moon. Her lips trembled for a while and I saw pearls of tears hanging on her eyelashes. We were experiencing a feeling of déjà vu!

Suddenly I felt as if I was rejuvenated. A sort of new charisma wakened within me. I jumped up and down with a new vigor and vitality. Some sort of a wonderful phenomenon was working in me by then. I was undergoing a kind of metamorphosis. My clothes fell down, like the withered slough of a snake, into the burning fire. I was turning into a new creature. My body began to shine like a newly sloughed serpent. I felt as if I was the first one in the generation of a new species. Ah, the wonderful mutation!

With an uncontrollable curiosity, I asked her in utter amazement: 'What's the name of this tree?'

There was a sad smile on her face. She breathed a long sigh, as if she had been completing the penance for a sin committed a long time before. Once again, there was that angelic smile on her face when she murmured: 'Don't you remember, it's the Tree of Life!'

As all my stripped-off clothes were consumed completely by the fire that burned brightly in front of the cave, she sighed as if she had relieved herself off a heavy burden which she had been carrying all these years. She slowly came towards me and put her hands around my neck. For a moment, she stared into my eyes. I looked into her bright eyes and felt a heavenly light passing into my eyes. Pressing her face against my hairy chest, she whispered and purred like a cat: 'Adam... Adam... Adam!'

It's all clear now, Adam! Here comes meaning for your life! All these days you lived for this discovery. Here's a chance to suffer your penance. The penance of a sin of which you are not aware of. A sin committed by your ancestors... and you have been doomed to bear the cross.

And once you feel that you have committed a sin... or a sort of unknown sense of guilt... you can't escape without compensation... and that's the penance... and there's no redemption without penance.

If Adam and Eve united in committing a sin, they must untie in finding a way out of it. Once you lost your immortality, you have to regain it. Therefore, the purpose of this human life is to regain that immortality... to regain that lost Paradise... at least the experience of it.

Adam, you're lucky! You have met your Eve! Now, it's time to realize the purpose of your life. Is it to reach excellence, as the Greeks say? Is it to join Para Brahma, as the Hindus say? To reach heaven, as the Semitic religions say? Whatever the aim, one thing is sure. Man wants to become immortal. How? Adam, now you begin your quest. It's high time to start your search.

Adam, first try to become a full man. You'll be a part of all that you have met, as Ulysses says, be it in the form of peoples, of places or of books. A myriad of writers, from the past masters to the contemporary quill-wielders, will be helpful to you. A myriad of events, sights and sounds will be of great inspiration to you. And the divine force in you will open new vents to knowledge and experience, and the divine light in you will open new outlets to express your personality. Let the Columns of Cloud and the Columns of Fire lead you!

Turn the pages of your diary, Adam Junior. See how far you've progressed in your aim. Let each page of your diary be a record of your genuine efforts... efforts to attain immortality.

On this New Year's Day, let me renew my efforts to realize my long time cherished wish to become immortal. I have to become immortal... nothing but immortal.

Many a man has become immortal through magnificent works of art and architecture. Painters and sculptors too became immortal. Are there human beings who do not wish to become immortal, at least, by placing black stones or white pebbles over their dead bodies, over their graves?

The easiest way to become immortal is to believe in a life after death. Almost all human beings around me believe in the immortality of their so-called souls. May I also accept that easy and effortless way?

There is nothing to exert one's efforts to believe in something irrational. Anybody can believe in anything. For instance, some believe that by drinking the blood of another, they can attain immortality. But all beliefs are as good as the imaginary axis of the planet earth. So I must look for another feasible way.

People like Homer, Valmiki, Shakespeare and Kalidas gained immortality in their own way. But how long should I wait to get that 'heaven-sent moment' of divine inspiration to compose great perennial literature? I burn the midnight oil in vain. And the result is only a blob of black sputum that I cough out every morning. Of course, through literature one can attain immortality. But the fate of a creative writer in between his ambition to become immortal and his reasonable animal instincts is really an obstacle.

People like Alexander, Napoleon, Hitler and Lincoln gained immortality through politics. They were successful in turning a lie into a truth through repetition. They could make unbelievable things believable through their oratory. What about me? My tongue is just a piece of cold meat. One becomes helpless under such predicaments.

Like all other great clever men of history, I too become god-fearing in the intoxication of helplessness. The Buddha and Krishna, the Christ and Mohammed, to name a few, are all immortal, aren't they? There was no scarcity of immortality for them as they were all either the incarnations or sons or prophets of God! What about me, a son of man, the legitimate son of a man and a woman?

Even thinkers, philosophers and scientists become immortal. Confucius, Marx, Einstein and Gandhi became immortal with their fancies. But they too are rare manifestations, and that I cannot expect to be.

To become immortal means to become God! Only God can create and God lives through his creations. For when God created man, he created him like himself. Therefore, human beings also began to create. His creations were also like himself. Thus, he also became immortal like God. 'You will be like God,' the snake said once.

Creation! Creations in art, architecture, in science and literature, in politics and religion. Creation that leads to production and reproduction. Nothing new but just the old wine in the new bottle. And thus, my ancestors became immortal through me. My grandfather became immortal through my father and my father through me.

I continue my search. I must seek the help of my partner in the process of acquiring immortality. And my partner will also gain immortality together with me. But who was the partner of God? And we believe that God is immortal. Of course, let the dichotomy prove it. Adam and Eve. Snake and Fruit. Tree of Knowledge and Tree of Life. Heaven and Paradise. God and Satan. Yes, Adam, you found your Eve at last! That's all! You gained a partner in the process of achieving immortality.

In fact, to become immortal, one should be in the good book of Fate. I have to please my fate with rites and rituals, with ceremonies and praises. Here, at last, my fate smiles on me. As she smiles charmingly, I faint into her hands... or fate herself faints at my smiles and falls into my hands.

I have to become immortal! Myself through my children, and my children through their children and through them my grandfather... and myself! All... all must be immortalized!

Blood boils in my veins for my immortality. On this day, Adam legalizes his partnership with Eve for immortality. But... can I make her immortal? Or can she make me immortal? Only time can prove it.

Cut! Cut! Stop, Adam!

No more diary-writing... it's dangerous! Your Eve will not tolerate it. Are you sure that she has that much sense of humor? Though it is the greatest quality needed for a happy married life.

But Adam, can you stop your diary-writing? When events, one after another, occur in life, how much of them can be kept in the folds of your memory? At least, you lose their accuracy.

No longer are you an individual! The more you try to develop your individuality, the more you wish to keep a record of it, and the more you move away from your partnership. And as diary-writing is purely a personal matter, it may create misunderstanding amongst couples if your partner has no sense of humor. And there shouldn't be anything that would create a gap in the partnership between a husband and wife.

Once you are a member of society, you become a representative of the society. Or other members of the society represent you and, therefore, your story becomes their story and their stories become your story. Their experience is your own experience. And so, Adam, you are not alone. What about the masses of experience your friends have? Let them say it so that you can share their experience and become part of it.

You are only one amongst the crowd... the crowd... the smell... the sweat... the bodies... the sex... the children... the members of your family... the friends... the relatives... the strangers... the grandchildren... the great grandchildren... and, again, Adam. Adam, the lonely man.

It's true, Adam, that you're only an unimportant speck in the vast ocean of human population. But you can't go on like that. Once you were only part of the crowd. But now you've discovered your partner, thereby, half of your life's mission is over, and you've legalized that partnership. Therefore, both of you are registered members of society. Both of you have responsibilities to each other and also towards other members of society. No longer are you free. You've been chained, Adam, chained with a myriad of relationships!

Come back to reality. Realize the fact of human life on this earth. No longer are you in the Garden of Eden. Fruits won't grow as such in this Garden of Eden. You have to work hard. Your Eve can't pluck fruits as such. Unless they are the fruits of her own garden. She can't fetch fruits from her neighbor's garden. Adam, it's your duty to bring fruits for her. You're supposed to find daily bread for her. You have to care for the physical immortality first. Then, think about the spiritual immortality.

Adam, it's too late for you to think over the consequences of your rash decision. You found your Eve and made her yours. You thought of it as a natural course of an event. But have you thought about your obligations to her, in particular, and your responsibilities to the family, in general?

Of course, at first, you thought that it was quite easy for you, a well-qualified person, to find the means of a reasonable livelihood. But qualifications and talents have no market here, unless you bribe others to accept you... to discover you.

A few days, weeks or months, she may tolerate your helplessness. Then, she may think of gathering fruits and bread herself. And it's easier to sell a woman's talents than a man's. For her, the talents of the brawn and the brain are of equal value. She even suggests to you about her sale-value, and even seeks your opinion on it.

Here, real despair comes to you. You're compelled to think about the meaninglessness of life. You become too cruel in a world of injustice. Your animal instincts are aroused. You wish to destroy everything; you wish to kill everyone. The spirit of Cain works in you for a moment; and you're tempted to justify the blood of Abel. Yes! This is the situation in which 'God grieved at his heart for he had made man on earth.' But where's that God who created me? Stole my rib bone and made Eve. Am I not hearing the words of God: 'My spirit shall not always strive with man, for that he also is flesh!'

Adam, you're of flesh! And flesh must achieve the needs of flesh. Think of Eve. Don't forget that love covereth a multitude of sins. But how long can you depend on flesh, the mortal flesh?

You live in a society that depends on a barter system. If you give something, in return, you'll get something. You give your sweat; you get your bread. And, of course, you are ready to give your sweat but nobody is there to buy it or exchange it for a piece of bread. That's this world. What a pity!

Sometimes they may not need your sweat at all. Then you may give your blood. They may not buy your sweat or blood; then, you give your head. Think, Adam! Think about the power of your head. You have to feed your Eve! Try to barter your brain for bread… which can be shared by both of you.

Try to find a place where people need your talents. Scan the opportunity pages of the newspapers. Check the columns of employment bulletins. Send applications one after another. Don't be desperate when they reject your applications. Try again! And again! This is not a place for the desperate and the dejected. Remember only the fittest can survive here.

Well, all these are easier to say. Sometimes you'll be at the end of your tether. Then you may think about putting an end to your life. You can jump into a deep well and drown to death. Or you can hang yourself to death. Or you can drink poison or swallow sleeping pills and die.

But anybody can do that! You may be tempted to do any such inhuman deed. Who's there to prevent you? But Adam, don't forget your partner. Think of her penance and the agony of her solitude. Perhaps, a savior may appear quite unexpectedly and…

But how long could one live in a world of myths? How long could one depend on the fruits of the Tree of Knowledge? Those were fruits of food for your mind, of course. But what about the food for your body? How long could sheer optimism help you to prolong your life?

Adam, come to the modern world of reality. Your Eve can no longer live in the wilderness of the Garden of Eden. She may prefer the company of the society ladies who spend their time in clubs, parlors and saloons. And I, Adam Junior, become forlorn. Only confessions can relieve me from my sense of guilt.

I was at the end of my tether! I opened the packet and counted the sleeping pills in it. They corresponded to my age; one tablet for each year.

Yes! It was time to end my too long journey. These years were very, very long to me though I forgot to live. Nobody was here to mourn my death. Perhaps, my wife would shed a few drops of tears. But Time the Healer would bring consolation to her and she too would forget this unwanted element.

I looked at the glass full of sweet milk brought by her, for it was her routine from the time of our staying together onwards. I put the sleeping pills, one by one, into the glass, and stirred it. Then I waited for the heaven-sent moment to drink it.

I needed a moment's super courage to commit suicide. Many a time I had tried to commit suicide but, alas, I was not a brave man. Without getting some peace of mind, how could one commit suicide? Whenever I tried to do that heavenly act, an immediate distraction would occur before me like an ill-omen.

I like to commit suicide in a lovely way. To die in the midst of sleep is the happiest thing one could expect in human life. So many times Yama, the God of Death, appeared before me in the form of sleeping tablets. But he was always reluctant to welcome this unfortunate creature to his dark world. It was a tragedy with me that whenever I decided to do a brave act, an immediate problem would rise before me like a fence of barbed wire.

On the previous day, she said to me: 'Oh, dear! You are a fool!'

Yes! I admitted it. It was not my fault that I was born on All Fools Day, the first of April. And April is the best month. I was a born fool, I wanted to live like a fool and I wished to die like a fool. I knew that a fool's coxcomb is far greater than a king's crown.

She struck her beautiful right palm on her forehead and cried: 'Oh, my goodness! Who gave you this royal name; it ought to be 'Beggar'!'

Yes! I admitted it too. I was a beggar and I knocked at each and every door to get a job. All of them turned me out. Some of them sympathized with me; others advised me to start a small-scale industry. Some others laughed at me and asked me to join politics; and few others threatened me. Wasn't I a beggar?

I looked at the latest letter sent by my mother. She wrote: 'Believe in God, my son. He will help you.'

Yes! I admitted it. Many a time God appeared before me in the form of a cup of tea or a piece of bread or in the figure of an interview card. On a hot summer day, when I was wandering through the streets of an ancient city in search of a job, God appeared before me in the form of a cup of tea. Again, when I was a hungry, ticketless traveler on a train, He appeared before me somewhere in the central part of this country, in the form of a packet of cooked rice. And what about those bundles of interview cards which were sacredly kept in my file? They were pages from the Bible for me! They helped me at least to prolong my life a bit more.

Once my father said: 'It's the fault with your horoscope,

my child. You have to suffer all these misfortunes up to the age of thirty five. Then the stars will shower blessings upon you.'

I couldn't admit it, however! Aries is not a bad star. I knew only one divine thing, the Goddess of Ill-luck. I had had a lot of experience with her, more than with any other gods or goddesses. She had two faces, as I experienced, one beautiful and the other an ugly one. She always looked at me with her ugly face. But, at the nick of an opportunity, she would smile at me, giving a glimpse of hope. Then, I attended my interviews as a rejuvenated man. But when the result came, to my utter distress, my goddess would show her ugly face once again. She continued this 'hide and seek' game for a number of years.

How long could one hang on to the threads of misfortune? All these years, my fancy cheated me much. My hopes burned me into ashes. I should have nipped them in the bud. Many a time, I had imagined that I would become the king of this country or even the emperor of the world. I had imagined that I could solve all the problems of the world with a magical snap of my fingers. But, alas, I was a fool, a born fool!

This world is not for fools. Neither for lovers and poets nor for madmen. I knew it and as I was a born fool, I had no other choice. I took the glass in my hand, collected a bit of courage and tried to drink the potion.

Oh, my Goddess Ill-luck! A knock came at my door, and I looked up cursing myself. She rushed excitedly into my room. She cried in ecstasy: 'Oh, my darling! How lucky you are! See this interview card?'

She pushed an interview card into my hands. Another incarnation of God! The beautiful face of my Goddess Ill-luck.

I said to her with a grave face: 'Just keep it in your hands. Tomorrow you may put it in my coffin!'

She stared at me. Then she noticed the glass filled with sweet milk and the empty packet of sleeping pills lying on my table.

'Oh, you fool! How dare you!' she shrieked and, then, threw the glass and milk through the window. A moment's silence, and then, she hid her face in her palms and sobbed bitterly.

I kept quiet, thinking about the unlucky man who turned back after touching the plough. God once again appeared before me in the form of an interview card so that I had to attend yet another interview.

Was it to prolong my life a bit more? Was it only to know that I was rejected by the interview Board? Was it to prepare another sweet potion? I didn't know.

You have to prolong your life, Adam! For the purpose of your life is to attain immortality. You have to stoop before your Eve, at times, to gain that goal. She may treat you like a dog, but don't feel ashamed because she herself is a cat.

Don't be so imaginative, Adam Junior. It's the fuming brain that brings dreams. Be practical about the realities of life. Don't write stories but only history, for history is stranger than fiction. Write the history of a writer in which the third person becomes the second or the first person.

He was a litterateur! And he was not willing to waste away his life worthlessly involved in momentary worldly pleasures, like other people who lived in and around him. Moreover, he had already realized that wants were the root causes of all sorrows and wants were unlimited. And that was the reason why he turned his attention fully towards creative writing which would give immortality to his own self!

And thus he had been spending his youth among those scattered books of literature and those half-finished papers either crushed to balls or torn into bits... in between the roof where spiders and lizards made their homes and the floor where cockroaches and mice played the hide and seek game.

Never did he care about the nuisance of spiders, lizards, cockroaches and mice in his room. But he became quite restless when snakes began to raise their hoods from among those books of literature, which adored more than his life, and from those bundles of his creative writings and those piles of papers in which he had scribbled down his fancies.

And one fine morning, enlightenment came upon that bookworm suddenly as he was engaged in his literary activities in the loneliness of his cloister. And thus, he realized the fact that if he had had a cat of his own, it would have protected him from those snakes that continuously disturbed his equanimity. Soon, he opened the door, came out of the privacy of his long-time closed room into the open air and began to look for a suitable cat.

He met a number of cats that belonged to different breeds and that varied in size and color. Some of them had beauty and charm but they were quite wild. Some others were quite tamed and domesticated but they were not beautiful. At last, his optimistic efforts gained success.

He found a charming, domesticated cat and brought her home. He felt as if he had the possession of the most valuable thing on earth. But he did not know at that time the truth that the nature of all cats was one and the same. However, both of them lived together in his room with co-operation and mutual love and respect.

And thus, the snakes that disturbed him all the time became food for the cat. And by then, the spiders and the lizards, the cockroaches and the mice in his room also ran away with fear. But he became totally confused when the cat began to interpret that whatever she did and whatsoever changes occurred after her arrival were all examples of her deep love towards her roommate and to show stubbornness in extracting from him the remuneration for each one of such instances.

Of course, he was very happy as the cat used to kill and eat, from time to time, the snakes that came out of the library books and from the bundles of his own literary manuscripts and danced before him with their raised hoods. But he was simultaneously sad at the fact that the spiders and the lizards, the cockroaches and the mice who gave inspiration to his creative writings ran away from his room, of course, being frightened by the cries of the cat.

However, in between the uncontrollable urge for creative writing and the absence of its motivation, he felt quite dejected. Being desperate at the wasteful passing of his life, he turned again towards his literary activities.

But whenever he attempted to do so, his cat would come near him and jump on his table with a purring sound of love making. She would turn everything upside down, strike his pen away with her paw, tear away his papers upon which he was writing and kick down the inkpot spilling the ink all over the table and on his clothes.

Many a time, when he was deeply immersed in meditation to get that 'heaven-sent moment' of real inspiration, his cat would come near his feet and rub her body against his legs with a murmuring of love or of some love-complaints. She would jump onto his lap and, sitting there with a full expression of security and satisfaction, dig her nails into the thick hair of his chest and scratch him lightly to sleep. And in situations like this, how could a poor litterateur get genuine inspiration or write real literature?

On certain other occasions when having felt really tired of reading and writing, he used to lift up that cat, for a change, and place her on his lap and tried to caress or rock her to sleep in order to relieve himself of the tension of writing.

In such situations, she would turn away pretending that she was very busy with a lot of other personal matters. And if he had insisted and applied a little pressure, she would attack him with tooth and nail and escape from his grip after giving him serious scratches and biting injuries. Could one change the instincts and inborn characteristics of a cat, just by changing her name to Eve?

As days passed, anger and sadness accumulated in him and he was in a sort of utter agony. In fact, he was in a dilemma, a kind if situation created when the restlessness caused by his inability to produce creative works and his unwillingness to inflict pain on the cat that for the first time entered his life and amalgamated into a single life.

One day, finding that he could not carry on with his life in such a pitiable manner, he attacked the cat physically, beat her for the first time and took her to a far away place and abandoned her there. But when he woke up the next morning, as the first auspicious sight of the day, he found the cat lying at his feet with closed eyes and murmuring something in an amicable tone.

Years passed and there was no change in the nature and character of the cat. She stayed with him killing and eating the snakes, from time to time, and by frightening and chasing away the spiders, the lizards, the cockroaches and the mice.

And whenever he started to write literature, the cat as a regular habit, came and disturbed him, as if it was her right to do so, and whenever he tried to caress her, she would wriggle away as usual from him in 'the most unkind' manner.

At last, he decided to leave all his efforts to become immortal through the means of literature. He finally realized the dictum: 'The end justifies the means!' He also realized the truth that he could become immortal by producing children of his own flesh and blood, as all the other people who lived in and around him did.

He tried to believe himself, just like all those great people who failed to achieve immortality through literature that a cat has nine lives and, therefore, by loving and serving the cat that lived as his roommate, becoming an inevitable part of his life, he could also gain nine lives together with her, here on this beautiful earth.

Alas! This is the fate of many a creative writer. Many ban the entrance of cats into their lives, and some others abandon the cats that entered into their lives as and when they ate the disturbing snakes and a few others kept them just for the sake of their immortality.

What meaning is there for immortality if there is no thrill in living? If one's efforts to attain immortality degrade the so-called dignity of human life, immortality becomes valueless. Of course, thrills are messengers of immortality. Lest, Adam, you should cry like T. S. Eliot: 'Where is the life you have lost in living?'

But what significance is there for immortality if man could not attain it independently, with out any external help? Man is created from dust and unto dust he returns. In other words, dust is mortal, man is dust and, therefore, man is mortal. Quite funny! Does it mean that at the time of his creation itself, even before he committed the original sin, God created him as a mortal being? Angels are created from light and devils from fire and, so, they are immortal. But man is created as mortal from dust and the story of the fallen man becomes unnatural.

Adam, man is basically an animal. It's society that created man from animals! And, therefore, he feels so relaxed when he returns to his fundamental instincts. He feels himself an animal and he considers other human beings animals. And so, if his mate is a cat, he himself becomes a cat or, perhaps, something superior, say a dog. And a cat's partner should be a dog. For it is a truth which is sacred and mysterious, like other sacred truths.

'When God created man, he created them dog and cat; and called them Adam!' Yes, Adam, so pitiable is human fate. But don't worry. It's just De Humana Physiognomonia. And, therefore, be happy. You have to bear the burden of such sacred truths. Call Eve, if you want. Let her help you carry the burden of such disgusting truths... to the grave.

The animal in man is too heavy to do away with. Yet man and woman adjust their life with each other, even at certain sub-human or anthromorphic situations.

Yes! He was just an ordinary dog! Nothing more; nothing less.

At first, it was a truth known only to him. Or he thought like that till the previous day. And how much he wished that his partner, the cat, should not come to know about that truth.

And that was the reason why he always behaved according to her likes and dislikes. He came running towards her when she just snapped her fingers. Wherever she went, he followed her like a watchdog. He ate deliciously the food, whatever it was, if it was given by her hands. He earnestly participated in all matters, personal or otherwise, but only in accordance with her plans.

When she decided to go somewhere alone, he would stay there watching her each movement anxiously but affectionately until she walked away from his eyes. He would guard the house and wait for her without even a blink of his eyes, and straining his ears for the sound of her light foot-falls when she returned. When she appeared, he would hop around her with a sort of uncontrollable rapture and behaved even quite awkwardly as if he did not know how to express his joy and pleasure.

He loved her; he respected, obeyed and feared her. What else could anyone expect from a faithful dog?

He tried to be happy in her happiness and to be sad in her

sadness. He did not forget to walk with her, to sleep with her, to encourage her and to give her thrill and delight, by presenting all sorts of calisthenics.

For he knew himself that he was only an ordinary dog. But on the previous day, all of a sudden, he was shocked to the core, as and when he happened to realize that from the very beginning itself she had been aware of that truth which he had been keeping all these years with him as a closely guarded secret.

Wasn't it because of that reason that she always beckoned him to help her or to nurse her whenever she desired? Yes! All these years!

He had to stand near her with a bowed head when she wanted to pat or caress him. He had to wait outside the room when she wanted to sit alone. He had to wake up quickly even from his deep sleep if she needed him. And never did she allow him to disturb her when she was sleeping.

Yes! It was a truth known to both of them alike that he was only an ordinary dog. And that was the reason why he stood smiling when she loved, scolded, punished or caressed him.

Oh, Adam! Don't be disheartened by such bitter experiences. Once, your forefather allowed his wife to go away from his side. She was tempted by the snake and, in turn, he was tempted by her. Thus, all the three were ousted from the Garden of Eden. And, there onwards, Adam, you became Eve's watchdog. These are all part of the game. If she can become a cat, why can't you become a dog?

If a husband can call his wife a cat, a wife can call her husband a dog. In such situations, a dog becomes the husband of a cat, and life becomes quite tolerable. Adam, forget everything else. Think of your duty as a watchdog. Your Eve expects your protection and, therefore, you have to accept the fact. It's a fact that only the two of you know. And so, keep it between you and your Eve.

Married life is a sort of 'hide and seek' game. Sometimes, you'll be the police and she'll be the thief. And other times, you'll be the thief and she'll be the police. Life goes on like that. Therefore be patient. Or everything's spoiled. Think of patience as the key-word to conjugal success. And humility and discernment add sweetness, if they are required. Once you feel fed up with sweet pudding, why not a touch of sour pickles... so that you can have more of that sweet pudding!

One relationship leads to another. Once the man woman relationship is legalized, it leads to a number of other relationships. The relatives of the husband and of the wife, especially the in-laws, make family life highly complicated. Of course, all such relationships help mutually to a certain extent. At the same time, they may develop themselves into bondages. Adam, you can't live here a life of the Eden Garden. Your life is interconnected just like the planets in the galaxy. You can't survive yourself.

Yes, Adam, reluctant birds will suffer. Why are you still afraid to face reality? Make the first move with full confidence. Faith and hope will be your companions.

But, remember, that fear goes with faith, side by side. Fear was the beginning of wisdom as it spurred man to quench his curiosity. At the same time, fear was also the beginning of ignorance, as it led man to a myriad of foolish beliefs, which later turned into, what we call religions.

It is said that God created Man and Man created religions. And in his eagerness to please God, he attempts all sorts of endeavors, fair or foul, even at the risk of breaking human relationships, as his belief is the outcome of his pure selfishness.

Out of man's power of creativity came thousands of fantastic ideas which later became the accepted, unquestionable rites, orgies and ceremonies of all religions. Men and women are so blind in their religious beliefs that they are forced to ignore even the happiness of co-existence.

There are the Hindus, the Greeks, the Christians, the Buddhists, the Sikhs, the Muslims, the Mormons and the Bahais. All rivers flow into the ocean, as Lord Krishna says; and the goals of different religions are one and the same. But each religion in itself is fanatic. Each believer is a fundamentalist. If man tries to protect his God, he is the creator of that God. For him, God is someone to be protected by him. What an idea, Adam. You have to live amongst those creators and protectors of God. You are incapable of correcting them for they are incorrigible to the core. So, you have to live a life, sandwiched between tweedledum and tweedledee.

Man is an emotional animal. Sometimes even irrational ideas and notions create strange emotions in him. Then he lives in a make-believe world and acts accordingly. This leads to conflicts and quarrels, both in his family life and in his social life. Quarrels and differences of opinion are inevitable in family life as well as in social life. Light exchanges of hot words and slight expressions of anger may enhance the strength of the relationship in conjugal life. But in social life, they may lead to further controversies and conflicts. Nobody can hate a person who repeatedly argues that two plus two equals four, because there's knowledge in mathematics. All quarrels are caused by opinions, and when one is not sure about the correctness of his opinion.

Even in controversial situations, one can maintain good relationships. Minor quarrels enhance the sweetness of conjugal life, they say. But religious belief is something deep-rooted and so a quarrel over such issues ends up in drastic, unpredictable results. Religion and politics are based on opinions and, therefore, a dispute over them will result in riots, fighting and massacres. Such disputes will not arouse sympathy in the hearts of the people as the believers themselves do not know whether what they believe is true or not. Opinion has nothing to do with knowledge and, so, religious and political opinions keep man under ignorance.

Remember, Adam, love is Truth! Truth is Wisdom! All definitions for these abstract words are based on knowledge and experience. All quarrels are subsided when there is real love. Those silly quarrels and misunderstandings amongst married people will bring real blessings if the persons concerned show a bit of patience and humility.

But Man is an Animal! A marriage is often the result of momentary attractions related to sex, sympathy, beauty, education, health, wealth, tradition or custom. The meeting of the man and the woman might have been an accident or merely a coincidence.

Adam, situations that lead to a marriage may be very funny and highly ridiculous, perhaps. But real understanding amongst the couples and proper communication between the husbands and wives will make their lives highly successful. There will be a secret behind the success of every married couple. As it is a part of wisdom, one can't disclose it in public. Though nothing is strange in it.

But, Adam, all these years you thought that Eve was your possession. You loved her because you thought that she was part of your body. Could you love her if she was not a part of your body? The answer is evident. You are so possessive and self-assertive that you didn't care for her individuality. You couldn't think of her personality apart from your own personality. You utilized her talents just for your own pleasure, convenience and supremacy over her. You're a sinner, Adam!

Now, think in the other way. Your Eve is too possessive and she tries to dominate over you. She thinks that you are her own possession. She realized that without her, Adam cannot become immortal. She knows your weaknesses, and she makes use of them for her pleasure, convenience and supremacy over you. You become a puppet, a mere play thing, in her hands.

Now she scolds you, advises you, guides you, warns you and teases you. When you are restlessly waiting for the heavenly inspiration to write down a new piece of creative literature, you suddenly hear the bangle-sound of her complaints. With your paint and brush, you try to recapture some forgotten shades of a dream, and then, her shouts or alarms break the thread of your fancy's net. And you suffer all these as a punishment for your recklessness in eating the forbidden fruit!

You feel that there's some reason in her words, though you aren't ready to accept it fully. You continue your search for a living, with more determination. Your Eve is hungry, and it's your duty to bring food for her. Forget your so-called principles and get her bread, Adam. Ethics can't quench her thirst. Get bread and water through fair or foul means.

A change comes to you. You took the decision and you can't turn back so easily. Then, chances are opened before you, one after another. Her warnings and scolding made you a man. They helped you to break away the chrysalis in which you were hiding. She even threatened that she would go to the streets and see whether she could earn her bread. No, Eve! Don't try to prove your own value. Every snake waits for such an opportunity.

Adam, take it as a challenge against your manliness. When the question of your own existence comes, you decide to snatch the first opportunity. Then, positions, one after another, queue-up for you. Here you must be careful before making a selection. You are at a junction, you are free to choose and you have to choose. Of course, if you have to choose from what is not in your power, you will not be blamed. But here you have to choose from what is in your power, your selection or rejection decides your future.

Why not consider the profession of a journalist? Instead of becoming a king with the burden of a crown on your head, it is better to become the king-maker. Journalists deal with history and with current events; they know the mind of the people and they can format their mind. While living in the present, you analyze the past, study the present meticulously and present what happens around you in accordance with the needs of the people. You realize that the pen is mightier than the sword! You can be a freelance journalist and write on any subject under the sun. But you have to burn much midnight oil. If you cannot find someone to publish what you write, you will be at a stake. You must be discovered by someone. Once you get acceptance, your words have value and validity. You will become powerful enough to control the affairs of the government. But the publishers around you have no noble intentions. They are mere businessmen who sell your sweat for their profit. You believe in the principle of Truth, the only Whole Truth. But they define and interpret Truth in a different way: Tell the Truth; only the Truth necessary for our profit! How can you keep your personality under such severe instructions? It's quite risky to your exclusive individuality.

What about the profession of a clerk or in the service of administration? You can become an important person in the operation of the government. You may be the key-nail in that great machine! But you will be under a politician who is elected to a higher position by the people who are befooled by his harangues. All your talents are sold just for his survival. Those ministers, who stand like servants before a journalist, become masters of an administrative officer. Day in and day out, you toil for their pleasure of being in power. Of course, if you are clever, you can shine; the shining of the cloud that moves close to the sun. Can you stoop to that level?

What about a lawyer's profession? You wear the black gown, in the high expectation of delivering justice to the members of society who badly need it. But you have to interpret law; and the goddess of justice is blindfolded! You have to manipulate the sections and clauses of law and interpret them in accordance with the needs of your clients. Sometimes, even you have to prove things against your conscience. But that's justice for a lawyer. Look into the pocket of your client and decide your rate. Different rates for different clients; different rates for the same point of law! But, Adam, how could you adjust with 'uneven laws'? Of course, your conscience always made you a coward.

Why can't you become a priest, and later a bishop, as your parents suggested or hoped, or at least a preacher without any ecclesiastical 'hands-placing on your head by a higher priest'? Then you will get social status, money and power, of course, a sort of pseudo-power. And the charisma of the holy cassock covers a multitude of inabilities and sins. But you have to preach those things which you really cannot believe. You must take it as a mere profession and insist the ideas, which you know irrational, on others. But how long can you manage your life like that? Can you degrade your noble birth to such a level? It's a sin, Adam! It's an unpardonable sin, a sin against your own soul!

Well, why don't you choose the profession of a teacher or professor? It's always better to be a teacher, if you don't care for luxuries which other professions may offer. Moreover, a teacher is a preacher too. And it is the experience that makes a real teacher. You have sufficient experience; and your experience is not the experience which others claim, for their experience is similar to the experience of brushing one's teeth!

You are different from others and your experience is unique. In a teacher's profession, one can enjoy unlimited freedom. In a classroom, you are the king. And when you become a professor, your obligations are lesser, and you can relax the whole of your life with a job that gives higher satisfaction and reasonable remuneration to manage yourself and your family. Moreover, society has much faith in a teacher and they respect him. With their support, he can grow to any level, as their representative in the local governing bodies or as a member in the Legislative Assembly or as a member in the Parliament. If fortune favors, sky is the limit for his growth. You can even become one of their rulers.

When the options are innumerable, from that of becoming a beggar to that of becoming an emperor, it's natural that you'll be confused. Don't think that anybody can beg or rule. Both professions need specific talents and timely luck. In this world beggars select to rule and emperors select to beg. Each one enjoys his realm! At the same time, ambition leads to dissatisfaction and you look forward to other realms. And you feel others are happier than you. This jealousy prompts you to select power; the maximum possible power. And once you immerse in power, it blinds you to the core.

No more second thoughts, Adam. Now, you get a position, you get money and you get power. You become the ruler of a realm where no one could interfere or question your decisions. And then you find a smile on your Eve's face. But was that smile evidence of consent on her part to give immortality to you?

Mornings and evenings come and go; months and years pass one by one. Adam, you are still far away from your destination. Your goal in family life is still a mirage for you. You desperately crave for immortality. And it is only through your Eve that you can acquire it! Of course, it's your own option, and you have to face the consequences of it.

Your Eve has her own excuses. She wants to postpone her conceiving. She is afraid that it would reduce her beauty, damage her personality or harm her individuality. Or she needs more time to stand on her legs, to enjoy the easiness of youth and to relax without burdens of life. She thinks that to conceive a child will make her a slave to her husband, or a prisoner to the family for the rest of her life.

At times, she even becomes hysteric and shrieks: 'Oh! Why I alone should suffer? Every month the horror of a bloody week! Once it stops, the weeks of the swelling womb! The fattening of the body; the loosening of the muscles! The ugliness and disability of a human body! Then the travail, the delivery, the breast feeding and the nurturing of the child! Oh, my God! Why I alone should suffer all these?'

Other times, she weeps with a broken heart: 'God! Why did you create me? Why this life of misery for me on earth? If you give me another life on this earth, it should not be as a woman! Never again the life of a woman!'

Oh, no! Don't think like that, dear Eve. In fact, you are the greatest creation on this earth. Without you, this world will not survive. Human beings must fill this world, like stars in the sky or sands on the shore; and that's the will of God. For that, you are needed. Adam becomes quite insignificant before you, oh Eve.

She ignores your consolation and stares at the heavens and murmurs: 'You betrayed me, God! You made me believe that all these are the consequences of my sin, the eating of the forbidden fruit! No! Not at all! You have pre-planned everything! Otherwise, why did You make a womb in my body at the time of my creation, much earlier to my fall? The forbidden tree, the snake, the fall and the curses on me – all were mere farce! You betrayed me God, You betrayed Eve, the best of your human creations! You sinned against me! And for every sin, there's punishment! If so, your betrayal of Eve will be repaid in the same coin! I'll make my Adam repay it! He will betray you, and You will be redeemed and freed from your sin!'

Oh, Eve! It's heresy! Be humble before God. Humility and patience are the only keys to happiness. Accept the fact that life is quite miserable on this earth and the success of human life depends on how happy it can be made. No gains without pains, my dear!

Or, sometimes, she may even be thinking in an unnatural way: 'Oh God! Am I the rib bone of this Adam? Didn't I commit a blunder in my choice, if the choice is mine? Am I really belonging to some other Adam? Or even Adams?'

'Or why should I be with an Adam? Always living with him, caring for his strange likes and dislikes, taking into my body his stinking sperm, carrying his child in my womb for about a year and finally delivering a child to him? And, thereby, the natural texture and shape of my whole body is changed into something disgusting?'

'Oh, why don't I live alone as a single entity? Is it mandatory on the part of a woman that her life will become full only with an Adam? Don't I have the freedom to attain my own immortality without depending on a male, or on another individual as the case may be?'

'Or why not live with another Eve who is equal to me in every way? The natural and physiological domination and overpowering of a male on a female is intolerable! At least, physically a male may not be equal to me and, therefore, there's a male domination and that in itself is a sort of submission. Am I supposed to bear that injustice throughout my life?'

Oh, Eve! Control yourself! Don't play with your whims

and fancies to that extreme. Did I ever curtail your freedom of individuality? Did I ever try to keep you like a slave? When you decided to go to another part of the Garden of Eden, far away from my presence, and to manage yourself there, did I prevent you? I had full confidence in your abilities then. But when you met the snake, you forgot your Adam for a moment. If that forbidden fruit had only provided you equality with Adam, would you have consumed it? Instead, when the snake promised you equality with God, my Creator, you were really tempted. That was your sin! As a woman, you wished to become equal to God, and not equal to man. You think only in two extremes, either as an inferior being or as a superior one. You can't think in equal terms; and you are fully aware of the reasons for your inferiority and your superiority.

And my sin was that I risked my life, unlike other creatures in the Garden of Eden, and decided to die with you, even ignoring for a moment the grace of my Creator. Thereby, I became equal to you, in life and in death! For that sin, I am ready to stoop to any level, for without your consent I have no immortality. Or else, I should be an animal, barbarous enough to ignore the individuality of a female. Come, dear Eve, let's come to a consensus.

Oh, I am fed up arguing with you. Only God can answer your questions and clear your doubts. Adam, you fail miserably here.

Remember Adam, immortality cannot be attained so easily. You selected the easiest way but, there too, it's the fate that decided the matter. All your calculations and confidence go wrong until you fall down and surrender yourself at the mercy of your fate.

Months and years pass. Adam accuses Eve; Eve accuses Adam. Both knew that each of them was powerful enough to produce a new generation. But unknown reasons postpone their desires. Uncertainty brings in darkness. With dejected hearts, both of you decide to subjugate unconditionally before the foul-play of your fate.

The pheasant-crow waits for the hatching of its eggs, in vain. But I must somehow hatch my eggs. From where will I get the blue-koduveli that can hatch my eggs? Should I go down into the darkness of some unused wells to gather that magical herb? God! You blessed me with eggs but they waste away being unfertilized. Don't be desperate, Adam. Have confidence on the power of the fish-head.

Suddenly, a flash of hope kindles the fires of hope within you. The dream of immortality once again enthralls you. Both of you were thrilled at that new experience and both of you sang and danced in ecstasy. You began to feel real conjugal bliss. You were ready to sacrifice each other for even simple and minute pleasures and happiness.

Then began the waiting for the child, the fruit of your unison. Both of you started counting days, weeks and months, impatiently. You watched her with pride; she looked at you with honor. When was that day in which your mortality transforms into immortality?

You wait outside the labor-room. You walk a thousand times, to and fro, along the corridor, like a caged lion. You count the mosaic tiles on the floor; you count the number of steps you place, from one end to the other end of the verandah. You pray to every angel and every saint. And minutes crawl like hours.

Your sweetheart is suffering labor pain. In pain thou shalt bring forth children. The curse of God still hangs upon her. But how could a husband ignore the responsibility in giving his wife this pain? You hear her shrieks of travail, in her efforts to give you immortality. Adam, your heart beats fast with agony and anxiety. Your mind is full of tension; and the muscles of your body turn tight.

All of a sudden, you hear a cry from the labor-room. A new voice but it seems quite familiar to you. As if you heard that cry many times in your dreams. You recognize that voice of consolation, and suddenly, you feel quite relaxed. What remains with you is just curiosity.

Then a nurse brings a small bundle of a thick towel, at the half-opened door of the labor-room. You stretch your neck like a giraffe, and look into the small opening among the folds of the towel, delicately carried by the nurse. A flash of thrill and delight! You see the tiny face of a child, blinking at the unfamiliar sunlight, but vaguely looking into your eyes. For a moment you forget everything else, and feel yourself immortalized. You heave a hot sigh of relief. Life becomes worthy of living. Life becomes truly meaningful and you realize new meanings for your mortal life.

Adam, here onwards you toil not merely for bread and water for you and your Eve. You have to work hard and harder for your progeny. You feel your burden light; you feel the sweat on your forehead sweet. 'Behold, the Man has become as one of us!' The voice of God echoes in your ears, and a smile of victory hangs upon your lips.

Days, weeks, months and years pass, watching the growth of your child, from a tiny, wriggling object into a perfect person of its own individuality, a blend of you and your Eve, a replica of your own self.

You feel that the well-being of the family is safe in the hands of your Eve. She is fully capable of managing all the domestic affairs as well as maintaining the relationship with other members of your family, other relatives and neighbors.

You slowly concentrate on social work. Of course, you have responsibilities to the society in which you live. But once you get chances to dominate over other members of the society, you forget your responsibility towards your wife and children. Maybe you are too busy dealing with the problems of your fellow-beings. But that's not an excuse to ignore the problems of the members of your own family!

Adam, you're happy or you try to find happiness in future gains. You prepare plans and schemes to attain something greater in the future. But don't think of your Eve in the same stream of thinking. She always prefers immediate pleasures. She never cares for what happens in the future. That's her nature from the Garden of Eden onwards. 'Let's enjoy life now!' she says. Of course, where life is uncertain, can we make long-term plans? Can we think that there's light at the other end of this dark lane? But Adam, the success of life depends on its sum-total. When you make calculations, it may not be as successful as you expected it. That's the case with every so-called immortal personality you find in history. Slow and steady, wins the race! But you are disappointed when your Eve thinks of immediate pleasures. Of course, they're silly but you also need it for your survival.

And remember, Adam, life acquires meaning quite accidentally. It may be an unexpected friendly encounter or an expression of sympathy or a sexual attraction. But the outcome may be unexpected. It may change human lives. It may even change human destiny! Miracles will happen at unexpected moments. What you can do is wait for that blessed moments... wait patiently.

If accidents can unite persons into a happy family life, they can also break happy families and separate persons. Adam, just an accident of eating the forbidden fruit led to the loss of your happiness in the Garden of Eden. Similar accidents may be repeated and you and your family may lose happiness quite unexpectedly.

Such accidents may occur at the bus-stops, railway stations

or aerodromes. Whether a name is given or not to a person whom you meet, things will happen as it should happen. Adam, open your diary and see what you scribbled on its pages. Of course, you never cared for the warning not to write diary notes.

I was walking towards the synagogue. Being so deeply immersed in thoughts, I paid no heed for those things that occurred around me. And no need to say that it was Shabbat! For it was only on Shabbat that many of us went to the synagogue. We used to go to temples, synagogues, churches, mosques and gurudwaras in search of God. For we were like the musk-deer that wandered all over the forest in search of the origin of its musk, being ignorant of the fact that it was in its body itself, to be particular at its groin. And another reason was that Shabbats were holidays. Wasn't it on those days that we used to go shopping or see movies or visit our relatives, as they were days in which it was not necessary for us to go for work?

And that might be the reason - or it might be because I was too anxious and worried about the existence of the synagogue and about the future of God – why I did not notice one of my neighbor-girls who walked just ahead of me. Perhaps she too was drowned like me in some deep thoughts!

Her name was Ms. Whore or Ms. Prostitute; or it was in such names our natives, the so-called elite or illiterate citizens, respectively, called her in accordance with their financial status! Whatsoever, it was she who greeted me first and, of course, I returned her greetings, and we together walked towards the front of the synagogue. For was it not there that the bus which went to the city stopped to collect those who did not go to the synagogue? And without entering into the bus which stopped every morning in front of the synagogue, nobody could go to the city where they used to shop or see movies or visit their relatives!

Though both of us were walking along the road, deeply engrossed in our own thoughts, perhaps thoughts on unknown and unnatural things, and even without least attention to whatever happened around us, we were quite aware of the electric current, as the third-rate quill-wielders of the pulp literature used to describe, that passed from one person to another due to the mutual unintentional friction of our bodies!

When I asked her, of course quite foolishly, the reason for that permanent expression of sorrow on her face, she replied: 'I don't know exactly whether the expression on my face is sorrow or not! But what other expression should be there on my face as I am a person who walks in the vacuity between the sole truths of birth and death, with a body smeared by the stains of sin that were thrown at or imposed upon me by circumstances? And I know that you too are incapable of giving another name for that so-called expression on my face!'

As we were walking silently, fixing our eyes at the other end of the road, her side conducted heat to me through my elbow and my fingers that heedlessly tangled among her fingers. When pedestrians who were familiar to us came towards us from the opposite direction, I realized how she moved away from me with a shudder and how she tried to shake away her palm from the knot of my fingers.

I asked her quite innocently how her name happened to be Whore or Prostitute. She said: 'What's there to be surprised when a woman is called Whore or Prostitute if she had been raped by four persons on four different occasions?'

She continued: 'The first one was our University Professor who raped me in the loneliness of the department and recommended my name for a doctorate degree at the cost of my virginity!'

After a long sigh, she said: 'When his wife came to know

about this, she asked her brother who was a policeman to arrest me. In the loneliness of the lock-up room of the police station, he raped me and reassured that I had lost my virginity!'

She continued: 'Later in the loneliness of the legal office, the advocate raped me and argued in the court that I would not have lost my virginity!'

She stopped for a while. Taking a deep breath, she said: 'On the previous day of delivering the verdict, the judge raped me in the loneliness of his chamber and declared that I had not lost my virginity. And, thus, as a woman who regained her virginity, I live only to be called Whore or Prostitute!'

When she was telling me her story, I felt a sort of surprise rather than mere sorrow. I was thinking only about the electric current that passed from her body to me through the elbow of my left arm and also about the heat that it produced in me. And I gave more importance to the fact that she was 'a woman raped by four persons on four different occasions' rather than to 'a woman happened to be called Whore or Prostitute'!

I began to talk to her in a consoling and pleasing tone: 'Rape by professionals like Professors, Policemen, Advocates and Judges is a common phenomenon in our society! Moreover, if both the man and the woman get at least a moment of mutual pleasure, a rape may not become such a big crime! Truly speaking, it is disappointment of not getting a chance or the jealousy towards those who got the opportunity that appears on the faces of the people like us in the form of moral indignation. We are all just camouflaged philanthropists of a hypocritical society!'

She suddenly turned her face and stared into my eyes! Then, as if nothing happened, she walked forward and said in a hushed voice: 'If you don't say it to anyone else, even to your wife, I shall tell you a secret. I am suffering from a very serious sexually transmitted disease!'

I was shocked and I stood there for a moment like a dead body! I visualized how my happy married life was going to be contaminated with poison. And, then, we walked to the bus-stop at the front of the synagogue, just like two strangers. And there at the bus-stop, I found my relatives and relatives-in-law, standing incapable of taking a decision whether to go to the synagogue or to the market.

My wife stood there silently staring at me, who dared to walk together with a woman named Whore or Prostitute towards the bus-stop at the front of the synagogue! My brother turned his back to me as if it was shameful even to look at my face. My wife's mother suppressing her sobs cast a painful look at me with eyes overflowing with tears. My own mother who delivered me, and brought me up with her own breast-milk was crying and cursing me as usual. My wife's grandmother who was deaf with age was looking at me in an unbelievable manner. My own grandmother who was old and blind with age was straining her ears without knowing the meaning of the sudden silence that occurred at my arrival. I stood in front of the synagogue for a moment without knowing what to do!

Soon the line-bus to the city came like a tempest and stopped with a screech at the front of the synagogue. My neighbor, friend or comrade whom they called Whore or Prostitute slowly walked with a bent-head, as if she was in deep thought or meditation, towards the deserted synagogue.

My relatives and relatives-in-law stood there in utter confusion, thinking whether to go to the city or to the synagogue. For a moment, I too was incapable of deciding whether to go shopping or to see a movie or to call at my friends in the city.

Then, within a split-second, I jumped onto the bus that had already begun to move, and dissolved in its crowd's non-entity.

What an escapist you are, Adam? You don't know whether your Eve will continue to wait for you. You don't know whether the girl whom you met on the way was the same girl whom you met somewhere in a train or in the temple complex of Khajaraho. How strange human behavior is!

Adam, this is life! Atrocities against women are given wider publicity because such news is sensational. In fact, everyone who is involved in the handling of such cases gets a sort of sadistic or vicarious pleasure. People express great indignation on such matters but its all part of their hypocrisy. Do you think that people have any real sympathy towards a raped girl? Or a girl tempted by the snake in the Garden of Eden? Never! It's a sort of camouflaged indignation they project. They ask: 'Can you thread a moving needle?'

There are people who sympathize with the sad life of prostitutes. But in their heart, you can see a flash of curiosity or jealousy. They laugh in their hearts. They support the laws of morality because they don't get opportunities otherwise. And if you show some real sympathy, your relatives will become suspicious of you.

Adam, at least you're greater than others. You had a lot of opportunities but you could resist your temptations. You have to answer only to your conscience. And don't care about what others say or think about you. Even if it's your Eve!

Move on with confidence. Nobody can change your fate. Adam, your fate is marked. It's all fixed even before your creation, so your birth, life and death are part of an unchangeable scheme. Some people may believe that one's fate is marked six days after his birth but whether it is written before birth or after birth is unimportant. Remember the saying in Hindu philosophy:

Bidhena jo likh diya chatti rat ke ank /
Ratti ghatte na til bede rahu re jeev nishank //

Be fearless, feel free and be at ease, for you are bound to
meet the fate that has been written on the sixth day of your
birth by the Fate-maker, and you can't change it by a sesame
seed even! So, Adam, have confidence and don't feel disturbed
of anything happening in your life.

You may become restless at the wrong notions of others.
You want to serve society and find solutions to the injustice
suffered by your fellow human beings. But as you try to do so,
opposition comes even from unexpected quarters. Your
neighbors, friends, relatives and even your wife turn against
you. In your zeal to uplift society, you ignore such oppositions.
Then, you may wish to wipe off those who stand in your way
of justice. You may become too cruel in removing the
obstacles in your way, especially, if you get the power and
position to do so.

When you get power, you gradually become addicted to it.
The more prominence you achieved, the more social
involvement you welcomed. Power is a magic drug, once you
begin to enjoy it, you can't escape from its charm. Gradually,
in order to attain more power or to retain the power you
attained, you embark upon new tactics. You feel all those who
try to control or degrade your power are your enemies. Even
you think that your superiors and, at times, your friends too are
your enemies. And the new tactics and strategies you evolved
lead you to take up any action, sometimes, very cruel and
inhuman actions!

In fact, you get a sort of pleasure out of it. It's like the
pleasure a person enjoys while killing mosquitoes! You know
that mosquitoes are your enemies. They come one after
another, some hide in the corner of your room, a few fly around

you with a song, and others attack you directly. You know that all of them desire your blood, or you believe so.

At first you have limited power to destroy them. So you decide to make consensus with them. If they become too disturbing or ferocious, you use your hands and slap them to death. Sometimes, you drive them away with a simple wave of your hand. Or you may shrug your shoulders, when a drastic attack is operated, and you just go inside your mosquito net and sleep peacefully.

But everything changes as you get a promotion so that you can use a plastic swatter! You realize that you can't kill flying mosquitoes with a plastic swatter. Then, you move by the side of the walls, and kill those poor mosquitoes who take rest. You kill even those non-violent mosquitoes one by one, and feel the greatness of triumph. But, remember that you can't destroy the active mosquitoes with a manually operated swatter. You can frighten them away by waving the swatter, but of no use. You, finally, crawl into your mosquito net and feel safe in it. Yet, even in your dreams, you prepare some new schemes to destroy all those enemies.

At last, you get another promotion, and that means more power and more enemies. The attaining of an electronic swatter changes your whole attitude towards life. You realize that all the mosquitoes can be killed with this new instrument, whether they are resting on the walls and cupboards or hiding in a corner of your room or singing around you or attacking you directly.

You enter the room, the mosquitoes swarm around you as usual. You switch on the electronic swatter, and almost all of them are shot dead within a minute. But, from every dead mosquito, thousands will rise up. And you kill each mosquito that comes towards you, with a light swing of your bat.

Bam! Bam! Or Tuk! Tuk! You shoot them one after

another. You feel a sort of music in the shooting sound. An odor comes out from the swatter, which intoxicates you. Then you continue your ping-pong till the odor of death intensifies.

At first, they come in groups, and you kill them all. Then, they come one by one, and you kill them one by one. Sometimes, they fly straight into your electronic swatter, like members of some suicide squad, and meet their instant deaths! At times, you move towards their hideouts and kill them. Some innocent and non-violent mosquitoes, even those vegetarians who feed on leaves and banana peels, are also killed in the operation, and you consider it part of the normal course of action.

Some of them escape your attack, and you allow them to escape, for you know that they will come back another day and fall into your trap. Finally, you think that the operation is a hundred percent successful. You feel tired and retire into your mosquito net. During your sleep, you continue to scheme new massacres for the next day.

Adam, remember that one can't do away with all their enemies! In fact, they are not really your enemies. Like you, they too blindly believe in certain so-called principles. They are ready to die for their principles. They are like honeybees destined to be drowned in their own honey. And, in this world, there will be no end for martyrs, as far as they believe martyrdom as the purpose of life. Some become martyrs in accidents; some others deliberately walk into martyrdom.

In fact, it was not solely your mistake. Once fed up with cruelty, you decide to put down your weapon and, suddenly, thinking that it was your weakness, the enemies launch their fresh attack. And you can't help taking the weapon again. But how long can you operate such cruel genocides? Remember, thousands will rise up from each drop of blood.

Of course, you became one of the rulers of society by

chance. And your opposing people too wait for their chance. You fight for your survival and they fight for theirs. And you think that there's a flood after you! Remember that the world will continue as usual, and history will laugh at your self-assertiveness. Even in your absence, society will be guided by others who are, perhaps, better than you, and things will go on smoothly like this till Doom's Day.

But is to acquire power and try every means to retain it a crime or a sin? Isn't power a basic need of man like air and water? There are people who think that air, water, food, sex, shelter and clothing are the only basic needs of man. But they were the basic needs of the primitive man. In fact, most of them are mere basic needs of animals.

Is man not different from animal? If he is different, the list of his basic needs should be lengthened. If man is an advanced creature, his basic needs also should be advanced or modified ones. Instead of mere air and water, they must be fresh air and fresh water. What about delicious food and magnificent shelter as basic needs for man? If sex for reproduction is a basic need of animals, sex for pleasure is the basic need of man! What about attractive clothing rather than something that gives protection from cold? Isn't family life a basic need for man? Why can't we include various entertainments that boost human life in the list of basic needs? What about things like tobacco and alcohol which stimulate man's enthusiasm for life? And, last but not least, what about power? All these are really the genuine basic needs of man. Then, Adam, you are not a sinner. You only desired those things which are necessary and inevitable for a real human being.

Of course, there are human beings who live like animals. They think that simply to live is the purpose of life! At times, circumstances compel man to live like animals but such a life is not what is expected of man. He must live like a human

162

being, and that's what God expects from him.

Of course, man can avoid almost all his basic needs and live. There are people, in our great stories and sagas, who lived even without air, water or food. Human beings can lead a life of complete renunciation, rejecting even all the basic needs. But that's not a natural way of living. Then, you are torturing your body. Many of our religions insist various ways of such body-torturing, from mild fasting to severe mutilation of the God-given body. But no philosophy or theology should stand against the basic aspirations of the human mind.

And if man's deliberate adjustments with his circumstances or his un-natural aspirations and vaulting ambitions bring him sorrow and despair, that's part of the game; he is doomed to face them as part of his fate.

Then, Adam, do you think that man is chained to his fate; is he a predestined creation? Can he not break the shackles of fate imposed upon him? If so, human life itself will become meaningless. Why can't you separate fate from that span of life between birth and death? Aren't birth and death the only unquestionable facts of fate bestowed upon you? In between birth and death, man is supposed to make up his life. Failure and success of life depend on circumstances. And when man fails to manipulate his circumstances, life becomes a burden for him. Then, man may think of death, the ordinary death in the form of a birth without death or the best death in the form of a glorious martyrdom.

But Adam, isn't it true that you forgot yourself in the craze for power and wealth? It's high-time to realize your own limitations but you will never. You became too cruel. You continue to create martyrs until you yourself become a martyr. Once you blindly follow a dogma or principle, you don't care about friendly or other blood-relationships. You are prepared to betray your intimate friends and followers and, even, your own master. Of course, you have your way, and your master has his. And what can you do, if the master wants to become a martyr for the philosophy he upholds… or if he requests you to elevate him to the position of a martyr?

You call me Judas, a betrayer of my master? But how could I prove that my master wished to become a martyr and, even, indirectly requested me to help him? In the fullness of Time, everything will be proved.

How funny it was! Adam, you tried to achieve power and you gained it; but the more power you gained, and the more you felt impotent. You fell into the trap made by your master. He promised you greater power and you believed it. Of course, there are various levels of power like physical power, mental power or spiritual power and so on, and he knew best. Your master knew the secret of power and of its excellence. He knew that martyrdom was the best way to achieve immortality. And he deliberately made you a pawn in the game.

Don't you feel a vacuity in your mind, as you stand quite depressed, on this deserted mountain slope? Mountains and valleys are refreshing and invigorating; they give you new ideas and strength for your future activities. Your master used to go to the mounts and return with greater energy. But now, you feel a kind of indifference, a sense of loss, an experience which one undergoes when all those dreams fondled throughout life were dried and withered. The mental condition of a lonely traveler who finds his way completely blocked that he cannot go either forward or backward!

From the distant Calvary Mount, the uproar of the crazy people flows down to the valley where I stand, waiting for the white smoke. Won't my master, at least at this last moment, reveal his real divine power and come out of the mess as the King of Kings? Can't he, who fed the five thousand with five breads, create a large army from the stones and thorny bushes of Calvary? How great it would be if he broke forever the yoke of slavery imposed on these poor human beings?

Perhaps, he deliberately accepts crucifixion in a calm and peaceful manner? But I can't think of such a situation! For he is the Messiah, born with all the strength of breaking the chains of mortality, to establish an empire! Can these worms and vermin of men crucify such a divine being? No, never!

Are his words really true? He said that he would be crucified, but on the third day he would resurrect. If his words are true, the whole world will think of me as a barbarian who betrayed his master. Will there be a person, realizing my sincerity, enter into my heart and find out the truth? Even my friends, my colleagues in the Nationalist Movement, will mock me! Nobody will suspect the other zealots who have been working with me, and they too will isolate and hate me! Today, I am alone, for as their leader, I volunteered to betray my master.

Whatever I attempt, will come to an utter failure, and that's my fate. Never did my dreams blossom or my desires become fulfilled. As I was the favorite of my master, all his other disciples despised me. They looked down upon me and ignored me as I did not belong to their native place. My master knew it and that was the reason why he made me his treasurer and gave me the highest position among the group. And I was always keeping sufficient money in the leather pouch hidden in the inner pocket of my gown. I was always very particular in distributing the money in accordance with the need of each one of the disciples. But they always watched me with envy, jealousy and malice!

Of course, money was not at all a problem for my master. Weren't the wealthy people of the country, his secret disciples, ready to give whatever amount he needed? There were people prepared to wash his feet with highly expensive perfumes.

How much money could we collect if those perfumes were resold in the market? Could penury affect a person who is capable of taking sovereigns even from the mouth of fish? I was always with my master and I never suspected his divine power.

However, I could never adjust myself to go with the ways of most of his disciples who were mere illiterate fishermen hailing from the villages. For, I had my own clear principles and motives in joining with my master. The complete emancipation of the people was my great dream. Was it mere vaulting ambition of a megalomaniac? In fact, I joined him for the fulfillment of my long cherished dream for freedom of the people.

Of course, I was an extremist who took an oath to drive out all the evil forces under which the people suffered. And as a zealot, I could never tolerate the pacific approach and the very slow attitude of my master. Many a time, I expressed my dissent directly to the master, but then, he either warned me or scolded me. Well! Among his followers, I was the 'ho heis thon dhodeka', the leading disciple! Didn't he give that position to me just to console me, or rather, to control me? And I was kept out from my master's 'dearest trio', his so-called conscience keepers.

My master was very careful in giving the most important seat during the feast. On the seat where three people could sit, he gave only his right side for even one of his dearest disciples. My master asked me to sit on his left side so that he could lean on his left hand and give me bread with his right hand. And wasn't it our tradition to serve and honor the chief guest? Was there any disciple amongst us who did not desire to sit on the left side of the host, our master?

Though my master knew the thoughts that passed through my mind, during that feast, he did not prevent me from action;

he was giving me a silent permission. And no one cared or knew the secret words exchanged between us. However, I noticed the face of his dearest disciple, who sat on his right on the same seat with me and my master, turning pale and ghastly, when I dipped my piece of unleavened bread together with my master into the 'sharoshet' made from sweet fruits and bitter roots.

Was a kind of evil spirit entering into me when my master lovingly offered me a piece of bread dipped in sharoth? But there was no time for me, then, to ponder over such matters. Wasn't I a person who took the firm decision to adopt any drastic means for a greater end? I could not find any other means to save my master from his slow attitude. I knew that his lack of hurriedness would shatter the spirit of nationalism amongst us and, thereby, make us fall into an everlasting slavery.

Even now, the bitterness of the bread which I ate on the previous day, lingers on my tongue. The earlier I could hurl away the yoke from the shoulders of my people, the better. My master performed miracles only when he was compelled to do so, only when it was inevitable, and it was my duty to create an inevitable situation for him. I was quite sure that if my master was trapped, he, who had healed the sick and made the dead rise up into life, would destroy the enemies with his divine powers. And as a person who always walked with him, I knew that my master would do miracles if only situations demanded them.

When I went out during the feast, with a clear purpose, nobody prevented me. If my master had revealed why I went out, other disciples would have prevented me. And my master's silent permission heightened my confidence. Of course, other disciples thought that I, who always kept the purse with me, was going out to distribute money to the poor as it was a common practice on such feasts.

While conspiring with the enemies, I was feeling a sort of bliss, in the hope of the imminent emancipation of my people. I expected that it would happen on the day in the previous week, when the people roared 'hosanna' to my master and led him to the capital city. But then, my master ignored my long cherished dream and also the hope of the people. He always hesitated to grow and act up to my expectations. Or has he some other scheme of his own? Well! There onwards, I was in a pledge to take rest only after making him the sole ruler of our people, by giving him the scepter and the crown with my own hands.

I knew that a huge amount would be given to the person who pointed out my master. But I was not greedy and I took from the enemies only thirty pieces of silver, the formal amount to make an agreement legal; for my aim was not to earn wealth. And that too I threw at the faces of those who made agreement with me. And that also was the reason why I did not even go to the court as a witness against my master. I had the full confidence that my master would break the head of the enemies with his wonderful divine power.

I also knew that the owner of the private garden on Mount Olive was a secret disciple of my master and that, after the feast, my master together with others would go there for prayer. I told the enemies a sign to recognize my master. I knew that on such full-moon nights, if the soldiers arrested someone else instead of my master, all my efforts would become worthless, and my dream for the emancipation of the people would burn into ashes.

During that cursed night of yesterday, I betrayed my master with a kiss. When my master embraced me, sincerity was overflowing from my eyes. My heart was murmuring to him: 'My dearest master! I am giving you a golden opportunity to destroy all our enemies! Please, don't hesitate to reveal your divine power! Master! Please, don't put me into another ordeal!' And my master, who knew the thoughts and feelings of my heart, was just looking into my eyes with a smile of understanding.

I expected that my kiss would make my master valiant. In fact, through my kiss, I was pouring into my master my courage, enthusiasm and zeal to break the yoke of slavery. I blindly believed that he would release his divine power, even at that decisive moment, and that was the reason why I attempted the great sin of betraying one's master.

Am I being known as a sinner for betraying innocent blood? Will my detailed plan, erected on my dreams, crumble into pieces? Are my hopes withering away to nothingness?

No more uproar from Calvary! Darkness is spreading everywhere. Only the sobbing of women strains into this mountain slope, together with the waves of the wind. My God! Are my plans going to be mere castles in the air? Yes! If my master dies, there is no more life for me.

The Calvary is silent. The picture becomes clearer to me. Oh! What a farce is this human life? Who am I? What's the meaning of my human birth? Yes! We are mere mud-vessels, taken shape in the hands of our Creator. Mere clay-pots to be broken at any moment.

Will my sins be forgiven? Will I get redemption from my inevitable sins? Give me my punishment! I am ready to suffer all the consequences of my sin. Let the people stone me to death. Let them throw me into the vast and furious ocean. Let the blue whale swallow me and, then, throw me up onto some deserted shore. Let my body be scorched by the burning sun. Let the worms eat away the plants that give me shade.

Ah! It's my craze for power that led me to this fall. I must resign my job. I must come out from my ivory tower; I must resign from life itself! I am ready to die for my sins, but is death just a punishment for my sins? Adam, you are the Judas; you are the synonym for betrayal. Like the legendary hero who betrayed his master, I must undergo the punishment of burning in the husk-fire. Adam, a more severe punishment is waiting for you.

It's your ego that trapped you. You became a maniac as well as a phobiac at the same time! Once you are in power, you are reluctant to leave it. Power is a drug to which you become addicted very quickly. Beware of its intoxication, Adam! The problem is that you do not know when to leave it. You clutch on to the chair, thinking that you are still capable of handling the power. You see signs of your inability but fail to recognize them. You get suggestions of incapability from many corners but ignore them. You tighten your grip on the chair thinking that you alone can handle the power bestowed upon you. Of course, there's pleasure in continuing in power, and in watching others restlessly move around you in their utter helplessness. You still maintain a sort of confidence. It is just like the confidence of the male who attempts another intercourse, immediately after the ejaculation. The erection lasts a few more seconds, of course, but only for a few moments and you have to retire disheartened and dissatisfied.

You desperately try to attack. Your efforts are like the attempts of the red ant; one wishes to save the ant and not to kill it but it goes on climbing on the body, irritating one to the core so that, finally, one is tempted to kill it. That's the situation you create for others.

It's fear, Adam, that forces you to keep on your grip on the chair. You are really afraid of yourself, afraid of what will happen to you in the future. You may be punished for your atrocities or negligence, for anybody can find fault with others but himself. You may be ignored by the members of society whom you served by sacrificing even the pleasures of your private life, for they are too busy with their own life. You may die 'unsung and un-honored', as one among the thousands who perish every day.

But, remember, horrible is the fate of a dictator who fails to retire from his public life at the right time! Even if you are punished, jailed or executed, don't worry, you will be a martyr. Those who can create martyrs must become a martyr. And martyrdom is the easiest way to become immortal. Every human being must die one day; if so, why not accept martyrdom, the most elegant way of death? Remember, the honeybees drown in their own honey too. What a graceful death. You'll be considered a martyr, and that's the final goal of every human birth.

Well! Are you so fortunate to gain that greatness of death? One day you'll come out from your make-believe world. Once you leave your position, you'll lose your power and authority. You return home, completely exhausted of a life-long struggle, expecting to lead a peaceful life with the members of your family. Then, you realize that many of your neighbors cannot recognize you, and those who recognize you, keep a distance. Most of your relatives with whom you had intimacy passed away, and others fail to develop intimacy with you. Your children are now grown-up citizens, and they find less time to spend with you.

And your dearest Eve, with whom you entrusted your domestic self, is quite estranged from you. In your absence, she felt much monotony, and she found her own ways to entertain herself. It was from you that she learned the pleasure of social work. At first, it began just for time-pass, but soon she was addicted to it, and found it impossible to return to her earlier way of life.

Of course, Eve, you were always like this. You always took decisions according to your will or did something as you wished and, then, tried to convince me in your own charming ways the propriety of your decisions and actions. In the Garden of Eden you yourself took the decision and acted accordingly and, then, came to me with your justifications. You put me in a dilemma where the choice for me was either of the two extremes, to leave you and live forever or to live with you and die forever! I pretended as if I agreed with your decisions and, thereafter, continued to do so with all your decisions. And you thought of it as something obligatory or mandatory on my part. But if I was tempted by the snake, would you have agreed with me to share the sin?

In the Garden of Eden, don't you remember Eve, you deserted me for a while to attain more power for yourself, and you returned to me as a sinner? Was I not ready to bear all the punishments for your sin together with you? But now, when I deserted you for a while to attain more power for myself, and I returned to you as a sinner, you are not ready to bear the punishments for my sin together with me! You were not ready even to wait a bit longer for my return, instead you left me forlorn; and that's your basic nature.

Adam, now you are in a dilemma. You have to find your own means of engagement. You can go to the theatre or to the market or to some clubs. But they are expensive places. The least expensive places are, perhaps, temples, churches, mosques, gurudwaras and synagogues. Of course, they won't admit you into their core committee. But there, people will respect you, as far as you stick to one of them. Beware, Adam, you must identify only with one of them, or else, you'll land in trouble.

And what do you think about the life of Eve? Once you are chained to domestic duties, your life becomes too miserable at home. You feel you have nothing to do for the success of life. In the Garden of Eden, you were very active and you took decisions yourself. But here, your talents are wasted and you feel insignificant. Of course, you felt the same thing at Eden, and your quick decision led to this peril of a human life.

Your Adam is too busy with responsibilities... obligations which you can't understand. There was a time when he thought of you as the sole source of power. But now he discovered the real power, the power of the head. You aren't getting the same love and affection which he used to give you. Even his love-making itself, at times, becomes quite formal. You wanted him to be with you always, talking about daily trivial affairs, consoling you in your silly ailments and worries. Of course, your body needs the tender caressing of his hands. Your heart desires his soothing words.

Has he gone far ahead of you? Has he become too unreachable for you? But it was all for your happiness... for the well-being of the family... for a better, comfortable life in the future.

But you feel so dejected and sad at the waste of your talents. You think you've hidden the single sovereign under earth so that you can't give it back doubled.

Well! If you feel so disappointed with your domestic life, why can't you serve others? Extend your work to other parts of this Garden of Eden. Our society needs unselfish persons like you. God created man with a single motif. But from the time of the Tower of Babel, there have been differences of opinions, principles, theories, dogmas and practices. Why can't you try to unite them?

But Eve, beware! It's like going away to another part of the Garden of Eden to tend the plants wildly growing there. You feel that our casual talks and smiles waste much time. But remember that man is created not just for toiling but for enjoying the simple things in life. Happiness is not a rare and big gem for which you search throughout your life and fail to find! It is a collection of very tiny glittering stones, likely to be ignored, which you gather on your long way, keeping them secretly in your palms.

Who could predict the fate of a human being? We think of everything in a positive way but the result is negative. We expect success and we get failure. But the failure is too drastic that even you may lose your paradise. Eve, if you lose your paradise, it'll be a loss for your Adam too!

Alright! You can go to the midst of these people with religious diversities. Your Adam is fed up with their irrational arguments. How could I become a member of a particular religious or political organization?

Adam, you learned everything about every religion. You know each religion's merits and demerits. And you know that there was nothing to be proud of being born into a particular religion, as your birth itself is beyond your limits. But how could you continue in a religion, once you knew its ideological drawbacks?

Then you were selfish! You wanted to have some identity, perhaps, a better identity, and you chose to remain where you were born and brought up. Of course, you betrayed your conscience, but there was no choice.

Your Eve was also born and brought up in a particular family, in a particular community of a particular religion. She maintained an equal closeness to all religions, unlike you who kept an equal distance from them. She loved and respected all religions, their dogmas and theories, their rites and ceremonies, their customs and practices, their holy days and festivals as well as their fasting and feastings, perhaps by the virtue of her previous births.

She learned that every religion came to this world not to make any fundamental changes in the beliefs and practices but to renew or replace them. She knew that all religions underwent changes for their survival over the passage of time, even without the knowledge of their believers and leaders. She lived in the midst of many religions like the Hindu, the Buddhist, the Jewish, the Christian, the Islam, the Sikh, the Parsi and what not, with a myriad of denominations in each one of them. She realized that the aim of every religion is the immortality of its believers, and each expected it to attain through God whom they named differently. She argued that God is eternal, omnipotent, omniscient, omnipresent and almighty, and the variety of names given to Him is immaterial and irrelevant. In fact, she insisted tolerance and reciprocal respect among them, and considered love and sympathy for the whole of humanity the mission of her life.

She realized that all festivals, celebrated by each religion, helped man to express his instinctive emotions and through that he could gain pleasure and happiness in a life full of misery and sorrow. She believed that the ideas like the Moksha, the Nirvana or the Salvation propounded by the Great are but one and the same, which should be attained while we live on this earth, and not after death. She knew that every religious organization performed sacrifices and prayers, literally or symbolically. Every religious leader conducted various sorts of calisthenics in the name of God which gave the observers a kind of physical or psychological entertainment. She believed that religious belief is an individual affair, and if religions fail to develop philanthropic sentiments, awareness of social life and self-control among its members, such religions will pave the way for the end of human life on the face of earth.

She knew that all the people of the world would never come under a single religion, and never forget their language and accept one single language, as it is unnatural. She felt much sorrow at the activities of some religious believers who tried to destroy other religions for the sake of their own survival. Her heart always struggled to free herself from the slavery imposed by religions on their helpless believers. However, she felt some solace while observing the fact that all religions celebrated their festivals. And all their ceremonies and festivals gave her a heavenly delight. She was happy to see that each religion celebrated its festival each month, one after another, and there was not a single month without a festival.

Unfortunately, this sort of free thinking was not allowed by any religion. It was her own community that avoided her first. As she began to respect the holy days of other religions, her own people began to look at her with suspicion. And once she was ignored by her own community, other religions were not ready to accept her. She wished to join one or the other religion, but they all turned her away. Of course, it was all a racket. When she realized the fact, it was too late. By that time, she became incapable of living without festivals.

As things were going on like that, one day the believers of various religions decided to arrange their festivals on a single day, and this made her suspicious of their aims. Her heart murmured to her that their intention was not fair and their decision was not a coincidence but a deliberate one. She knew that, even though the purpose of all festivals was one and the same, there must be some obscurity when they all gather in their own quarters and conduct separate holy processions, contesting each other by blocking traffic. Of course, such religious processions gave outlets for the anti-social instincts in man, his megalomaniac tendencies and his natural urge to break the laws of discipline imposed on him, as they were arranged in the name of God.

To cut the tale shorter, first she went to participate in a procession arranged by Christians, which she considered a birth right. But they chased her away, accusing her of co-operating with other religions. Then she went to join a procession conducted by the Muslims but they also drove her away as if she was an ugly animal, born and brought up in another religion.

One after another, she attempted to participate in different processions arranged by different religions, and when they all turned her away, she went to join a procession conducted by Hindus. She always considered the Hindu religion as the mother of all religious philosophies and respected it, as it could survive the test of time. But the participants in the procession, separated themselves into Brahmins, Shaivas, Vaishnavas and a myriad of other denominations, and each group attacked her. They chased her like wolves behind a young lamb.

They threw stones at her, as if she was a stray mad dog. In order to save herself, she ran towards the temple of the Mother Universe, which was believed to be a shelter for all living and non-living creations of this universe. But those crazy, self-assertive blind believers continued to throw stones at her!

'Sacrifice her! Burn her! Throw stones at her! Crucify her! Cut her throat with a sword! Pierce her heart with a trident!' She could hear only the cries and shouts of those who followed her. She noticed the fact that amongst those who demanded her blood, there were people from all religious groups. They were all united in the booze of their festivals, in the intoxication of so-called spirituality.

She fell down before the holy shrine. She felt her hot blood ooze out from her head as it was wetting the holy pedestal of Mother Universe, and the sanctum sanctorum was overflowing with her life-blood. She slowly slipped into the fact that she too became a part of that festival sacrifice.

From time immemorial, human beings were performing sacrifices on the altar to please God. But human sacrifice was the most primitive one. Yet they sacrificed my Eve. Does it mean that man is still primitive in his beliefs and practices? Or does it mean that man is returning to the old practices in his ignorance of God? Returning from the sacrifice of cooked food to uncooked food. From uncooked food to flowers... to fruits... and to vegetables. From vegetables to birds and animals. From animals to human sacrifice.

Oh, God! What an ignorant creature man is! You asked only the sacrifice of sweat. Thou shalt eat the bread with the sweat of thy forehead. But they ignored the significance of sweat in their laziness and began to sacrifice their urine, feces, semen and blood which are abominable to God. In the name of God, they sacrificed even parts of their body and made themselves invalid. Some cut off their thumbs or phallus, others pierced their earlobes and a few sacrificed the tip of the skin from their genital organs!

In every sacrifice, there is an element of cruelty and murder. Weren't they murdering my Eve? How many people massacred in the name of God? Hindus and Muslims, Muslims and Christians, Sunnis and Shias, Catholics and Protestants – all sacrificed each other in the name of God! And my Eve will be ignored as one among those millions.

Wasn't her death a sort of martyrdom? She might have deliberately offered to become a martyr. Didn't Lord Krishna know that he would die with the poisonous arrow of a hunter? Didn't Jesus know he would be crucified? Didn't Socrates know that he would die if he drank hemlock? Didn't my Eve know that all religious believers are crazy and blind in their faith?

But martyrdom itself is a suicide if the martyr deliberately accepts death. Walk into the Sarayu River and accept death by drowning in its waters is suicide, isn't it? Didn't my Eve know that it was suicidal to correct the foolishness of religious worshippers?

Oh, Eve! Come back! Come to life! Martyrdom is the last

refuge of the coward. To live here on this earth is important. Don't be a foolish follower of the so-called principles and philosophies. Of course, you can follow them if you are alone and single. But, remember, you are not alone, and you have more responsibility towards your Adam and your sons and daughters.

Eve, you forgot yourself for a moment. You forgot the sad plight your Adam has to lead on this earth. Of course, death is inevitable, but don't welcome death! Death may be physical, mental or spiritual. Blind beliefs lead to either of them.

Now your Adam is left alone! He was careless and irresponsible when you were with him. He didn't care for the day to day domestic affairs, as he knew that you could manage everything efficiently.

Adam, there was a time when you loved solitude. But now, loneliness appears to be hell for you. You feel that you are deprived of an important part of your body and soul. It's all part of your fate. Face all adverse situations with equanimity. What's done cannot be undone. What happened cannot be reverted. It's another phase in your life; as if experiencing another birth.

PART IV

$\mathbf{Y}$et again a birth?

All things born will die! Does it mean that there is only one birth and one death? Your ancestor Adam was not born but created and yet he died. Of course he faced many births in his life. Lucifer was created and he did not die. And he faced many deaths in his life. Adam, you have to face many births and many deaths during the short span of your life on this earth.

Suddenly you've become lonely once again. You feel as if much of your mission in life is over. No more you are a member in that society in which you have been an active part. Or perhaps it doesn't need you anymore. You feel as if you were a stranger in that familiar crowd.

Adam, you are now alone. You are a widower. Your Eve left you after giving to posterity whatever she could. Through your children you achieved immortality. As she left, you feel this earth null and void, once again.

This is another birth for you, Adam. Perhaps you've faced

more births, or deaths. The great flood is over and you are now left out somewhere on the shore like a rotten wooden log carried down all the way by the flood waters. It's time for you to begin your ascetic life. Of course, it's very difficult at first. Memories of worldly life will haunt you. But try your best to avoid them.

A leap from the present to the future is quite thrilling. Then it was adventurous to live in the future. But now you are destined to live in the past! Here you are compelled to make a leap from the present to the past. And life becomes bleak and dark for you.

This is the time for you to make the balance sheet of your profit–loss account. This is the time for you to make additions, subtractions, divisions and multiplications and to find out the net result.

Now you can smile over your gains and sigh over your losses. It's time to think about the meaningfulness and meaninglessness of your past actions. To think over the baselessness of your principles and the foolishness of your self-assertiveness. To observe the pros and cons of the make-believe world you created for yourself.

The death of your partner, reminds you about the truth and the inevitability of death. Adam, you can't escape from these truths. Be ready for it. For you don't know the time or hour; you don't know how it will come. But if it is inevitable and imminent, why should you worry about it, Adam?

This is the time for you to think over the generation gap. This is the time for you to engage in useless nostalgia. You have to live in a world of memories. You can think of the details of your past, analyze and evaluate, and patch up the broken ends.

No longer are you important in the new world. Everything will go on smoothly and in a better way even in your absence.

Don't be too happy about your achievements or too unhappy about your missed opportunities. Don't be too proud of your victories or too dejected at your failures. For you did everything to the satisfaction of your conscience. That's enough and that's all. You had a mission and you completed it. You did your duty, Adam! Now, don't flirt over its fruits. It is the next generation that should continue what you have left unfinished.

Don't worry about the coming days. Think of those good old days of delightful sights and sounds, of lovely touch and warmth. Do live in the past, face life with equanimity.

During the lonely small hours of the night... when the light snoring of my wife who slept nearby rose up... I used to read tragic stories... sitting very close to the kerosene lamp. And I sobbed sometimes quite uncontrollably.

Later... while lying down on the bed... expecting the arrival of Goddess Sleep... being quite exhausted of sobbing and suppressed cries... many a time I wet my pillows with hot tears... thinking of the cruelties that fate implements on poor human creatures.

On certain occasions... I cried silently, keeping my handkerchief to my mouth so as not to disturb my wife who soundly slept nearby. Many a time, I was frightened at the thought that my wife who was sleeping like an innocent child by the edge of the bed would wake up with a shudder and wonder whether I had gone insane.

I agree that these were, nay, still are, my drawbacks. Perhaps the tragic flaw in my character... the frailties of my nature. But am I to be blamed if I feel sadness and pain, or if I become moody and worried of, and turn frightened or dejected in a natural way while reading the news about murders and massacres, suicides and genocides, mass rapes and molestations, floods, droughts and famines, accidents and starvation deaths that fill up the pages of our news-dailies?

What else should I do but push on with my life like an abnormal creature that has no courage to face the stark realities of human life. And to live like a coward even in front of my wife who used to smile with understanding or laugh at my infirmities.

I knew that my mind was weak like the muscles of a heart-patient. The reading of each self-revealing article that appeared in the psychological and psychiatric periodicals confirmed the fact that I was supposed to be a mental patient! Or, at least, a psychiatric case! The only consolation for me was the words of Freud that all human beings are psychiatric cases in one way or the other.

I became quite aware of the seriousness of my mental weakness only when I overheard my son saying to his mother that he did not like to go to the cinema with me. Sitting in my private reading room, I overheard him complaining: 'Whenever there are tragic scenes in the film, father starts to cry aloud! People who sit in the front row will turn back and stare at us! What a shame!'

I heard his mother trying to justify my actions as well as console him: 'Your father is a simpleton, my son! He is as innocent as a dove, my child!'

How shameful it was! Was I a chicken-hearted fellow? How horrible was the situation in which a wife felt sympathy towards her husband on such matters! Well! Leave my case! But I was wondering more about the changes that were coming to my son as days passed.

All these years I've read tragic stories and watched tragic plays and films. It is said that tragedies have a purgative effect on our minds and they purify and prepare them so as to face the tragic realities of life courageously. But can I be blamed if Aristotle's Catharsis threw the gloves down at me?

However I was not ignoring the changes that occurred in my son. I still remember his first cry that came to my ears from the labor-room as it happened that very morning. Then I thought that he would have my own attitude towards melancholic matters. Well, it is natural that any new born babe will cry like him if he has seen the frightening face of birth. No wonder, when the midwife brought him to me, as I was anxiously waiting outside the labor-room, he sighed with a sort of relief and tried to smile at me with his eyes blinking in the day light. Or perhaps I felt so.

I remember those school-going days of my son. When we, his parents, engaged in some common husband-wife quarrels on some silly issues, tears filled his eyes and they overflowed and streamed down his cheeks. I also remember how he sobbed and cried like prince Siddhartha seeing mendicants in ragged clothes, extending their hands for alms. Of course, most of them had made their body appear disgusting with pussy sores and unhealed wounds. He believed their camouflaged appearance when they begged: 'Oh, Father! Oh, Mother! Give us alms! Give us something to eat! God will bless you!' Well, my son too was growing like his father, incapable of living in a camouflaged world.

It was when he studied in primary school that he saw for the first time the body of a murdered man. Kunju had killed Kutta just for an argument over five paisa while playing some card game. After a glance on the gory face and blood-clotted curls of Kutta, he returned home with a shriek and lied down on the bed for a week with high fever and delirium. All these I remember as if they happened a few days ago.

One day, while he was a student of the secondary school, I heard him say to his mother: 'Mom! I resigned from that Students' Movement! It is not because I have objections to their political ideology. I resigned because it was some of the leaders of our organization who had raped and killed a poor girl at a deserted rubber estate! After murdering her they also put some mud in her mouth! How brutal they were! Well, it's true that all great leaders are maniacs in one way or the other! But we must put them in jails when they begin to engage in inhuman activities!'

What he said was a hundred percent correct! How can a human being be so inhuman? So cruel? There was the photograph of that grotesque scene in the newspapers. It was sufficient even for a stone-hearted man to melt into tears. How sadistic some of these leaders and rulers are!

But changes came to him while he was a university student. One day returning from the college, he said: 'Papa! One of my friends presented the last scene of King Lear as part of our Arts Festival! King Lear who came to the stage carrying in his hands the body of his dead daughter and who died of a broken heart, in the excessive happiness of feeling a stir of life in her, attracted everybody! It was simply delightful!'

'Delightful!' I shuddered to the core. I remember how I felt my heart stop beating with heaviness even at the slight memory of that heart-breaking scene. How could he use the adjective delightful? Did it mean that his heart was undergoing the process of petrification? I tried to convince myself that he used the word delightful just by mistake or by coincidence.

It was then that the news with photographs of public punishments in certain Islamic countries came in the newspapers. I was thinking about the cruelty and the sadistic approach behind such laws. Criminals were flogged or even executed publicly and I always believed that such punishments were barbarous. But my son justified that system and said, 'Criminals deserve such punishments! If all the criminals escape punishment sometimes on the benefit of doubt or due to some clerical errors in the filing of a case, how could common people live without fear?'

I didn't react to his opinion. I knew that many of the murderers in our countries who were punished for life imprisonment used to come out just after a maximum period of seven or eight years.

While my son was studying at college, one of our neighbors, a tailor, was murdered by a carpenter, a classmate of my son's from the primary school. I came to know that my son stood very near to the dead body when the doctors conducted its post mortem. I asked him whether he was afraid of such a horrible thing. I shuddered when he replied in an easy-going manner: 'Aren't those who do the post mortem human beings too? Papa, you should have seen it! How easily the doctor hacked the chest of that dead tailor! And father, it isn't a big thing to open our skulls! First draw a line around the head with a sharp knife and then give one or two knocks on both the sides of the skull! That's all, and the top will come off like a cap! One should see a post mortem if he wants to learn something about the anatomy of a human body!'

I could only listen to his words with more fear than with surprise! On another occasion, when his grandmother who had been suffering from an ulcer was in the operation theatre and I was sitting on the mosaic floor of the hospital, outside, in a semi-conscious stage due to sadness and exhaustion, he received permission from the doctors to stand near the operating table and watch how his grandmother's stomach was split open! Only with shock and shudder do I remember that horrible situation!

Only with agony and despair did I read the newspaper that came daily with heart-breaking news like a thousand died in bombardments or in earthquakes or in cyclones. Then my son used to say: 'What's there to be sad about? According to the Malthusian theory in Economics, all these wars and natural calamities are the preventive steps taken by Nature against the considerable increase in population! And only when population attains its equilibrium, that the world will get its emancipation from these painful incidents!'

Whether Economics or any other sciences, I felt these naughty reactions of nature to control human population are too cruel and they always drowned me into utter sorrow and despair. Yet as days passed many a change occurred in me without my own knowledge even. At first my heart was in a benumbed state. That might be the reason why I felt a sort of indifference and placidity when my son wrote a letter to me from an Islamic country where he worked then, about the cruel and barbarous punishments given there to the criminals, publicly.

He wrote: 'Last day I went to see a public execution. The punishments here are not so cruel as we used to think earlier! On Friday afternoons, all the convicts to be punished are brought to a special place in front of the mosque. All convicts were given a kind of sedative medicine and were brought in a semi-conscious condition! To those, whose palms to be cut off, morphine injections are given on the wrist to make that part non- sensitive, and painless! With a small, sharp knife the wrist will be cut around and separated with a 'click' sound within a split second and the victim will be handed over to doctors who are waiting with an ambulance!'

He continued: 'Those convicts to be beheaded are brought to the place of execution in an unconscious condition under strong sedatives and in an exhausted state in which they cannot even make a cry! With a short, flat but heavy hatchet, the executioner gives only a slight strike at the back of the convict's neck! It's quite simple like that! As the connection between the brain and spinal cord is separated the convict will not feel even the slightest pain!'

His letter went on and on like that! I did not feel any emotion while reading that letter. Or was I also growing together with my son? I felt it in my heart. There were even signs of evidence.

On a subsequent day, I still remember, I went together with my wife to see a very famous tragedy. During tragic scenes, I saw my wife sob silently and press her handkerchief against her flowing eyes. When we reached home, she complained to me, with indignation rather than sadness: 'Look! Are you a human being? Your heart is nothing but stone! At those tragic scenes, all the spectators including myself burst into tears! But you, you alone, were smiling like a sadist!'

Hearing her words, I laughed aloud again and again. And I hoped that my son also would laugh, perhaps a bit louder, when he came to know about that incident.

How sad! Those days in which you felt the fragrance of your wife and those nights in which you heard the light breathing of your mate - all gone forever. How lonely you feel today, Adam.

But you have to suffer all these things. These days will be quite bad. Unbearable news will pierce your ears. Horrible things will happen around you. You must have a heart to bear such things. You must have a heart of stone! For only those whose hearts are petrified can live on this earth. They are the only fit persons to survive here. Oh, for a heart of stone.

Or how can we be sure that the coming generations are really different from the old ones? Their claim of a generation gap is just superficial, it seems. In fact, all novel attitudes are mere repetitions, steps to return to the old and, thus, to complete the cycle. Whether clockwise or anti-clockwise, we all have to reach the same beginning point. Well! Your forefathers thought that the earth was flat and they even killed those who opposed their belief. But that did not change the way of the planet. It means that the future generation hides somewhere amongst the past generations. I differed from my father just like my son differs from me, but my great grandfather and my great grandson must have similar attitudes to life.

My great grandfather had never traveled in any type of motor vehicle. He had been a permanent pedestrian and always preferred to travel on foot, irrespective of the distance, even at the age of four score and ten.

He had continuously reminded his sons: 'Look children! You shall not trust the machines for, in any case, no one can prophecy when they will deceive you. There is no doubt that they will cheat you one day.'

Then my grandfather had laughed at him and said: 'Father, whatever you want is readily available in this village itself. It won't take more than an hour's walk for you to get water, food or clothing, and even the rarest thing that helps you to prolong your life. But in order to get costly dress and delicacies which are inevitable for me, I must go to the town. Won't it take a minimum of two days if I go to the town and return home by walking all that distance?'

My grandfather really had gone to the town and returned home by motor vehicles. Of course, he had been trying to trust the machines.

Years might have passed after that incident and the situation being the same, one day my father informed my grandfather: 'Father, I have to go to the capital city. It'll take a minimum of four or five days if one goes by train. So I am planning to travel by plane.'

My grandfather's face turned ashen and he said hurriedly: 'Look, my son! You can trust all vehicles that move on land for the land is solid. But it certainly is dangerous to travel in the air or on water that moves and wavers endlessly.'

My father laughed aloud and did fly to the capital city. Later, in order to visit certain foreign countries, he even sailed in ships. But my father's face turned white like a sheet of paper when I myself made arrangements for space travel.

He told me with an air of pleading: 'My son! You can trust all earthly things. We can open new routes in the land, water and air. But you can't trust space, for it's dead sure that the vehicles traveling in space will deceive us.'

I laughed more loudly than my father used to do and did travel in space. It was only a week ago, or so it seems, that I returned home after my fifth trip to the moon!

Then, my face turned pale and bloodless with fear, as my son, fixing his eyes on me, said: 'Look, father! Whatever we want is quite available in this village itself. As human beings, it's our moral obligation to adjust with Nature by minimizing our wants. The more Man progresses, the less he can hold the reins of his needs. Whatever the situation, Man fundamentally must depend on Nature. We shall not put our trust wholly in machines, for no one can predict when they will deceive us. And there is no doubt that they will cheat you one day.'

Events have completed a full circle! I live to wonder whether I can see my great grandfather through my great grandson. Oh, what a fantastic imagination, Adam! You imagine wildly proving your beliefs, especially your religious beliefs. How funny!

But old generations give way for the new generations. Neither the old generations are totally old nor are the new generations totally new. There cannot be water-tight compartments, as social and religious traditions have chained them. Though it is the need of the age to break away from these religious customs which all have a foolish origin, the drugged new generation is incapable of doing so. Of course, they must have realized that old customs, rites and practices will lead them only to new customs, rites and practices. Yet the truth remains that all our religious traditions related to festivals and ceremonies can be traced to a cruel and malicious origin.

My dear Eve! They sacrificed you to cover the foolish aspects of their religions. How many times did we welcome their religious festivals? In the intoxication of their so-called divinity, they forget their humanitarianism. Oh, dear! How much did we enjoy those festivals and their colorful processions?

Eve! Don't you remember? Many a time we greeted Deepavali and Christmas as the festivals of light, and Onam and Eid as the festivals of food. Very many times we welcomed Holi, the festival of colors not as a mere festival but as a symbol of equality, fraternity and liberty. But we forgot that there is an element of revenge and brutality in all our festivals. Don't you remember the story of that old man, a former ruler of our country, which throws much light on the secret behind the malignity of a festival?

Every festival, Holi, Easter or Eid, has some bad features hidden behind the outward brightness. It is natural that Man as an animal is liable to corrupt all the good things of the world. But, does it mean that a religion can open the doors of opportunity for its crazy members for such corruptions, especially, when all religions claim some sort of a divine origin?

The malign force that took away your life, my dear Eve, is clear when that ruler from the old generation tells the story of his revenge, watching the new generation celebrating a festival.

Holi hei! Holi hoi! Holi hei!

They all cry in a frenzy mood.

My grandchildren are in high excitement and rapture. With thousands of colors smeared on their face and body, they dance and run here and there. They smile horribly and make faces at me like those barbarians who came out years ago from the thick forests of Africa. They shoot the colored water from the water guns onto my white clothes. Well! As you know, I have been wearing white clothes ever since I became one of the rulers of this country!

It was during that period that khaki dressed protectors of law and order, and the black-gowned tax collectors joined together and conducted the first horrible water-revolution in the history of this country against laborers and other members of the public. Of course, we have a number of revolutions named after the seven colors of the rainbow and after the five basic elements.

It is quite regretful that the people of this country often forget the strategic steps adopted during that revolution which lasted for six days. The black-gowned tax collectors went to every house of this country and collected as much money as possible through fair or foul methods. The khaki-dressed law-protectors helped them indirectly. They patrolled and roamed along the streets in their jeeps and splashed dirty water from the gutters onto the faces and clothes of the pedestrians. And the roads damaged by age and rainy seasons added spirit and enthusiasm to their revolutions.

Well! Evening passed and morning came - that was the sixth day of the revolution. As I was walking from my house to the Minister's Mansion, a jeep carrying a gang of the so-called protectors of law and order passed me. Only when the jeep disappeared at the other end of the road did I realize the fact that almost all the liquid, for it was not at all water, collected in a gutter in the road had splashed onto my dress! Wiping away the slime on my face and looking at it, I asked myself like the poet: 'Can this go on un-avenged, dear helpless victims?'

The decision of the laborers and of the tax-collectors was to conduct the revolution for six days and to take rest on the seventh day. But the laborers and the members of the public, who tolerated the so-called revolution for six days, only came out of their inertia on the seventh day!

Proletarians in their blue uniforms visited every house and collected as much money as possible through fair or foul method. The members of the public wearing white dress as a sign of their pretended purity ran helter skelter along the streets carrying dirty, colored water and stinking water from the gutters, in their pails, buckets and other household utensils. They baptized all the wretched people whom they saw on the street with that polluted water or, at times, even water mixed with cow-dung!

As I was going to the Minister's Mansion on that day, I too was dressed in my white clothing as usual, and they came running towards me. They did not spare even me, one of their beloved rulers! When they all left me, I wiped off the cow-dung from my face, and looking at it, I took an oath that I would not be consoled until all these were avenged.

All the intelligentsia in the country including myself stood agape in utter confusion without knowing the reason behind the eruption of anarchy in this country or understanding whether revolution or counter-revolution was justifiable. Then I realized that the best solution to the problem was to bring both groups to a consensus.

And thus, I invited the leaders of both the revolutionaries and the counter-revolutionaries and began our so-called 'summit' which led to the discovery of the root cause of the revolution and the counter-revolution in this country.

Accordingly, the root cause was that the so-called revolutionaries and counter revolutionaries had gained a sort of real sadistic pleasure and genuine satisfaction while splashing colored water onto the face and dress of others.

It was only by the evening of the seventh day that the

counter-revolutionaries could leak out this secret from their counterpart. Both groups boasted that it was Machiavelli who had pointed out the fact: 'End justifies means!'

In fact, the goals of the intelligentsia, including myself, were the prosperity, the grace and the satisfaction of the people of this country. To make it brief, I brought the revolutionaries and the counter revolutionaries to a consensus, of course, through non-violent and peaceful means.

They all agreed to the point that every year on a particular day, all of them would splash water on each other, and instead of slime and cow-dung, they would use different colored powders and inks. And thus, for the first time in history, the festival called 'Holi' began in this country. And my oath also was realized!!

And my grandchildren are in high excitement and rapture. They play splashing colored water with each other. They cry aloud in a frenzy mood: 'Holi hei! Holi hoi!'

Adam, don't be dejected! There's a sacrifice behind every ritual. Behind every traditional practice, there is also an element of revenge. Every custom, individual or social practice, started out of somebody's wicked or foolish mind. As the poet said: 'The mistake of yesterday would become today a custom for the people; and might become the science for tomorrow!'

But every festival is a sacrifice and every sacrifice is a festival. Then every human life is a festival and a sacrifice as well. Both festivals and sacrifices are occasions for celebration. Drink life to the lees.

If it is a festival let us celebrate it with a grand feast. You sit at the head of the table. Your children, grandchildren and great grandchildren sit around the dining table, like young olive plants. With great enthusiasm, they ask questions and you reply from your experience in a serious tone. They anxiously look at your face as if they are hearing a fairytale. You make jokes and they laugh heartily. You look around to see your wife bringing one more bowl of wine. And become angry at her absence. A lightning flashes through your heart! No more could your Eve bring drinks to you! She has gone forever! She has become a part of the festival with her sacrifice.

She sacrificed her life to give you one more festival. Think of your daughter and son. Your dear Eve offered them to you as precious gifts of perennial happiness. Your daughter gives you peace and prosperity; your son gives you pleasure and pride. You became immortal through them. Once you sacrificed your rib bone to get your Eve. Then she sacrificed her rib bone to get your children. Oh, Eve! How great it would have been if you had been with me until my last breath!

These superstitious sub-humans sacrificed my Eve for their pleasure. Is it for their pleasure alone? No! They wanted to please their God with the blood of my Eve. They are afraid of their self-created God; they are afraid of themselves.

Adam, in the Garden of Eden you walked with God. Both of you were friends. He loved you and you loved Him. He taught you that God is Love. But these religions of the world taught you that God is Fear. They created God according to their whims and fancies. They taught you to fear God rather than love God.

God! You created Man in your own image. You gave him the ability of creativity, of thinking and of imagination. You gave him reason and prudence. But these religions tried to chain his brain! They tried to put God in the shackles forged by their brains. God to them became a frightening monster. They ignored Your loving kindness. Of course, it was the result of Man's disobedience. When he disobeyed You, naturally, he became afraid of you.

God created Man, and that was the only religion then.

Adam and Eve, the first man and the first woman, were perfect human beings. They were naked, and Nature was naked to them. They lived in perfect harmony with God and Nature. But greed and lust made them selfish, and their selfishness led them towards their downfall. Once they began to exploit nature, by plucking out the fruits beyond their genuine need, and tried to acquire what was not allowed to them, they fell. Oh, what a fall! A fall from the status of perfect human beings to that of sub-human beings.

Then, Man created religions, in his helpless attempts to please God. He thought that religions could raise the sub-human beings to the status of super-human beings. Even Eve did the same thing. Instead of rising to the equal status of Adam, she wished to become equal to God. All these religions, which offer Man a higher status than that of a perfect man, follow the example of the snake. Let us be mere human beings rather than super-human beings.

Religions, with a myriad of their supernatural ideas like soul, spirit, ghost, hell and heaven, try to make man a sort of super man. But they became mere camps for the incorrigible sub-human beings. Of course, the snake too advocated a position equal to God. Dear Man! First try to become a perfect Man. If you cannot become a good man, how can you become a good Hindu, a good Christian or a good Muslim?

These religions say: 'Fear God, for fear of God is the beginning of wisdom!' In fact, fear of God is the beginning of ignorance. If human beings had been living in fear, they would not have made inventions in arts, sciences, literature and adventures. Why can't these religions say: 'Love God?' For the Age of Fear has gone forever and the Age of Love has dawned. Oh, Eve! If only your sacrifice could teach these blind people who grope for the black cat in utter darkness.

Forget all sentiments, Adam! Think only about

sensuousness. This divine gift cannot be enjoyed fully even in heaven. Utilize all the senses to the maximum benefit. For the five senses make a man, a full man. The sixth sense, perhaps, makes man great.

Remember, Adam, man is born from dust. And he returns to dust. But he is still a handful of dust while living if his senses are not working effectively.

Of all senses the sense of touch. Ah, for this most wonderful sense of man! In heaven do the human souls experience senses, at least, the five senses? If not can we call it a heaven? No doubt, in a Christian heaven, the souls will not enjoy sensuousness. In other heavens too the situation is more or less the same. Otherwise why should all these believers preach renunciation?

Once you are born and brought up in a family deep-rooted in religious customs, ceremonies and traditions, it is natural that even your subconscious mind is controlled by the religious notions of that particular religion.

Beware Adam! The wonderful experience of the five senses may not be effectively utilized by a person whose religion propagates renunciation of the senses. Alas! That was the fate of your friend. The pitiable destiny of people like him would be very miserable. What a waste of life! Once you feel the delight through any one of those senses, you can live for years in that memory. But even experience of certain strange delights would kindle your nostalgia.

The first stage of the story...

The childhood, quite restless and naughty. Pure innocence in the eyes. A sort of fully relaxed mind. The cool tender body. Light hair that moves in the gentle gale. Shades of feelings that amazements bring on the charming face. Limbs that move unnecessarily. All... all contributing to the wonderful legacy of childhood!

Fixing my eyes on the sweet mango fruits that she tightly held in her hands, very close to her heart, I asked her eagerly: 'I am very hungry; will you please give me a mango fruit?'

Naughtiness crept onto her lips and with a charming smile she said: 'I shall give you mango fruits, if you give me a kiss!'

I turned my face away with shyness and said: 'Then... I don't want your mango fruit!'

I walked away from her. She came forward and stopped me. She said in a low voice: 'Don't kiss me! Take these mango fruits; eat them till you have no more hunger!'

I took her mangoes. Rationality faded in my eyes. And there were the glittering pearls of tears in her innocent, black eyes.

The second stage of the story...

The youth, quite emotional and passionate... pure lust in the eyes! A sort of fully tensed mind. The hot, hard body. Soft hair that moves in the breeze. Different shades of excitement that desires bring on the beautiful face. Limbs that move only when necessary. All... all contributing to the wonderful legacy of youth.

Fixing my eyes on the glass of sweet coffee that she lightly held in her hand, I asked her eagerly: 'I am very thirsty; will you please give me some coffee?'

Passion crept onto her lips and with a lustful smile, she said: 'I shall give you coffee, if you give me a kiss!'

I turned my face away with arrogance and said: 'Then... I don't want your coffee.'

I walked away from her. She came towards me and stopped me. She said in a dejected tone: 'Don't kiss me! Take this coffee and drink it till you have no more thirst.'

I took the glass of coffee. Rationality faded in my eyes. And there was the glittering of tears in her lustful, red eyes.

The third stage of the story...

The old age, quite indifferent and placid. Pure maturity in the eyes. A sort of paralyzed mind. The cool, wrinkled body. Rough hair that moved in the wind. Shades of sadness that memories bring on the graceful face. Limbs that hesitate to move even for necessities. All... all contributing to the shocking legacy of old age.

Fixing my eyes on the sweet tobacco that she tightly held in her hands, I asked her eagerly: 'I feel a sort of satiety in the mouth, and will you please give me some tobacco leaf?'

Placidity crept onto her lips and with a sort of wry smile, she said: 'I shall give you some tobacco leaf, if you give me a kiss!'

I turned my face away with disgust and said: 'Then... I don't want your tobacco.'

I began to walk away from her. She came across me and stopped me. She said in a desperate tone: 'Don't kiss me! Take the tobacco and chew it till taste comes to your mouth!'

I took a piece of tobacco leaf. Rationality faded in my eyes. And there was the glittering of tears in her matured, white myopic eyes.

And the story doesn't end here... at least, as far as you are taught by the so-called protectors of morality that even kissing itself is a sin.

Don't say the truth! All the so-called believers will laugh at you. They will say: 'What a fool he is! He doesn't know that religion is something normal! It suggests ideas! Well, it's good to accept them. But if you can't, as usual, don't worry about it! You can make your own excuses!'

'Didn't you know, 'Eittilappadi payattilippadi'; in theory like that, in practice like this!'

How funny! Sheer hypocrites! They cheat themselves and cheat others. They ask us to do the impossible things; while they themselves do whatever they like.

Alas! Adam, they made a fool of you. And there's no end to human foolishness. We all suffer, trapped in between dogmas and their impracticability.

Oh Adam! What a fool you are! Like your friend, who lost the bliss of a kiss, you tried to make a theory out of everything. Even a kiss from the opposite sex becomes a taboo in your society. You thought that it was something sinful, something immoral or even something illegal. And see, how your friend lost the divine happiness that conveyed through the touching of two pairs of lips belonging to a man and a woman? And your philosophy was neither oriental nor occidental. You developed your own prejudices and ignored the simple, natural joys of human life. What a pity!

You suffered a lot, Adam, leading a life in between renunciation and sensuousness. And you could resist every temptation. How great! You listened to the call of your brain, and not of your heart. Of course, at times, the soft signals and signs tendered by your heart guided you. Then, you enjoyed the light music of love that strained through the vents of your heart.

Adam, now you are quite old and your senses are not fully working. But the memory of a thrill or a flash of delight guides you. That memory can reproduce the same thrill or delight, even in senility.

Nostalgia! What a wonderful feeling!

Once you are senile, once you feel physically inactive, play with your memories. Go for a look into the past and bring out those glimpses of experience. Smile and laugh or sob and cry. Really, old age is a wonderful pastime!!

Don't you feel the presence of that great monument of love and sensuousness? Those domes of love and minarets of sensuousness. Taj Mahal is no more a mansion or a building. It's an immortal symbol of that eternal experience of thrill and delight acquired from the real application of the divine senses.

In my childhood...

Keeping my shoes outside, I entered the mansion with waddling steps. As I moved from one corner to another, marble throbbed under my feet. I stood silently, feeling a sort unexplainable happiness aroused in me by that wonder-mansion. My heart was drowning into the sweet dreams that the magnificent future would bring to me.

The minarets that stood high up against the sky shined in the golden rays of the morning sun. Cypress trees danced and played in the cool breeze. Ripples smiled innocently in the blue waters of the Jumna. The eternal, cheerful song of a lovely bird strained towards me from some far away place. And the white marble stones were chanting the stories of love.

The arabesque with leaves and flowers, made of colorful stones, was quite attractive. The glittering of the gems was amazing! The cries of children echoed from the marble walls. Among those cries, mine too.

Nothing was there to think about as I stood alone at a deserted corner. Nothing was there to remember as I rolled on that smooth floor.

As I walked out, wearing my shoes again, I was thinking about the sweat drops that had fallen on the holy courtyard of that wonder-mansion... the sweat drops of thousands of men and women. And my mind chanted: 'A dream in marble!'

In my youth...

Keeping my shoes outside, I entered the monument with thrilling steps. As I moved from corner to corner, marble thrilled under my feet. I stood silently staring at the physical pleasure aroused in me by that wonder-mansion. My heart was drowning into the sweet thoughts of the magnificent present.

The minarets that stood silhouetted against the sky shone in the silver rays of the spring moon. Cypress trees thrilled and smiled in the cool breeze. Ripples giggled lustfully in the blue waters of the Jumna. The eternal love song of a lonely bird strained towards me from some far away place. And the white marble stones were chanting the stories of lust.

The arabesque with leaves and flowers made of colorful stones were quite wonderful. The value of the gems was amazing. The love songs of youngsters echoed from the marble walls. Among those songs, mine too.

There was a lot to think about as I stood alone at a deserted corner. But nothing was there to remember as I sat on that smooth floor.

As I walked out, wearing my shoes again, I was thinking about the blood drops that had fallen on the holy courtyard of that wonder-mansion... the blood drops of thousands of men and women. And my mind chanted: 'A revolution in marble!'

In my old age...

Keeping my shoes outside, I entered the mausoleum with shivering steps. As I moved from one corner to another, marble trembled under my feet. I stood silently staring at the philosophical thoughts aroused by that wonder-mansion. My heart was drowning into the sweet memories of the magnificent past.

The minarets that stood high up against the sky glittered in the golden rays of the setting sun. Cypress trees shuddered and shivered in the cool breeze. Ripples laughed frightfully in the blue waters of the Jumna. The eternal sad song of a lovely bird strained towards me from some far away place. And the white marble stones were chanting stories of sacrifice.

The arabesque with leaves and flowers made of colorful stones were quite unattractive. Neither the glittering nor the value of the multi-colored gems was amazing. The very old guardian cupped his palm over the right ear and sang: 'OMMMM!' His cry echoed from the marble walls. In that sound, mine too.

There was nothing to think about as I stood alone in a deserted corner. But much was there to remember as I lied on that smooth floor.

As I walked out, wearing my shoes again, I was thinking about those tear drops that had fallen on the holy courtyard of that wonder-mansion... the tear drops of thousands and thousands of men and women. And my mind chanted: 'An agony in marble!'

Taj Mahal! Its affect on the human mind differs, depending on the person concerned. It is a symbol of mystery for the child, of love for the youth and of sacrifice for the old. Perhaps something completely different for someone else.

It appeared like a beautiful statue, an idol of eternal love, placed in the temple of youngsters, and worshipped by lovers all over the world. Cypress trees were mixing different kinds of sorrows of separation on the palate of that symbol of love. The setting sun seemed to be an expert artist who showed his talent on that marble canvas. Like the mother cow that licked her calf sucking her udders and drinking milk, the ripples of River Jumna were fondling and singing a lullaby to her daughter, Taj Mahal. Or that mother, with her wavelets of white foam, might be adorning her little child, repeatedly, with silver anklets.

Man's desire to become immortal! While the poor keep a few pebbles at the top of their graves, the rich keep gems and marble. Indignation breaks out: 'Let the waters of Jumna rise up; and lick away this monument of kingship and imperialism!'

Even in the revolutionary's heart, some voice from inside, stops and intervenes the singer: 'Oh! No! How foolish you are! It tells us the greatness of love! It's magnificent, indeed! Sure, a poem in marble!'

Adam, you have tears hanging from your eyelids! Are you feeling the smoothness of the eternal marble on your fingers?

Just like touching the cheeks of your Eve? Memory of a love song disturbs your heart. But Adam, you are too old. Sentiments are not for old people. Face such facts with a wink of your eye. Wink and smile!

It's quite fun to think about the simple joys of life. Don't be too serious about life or else you may ignore the small gems of happiness. One cannot buy happiness; it must be sought and found. It must be found where it won't be found... and that's the art of living... the success of human life!

That's what the teacher had told you once. Adam, think of that. How happy was your past generation? They had problems but they tried to tackle them by reducing the seriousness of such situations, deliberately. They found joy in simple, usually unimportant events of their lives. After all, what is there left after death? My dear Adam, that teacher's story is very solacing, isn't it?

Whenever I was throwing the bread-pieces of wisdom into the ears of my students who sat before me with an unquenchable thirst for knowledge, I would turn myself into a matured old man... dispensing the unwanted crumbs of knowledge... standing in between the old writing table and the armless chair... in some unpopular room of the college.

And when, seeing me ascending the steps to the courtyard of my house with a confused tongue, chocked throat and tired legs, my love would come with a cup of steaming tea in her hand and a honey-flowing smile on her lips and then, and only then, would I turn myself into a passionate young man!

And when I was going with a brisk and cheerful body and a serious face to the old grandma who lived in my neighborhood, I would turn myself into an innocent child who always wished sincerely to acquire knowledge and wisdom.

But that morning, the great old grandma had breathed her last. The lifeless body of the grandma was laid on the bed, covering it up to the neck with a white shroud.

Everyone in the village called her grandma. A grand old woman of the village... with a mouth that touched the ears and the ears that touched the shoulders... according to the tradition of the old generation.

And she was lying on her bed... with a slightly pale and peaceful face. Surprisingly her left eye was tightly shut and her right eye was slightly opened. And I felt as if she was winking at me... even in death... with some meaningful idea being secretly conveyed to me.

It was a few months back that I left the crowd, and the noisy atmosphere, of the city and came to reside in that new house. As I was anxious to meet my neighbors, I went to the nearest house, the silence of which attracted me. And it was thus that I met that old grandma who was sitting on the verandah, with her legs stretched but keeping the right leg over the other, chewing her gums and flirting with silence.

She spoke with me about everything related to the history of that village and told me a lot of her personal stories as if I was her long-time friend. The story of her youngest son who came to visit her every weekend even through he was working in the capital city. The story of her only daughter who came at least once a month to enquire about her well-being even though she was living in a far away village, quite busily bearing the burden of a big family of her farmer husband. The story of her eldest son who, being anxious about his mother's health, came every year even though he was working somewhere in the snow-covered border areas of the country, wearing the olive-green uniform of a solider. And a hundred such similar stories.

As my simple acquaintance with that grand old woman turned into a sort of strong affection, I began to lisp and beg like a small child: 'Oh, dear old grandma! Won't you tell me another story?'

She would be squatting on the mat made of dried grass, spread on the verandah. Slowly she would take out a paper packet from the folds of her dress, a kind of dhoti tucked around her waist. She would take out a small vial of opium and open its lid very carefully. With the sharp tip of her pen-knife she would take out a tiny bit of opium and place it on her tongue. Ignoring the bitter taste of the drug, she licked and smacked it in a tempting manner that I had to ask her for a speck. That was the first and last time that I tasted that horrible thing, though she always smacked the tip of the knife like a child sucking a lollipop. Then she would smile showing her toothless gums like an innocent child which was a signal that the drug began to work on her and the story would soon come out. The story came out as if in a magical sense... the story of the meeting between the old grandma and the old grandpa... years ago.

Then, they were very small children. One day grandma was making garlands, putting white jasmine flowers one after another on a string, grandpa tried to frighten her by saying that the jasmine flowers were the white teeth of some vampire women. She, being really frightened, began to cry aloud and then grandpa winked at her closing his left eye and laughed aloud. Then grandma too winked at him back with her 'about-to-overflow eyes'. And she put the garland of the so-called vampire teeth around his neck. And thus months passed.

Grandpa was at home on vacation. Those summer holidays in the village. One day he was so angry at her that he did not even look at her. It was because grandma had not given him the fallen mango fruits collected when the wind blew and shook the huge native-mango tree. Then she winked at him with a naughty smile and gave him those sugary little mangoes. Grandpa took them and winked at her with a loud laugh. And thus months passed again.

On their first night of wedding, grandma was waiting at the corner of the bridal room with a heart throbbing with fear and anxiety. Grandpa entered the room silently, came towards the timid little bride and winked at her. Grandma shuddered for a moment without knowing what to do. After a second she too with fear and delicacy winked at him, and thus, a new life was building up with the 'give, take and share' relationship. And again months passed.

On the day in which grandma gave birth to his first boy-child, grandpa walked towards her bed, looked into her tired eyes and winked at her. Caressing the new born babe that slept by her side, grandma too winked at him. Days and months and years passed.

Grandma laughed like a child saying that all their little quarrels and common fights ended with mere winkings of eyes from either of them. Looking at grandma who was opening the paper packet that contained the opium vial and taking for a second time a speck of opium with the tip of her pen-knife, I tried to wink at her.

Later on another auspicious day, I squatted on the grass-mat spread on the floor and pleaded to her like a child: 'My dearest grandma, can't you say the rest of the story?'

Her dried eyes seemed to become wet for a moment. Fixing her eyes somewhere on a far away spot, she told me the rest of the story.

Grandpa was very seriously ill and death was fast approaching. Grandma looked after him like a nurse, or even like a mother nursing her little child. She was crying at the inevitable separation that would occur at any moment. Grandpa opened his eyes slowly and winked at her with a distorted smile. Grandma too winked as usual. But grandpa's left eye remained closed and his right eye remained opened... forever! When neighbors tried to rub down his eyes, grandma objected.

And till the white shroud fell on his face, grandpa's eyes continued to wink at her!

Licking the opium particle from the tip of the pen-knife, grandma said: 'I also want to die like that! I laughed aloud and winked at her! All these happened a few days ago! And now!'

I was chewing the guts of memories looking at the pale face of the grandma who kept her left eye closed and right eye opened in a sort of eternal winking. Her only daughter tried many a time to rub down the opened eyelid, as part of the tradition, but it remained the same. Till her face was covered with the white shroud, grandma continued to wink at grandpa who might be waiting for her somewhere in eternity. Somewhere beyond the horizon of human thoughts and feelings.

Oh, my goodness! What's happening to you, Adam? Why all these sentiments? All of a sudden sentiments rush to your mind. Your eyes fill with tears. And your lips tremble. Why?

Does it mean that you are becoming too old? The true domestic or conjugal life which you have been leading all these years has made you sentimental. Your wife... your children... your own wrinkled face. The old people around you. And the death... the unexpected death... for them and for you. Death that haunts you wherever you go.

Yes! Now you are really an old man! It's time to forget the past... the eventful past. Stop the nostalgia that comes to you even without your permission. Every piece of your memory drives you to tears... or sometimes to smiles, filled with tears. How sad! What a pity! You nostalgic fellow, Adam!

But remember, Adam, those experiments you have been conducting all these years. Didn't they give you much experience?

Life is full of experiments and we human beings are a sort of scientist. We continue our experiments to prove our foolish theories and principles. Many of us are mere objects for the experiments or sometimes the test-tubes, just the test-tubes that fade their colors or get scratches or break into pieces while facing the ordeals of experiments.

Adam, as the head of a family, you too had to conduct a lot of experiments. You too faced ordeals. At times, you yourself have become an object of an experiment! Your wife and even your children have experimented in the laboratories of life. Sometimes you may be successful, other times you will be a failure. When you succeed, all others are happy but when you fail they blame you, they hate you and finally you will be thrown out into the pile of garbage like a broken test-tube. And it brings a culmination to the toils of a life-long experiment.

Adam, aren't you that unfortunate scientist? The scientist who has been conducting experiments during his whole life... was watching everything suspiciously... always trying to discover something meaningful in meaningless things... ignoring all the precious moments of human life! And once you realize the truth, it has been too late... too late for at least one more experiment... too late for a last and final one.

Evening. In the horizon clouds lay scattered like the broken pieces of a glass test-tube... thrown away by someone... at the face of the evening sun. Those shapeless pieces have acquired their own figures... with the inerasable scars of some unknown failures. On their edges there are the reddish and yellowish stains of some acids and alkalis used in some failed experiments.

He surveyed the whole room. Perhaps he knew that he wouldn't get another chance. Combing back the curls of his tangled hair that curtained a part of his face, he stared into the test-tube... and heaved a deep sigh... like the last breath of a human creature.

Yes! Here's the last chapters of a generation that awaits its final fall... the culmination of an endless meditation of very many years... the winding up of an endless hard-work that continued for a long period... the sum total of the powers of trance that were achieved through eons of efforts. Here's the conclusion... here in this test-tube!

He watched every part of the room like a cat in a strange room. For a moment he stood enthralled by the silence of the room. He turned back as if he heard somebody move just near him. With a wry smile of vagueness, he called aloud: 'Eve!'

There... in the heavy silence of the room... from the thick darkness of the paths covered by a man's lifespan, there appear... the disfigured faces of the martyrs. They appear like images in a broken mirror. Yet very clearly they appear. Those numerous faces... of rats and rabbits and monkeys, the faces with stains of dried up tears. Their protuberant eyes stare at him... and among those faces, there is the face of his wife, nay, the face of the creature that shared his life for a long period. Like all those creatures... who became scapegoats for his experiments... the experiments for a better future. The faces of all those creatures... who sacrificed their lives on the Calvary of science.

Once again he looked at the contents of those test-tubes that would undergo tremendous changes within the next six hours. Six hours of evolution and the seventh hour for taking rest... eternal rest perhaps. For if there is no change for those objects of the experiment, definitely, there will be a change for the person who has been conducting these experiments.

He looked at the syringe filled with poison carefully kept on the table... that would bring the highest success to a person who failed completely... to a person who is thoroughly defeated in his long experiment of life. There was a dry smile of satisfaction on his face... a sort of weird distortion of his lips due to a feeling of persistent insufficiency.

Pulling out the chain-lock of the door that separated the laboratory from the rest of the house, he came out... as if from the hangover of a long sleep... as if from the obscurity of some strange dream... as if from the deep trance of a silent generation. Breaking the great secrecy of a termite-mound... breaking the chrysalis... coming out into a world of light and noise. He stood there in a shock watching the realities of a crazy, crowded and hurried world.

Through the clefts of the door that led to the adjacent room, the smell of marijuana strained out together with the sound of the slowly turning wheel of time: 'Dham maro dham!'

His heart began to palpitate uncontrollably. Eyelids began to blink as if to witness something ominous. As the eyes went into the room... the only daughter was lying there, exhausted of smoking too much, among those naked and half-naked human creatures. Her white fingers were groping in the darkness for those capsules of oblivion.

'Don't look through the keyhole!' He turned back, hearing the heavy voice. There stood the son's frail body. Representative of the latest generation.

In his red eyes, there was the sediment of intoxication. He felt as if he was melting in the fire of his son's eyes. And in his hand, there was the golden eagle that tried to fly up into a world of fancy. Inside the glass-eagle, there were the 'Lucky Drops' struggling to find new pastoral lands.

The bleating of the sheep that wander on the land of scarcity: 'At last you came out, didn't you? I always expected that you would come out one day! And that occurred today! Today I'll take out all the books from those shelves and sell them for their mere weight! I'll donate all your test-tubes and beakers to the vendor of used bottles! I'll throw away those stands, scales and balances to the owners of ghost farms! Then, I'll teach you to become a man... a real human being!'

To become a man! Did it mean that I was not at all a man? All these years I lived with one aim, one business and one purpose. Did that mean that I was not a man... not an ordinary human being?

The light waves of a laugh that was tangled in a dried and charred throat. The legs that tended to become paralyzed. Placing those legs one by one... dragging the weight of the body... moved along the dusty road... along the asphalted road... along the deserted streets... where the castrated bullocks, drawing their heavy carts, sprinkled urine and cow-dung all through the way... and when the hot wind, drying and powdering them, blew into the nostrils. He tried to sneeze aloud... as if to react spontaneously against this world.

On the beach. The beach where he had spent his childhood. A cool wind blows carrying the stench of white-meat. The chants of the women who sell their raw flesh. The muezzin of the foamy ripples that try again and again to reach the shore. The conch-sound of the black stones that suffocate among the roots of the banyan tree. The bell beats of the sand that is crushed under the feet of the passersby.

The pier that stretches into the vagueness of huge sea-waves. Its border railings and edge prevent human beings somewhere in the endlessness. Where the long road ends, where the journey comes to a standstill.

The planet called earth turned and turned continuously... and the six-hour period for evolution is completed. Turning back from the beach, moved along the deserted streets... along the asphalted road... along the dusty path... towards the house. Once again into the secrecy of the termite mound. Then entered the room. First, closed the door and locked it with the chain as usual. The planet called earth stopped for a moment showing the sixth hour.

While looking eagerly into the test-tube, flames of electric waves passed from the brain, through the spinal cord, into every part of the nervous system. The unchanged test-tube. The objects of the experiment remain without undergoing any evolution.

From the thick darkness… the eyes of rats, rabbits and monkeys stare. And among those, the eyes of a woman… yes, of a wife… nay… the tired eyes of a creature named Eve!

As the test-tube of a failure crushed under the pressure of the palm, the formulae of helplessness burned into flames… their faces turned brown and black. And the fingers moved towards the victory of the poisonous syringe… and the lips distorted themselves into a dry smile of eternal incompleteness and satiety.

The purpose of your life is served. You did whatever you felt fair and useful. You did your duty. And you expected the usual result… but in vain. And the realization comes a bit late. The success of life depends not on the result but on the way of living itself.

Human life is like that, Adam! Throughout your life, you try to do some experiment expecting positive results. Years pass in optimism. And when you realize your failure, you'll be late. You get no more time to start a fresh experiment and then… what's left for you is to leave everything for posterity and walk away with a pure, placid mind. Is it as simple as that?

What about the suffering you are supposed to undergo? Do you think that you have had sufficient suffering? Suffering is a sort of purgation. Everybody must pass through this purification ceremony… the ritual of pain… agony… rejection… dejection… hunger… insanity… wanderings… paralysis. It is all part of the game.

Yes, Adam, this is the right time for you to cry or laugh at the meaningfulness or meaninglessness of human life. Both are one and the same! One finds meaning in the meaninglessness and the other meaninglessness in the meaningfulness. Ah! Man is a patched fool!

It is the most worthy form of living and the inevitable death that puts an end to it. By believing in gods and in various forms of life after death, man tries to forget or pretends to ignore this fact. Those who properly utilized their senses made their lives worthy of living; for they could not find a similar or even a better form of life anywhere in heaven, hell or any other zones of the universe.

Here you can be free with your imagination. The meaningfulness and the meaninglessness of human life depend on this wonderful power of imagination. Based on this imagination, you cry or laugh at your fate as well as the fate of your fellow beings.

Those who think too seriously about their life, make it too miserable to themselves and to others. Because they think that other human beings are born here only to make their life worthy of living. And thus they become a sort of maniac as they suffer from a sort of paranoid illness. It makes them sadists without being unaware of that fact.

And once you are old, you think about such strange behaviors which you experienced in your life. And then cry or laugh at yourself or at others.

But! Oh, God! When did my failure begin? Where? How? What really happened in our conjugal life? What was our mistake, our sin? What estranged us so much? What made us look at each other suspiciously? Why did we think about each other with an inferiority complex or a superiority complex? What prompted us to go for the forbidden fruits?

Was it because of some mental disorder, as psychiatrists used to say? Was it because of the voice of education, as the sociologists used to say? In the Garden of Eden, education was a natural process and we learned all necessary subjects from

Nature. But here, we learned more, even unnecessary subjects, through artificial education and, thus cultivated differences in the name of equality. 'Concordia discord' was a mirage for human beings! Education taught us that man and woman are equal in every sense of the term. Of course, they are legally equal, socially equal and financially equal. They are intellectually equal or even spiritually equal, though most of our religions do not accept it. But were we equal physically? Were we equal emotionally? Were we equal in our sensitiveness? Were we equal in our sensuousness?

We have our own unique physical and emotional strengths. We have our exclusive sensitiveness and sensuousness. But aren't they different? Man tried to classify all fauna and flora into different species and sub-species based on their material features and not on their intellectual features. And human beings come under Homo sapiens. But man is a rational animal and this rationality varies from individual to individual. It is doubtless that certain exclusive rational features are common only amongst women and certain others are common only amongst men. Therefore, man is man and woman is woman; they are two different equal entities. And here, our argument on equality between man and woman becomes irrational.

Alas! Our education failed to teach us that man and woman can attain equality only through true love. It taught us to measure everything in legal and financial terms. Can anyone assess the value of sacrifice, humility and patience?

Even major religions stand at two extremes. While one preaches celibacy or, if necessary monogamy, the other one preaches involvement and, if necessary polygamy. While one considers marriage as a permanent heavenly alliance, the other one considers it as a temporary earthly arrangement. Of course, the latter still maintains their old tribal tradition.

Or are we supposed to enjoy the natural equality practiced

in certain African tribal cultures? There, men and women lead a sexual life similar to that of animals. Their courting and love-making are as innocent as that of young puppies playing under the warm sunlight. Men and women move hand in hand, touch or caress each other, scratch or press each other's body, without being aware of its sexual importance. If the woman gets pregnant, she delivers the child and either leaves it to the mercy of nature or brings it up with her. Men move from one woman to another just like the beetles from one flower to another. Women too seek new guys; when one city-bus goes, another comes.

But Eve! Is it what God expects from human beings? Animals, by nature, are free to mate but only during the allotted seasons. Human beings can do it irrespective of seasons. And moreover, they engage in sex not merely for reproduction. As rational beings, they are supposed to use their sexual gifts discriminatingly, with prudence. But too many voices of education have deafened our delicate sense and sensibility. And we failed to realize the meaning and purpose of conjugal life. We are really sinners!

God, you created us to enjoy the bliss of togetherness, to enjoy the moments of little pleasures and simple happiness in our day-to-day life. But we ignored it and thought that working in the garden was more important. We forgot the fact that work was only an incentive for a greater enjoyment of our conjugal life; like a pinch of sour-pickle during the course of a sweet porridge. We were too foolish to ignore that truth. That was our sin. We disobeyed your commands. We ate the forbidden fruits.

Everything was available in the Garden of Eden. Then we were really happy and felt satisfied with all those things basically needed for our life. Soon we desired for the luxury of the forbidden fruits. That was also our sin! One luxury led towards other luxuries. We desired more and more forbidden fruits of different Trees of Knowledge. Our wants became unlimited; and wants were the root-causes of sorrow. Our life became full of sorrow. We became dissatisfied creatures. The Garden of Eden was no longer a place of happiness for us. We were literally thrown out of our paradise!

There onwards we began to feel satiety. I went after the forbidden fruit of power and you ran after the forbidden fruit of social service. Both were fruits of the same Tree of Knowledge. But my option was deliberate, though mandatory to a certain extent, and therefore, it was a sin against the soul, an unpardonable one. I have to face the consequences and I am ready for it.

But, what about my Eve? She was forced to opt under the pressure of circumstances. Perhaps, I was the cause for it! And I am ready to suffer for her sin too! For why should my Eve suffer for the sin committed under a situation deliberately created by me?

My craze for work, money and power made me blind. I deserted the divine law of togetherness. Perhaps you always desired my presence with you? In my absence, you wished for some other engagement to keep in your social life. Perhaps you hated me and cursed me many times? You felt lethargic as you could not lead a life of inertia. I am sorry, my dear Eve! For you got the punishment first. What about my punishment?

No, Adam! Don't think like that! You committed no sin at all! What you did is only part of your married life. You did only what the responsibility of a husband demanded. Is that a sin? If it is a sin, it is beyond your limits. From childhood onwards, were you not taught that you were a born-sinner? If it is true, you must suffer for that sin of yours.

And what about the death of that female cat? Wasn't it a deliberate murder? Thou shalt not kill! And you disobeyed the sixth commandment of the Lord. In fact, you were trying to save the cat from the ditch into which it had fallen. As you were trying to save it, it misunderstood your intentions and attacked you. It bit your hand and even wounded your body with her teeth and nails. And you had no other option but to hurl it down against the wall, an action not amounting to murder. But it died or was killed and you have to face the punishment. Your body may be contaminated with rabies and you may die of water phobia, die without the ability to drink a drop of water, the most horrible form of death for a human being. She may take birth, again and again, to torment you, perhaps, all through her nine lives!

Oh, Adam, you imagine too much. You never wished to kill the cat. It just so happened! In fact, it was an act of self-defense and there's no need for a guilty conscience. You simply did what was necessary at the nick of that moment. So, don't ponder over such timid actions.

And you gave the most respectable burial for it too! You took the dead body in a plastic bag and carried it with prayer and chants to the funeral ground. It was a waste land where all the waste materials are carelessly thrown by people. And you placed its body in the large waste-bin as if the Parsi people place the dead body on the Tower of Silence. You came back, took your bath and completed your prayers. What else could you do, when fate acts beyond your expectations?

I admit that I am a sinner! I surrender to my fate! I am prepared for any sort of punishment! But why should my Eve suffer for my sin?

Some people like Pythagoras believed in the transformation of the human soul. Some Hindus in India believe in the rebirth of the human beings. If so, my dear Eve, you will take birth as another Eve on this Garden of Eden. For my sin, I offer you another option: 'I, Adam, hereby allow you to accept any other

Adam, in your next birth. I promise you that I will not claim you as my rib bone. And I will take my re-birth here in this beautiful Garden of Eden, as a worm without any rib bones, without any bones at all!'

'But, even then, I will miss you! I wish you would be my partner throughout all my rebirths, life after life. But I leave the choice to you. I should not be selfish and greedy. I am too old now to face this world alone. It would have been better, if you were here with me. But our fate decided the other way. My dear Eve! I am the old man whom fate allowed to live and suffer forever. But I have to leave this world of the madding crowds. Where should I go? Where will I get my punishment for the sin of being born here? Am I too old to be crucified? Is there anyone to crucify me, so that my life will be remembered forever?'

Adam, you can't escape like that! Of course, its time for your hermitage. Go to the wilderness and spend your days like a true hermit. But can you escape from the basic needs of life? Where did the sages go wrong?

You are an old man and you must undergo all the sufferings of the aged. Loneliness, hunger, senility, destitution, exhaustion, decrepitude and so on. And see whether you can die like that... like the hungry old man who always saw dreams.

The smoky eyes of the old man groped in and around the garbage bin and dug his fingers into the piled-up wastes of food. He chased away the street dogs that greedily licked the food-stained banana leaves used traditionally for serving food on auspicious days. The crows cried aloud and flew away leaving their droppings on the pile of waste-food-materials. And the fat temple oxen chewed the guts of food-stained banana leaves.

The old man pushed his skeleton fingers again and again

into the garbage bin. He began to gormandize those broken pieces of cooked vegetables and rice-grains that touched his fingers. He chewed and gulped down the bits of meat detached from half eaten, waste-bones, thrown away from some hotels. He kicked a stray dog that was licking the sore on his leg. He looked anxiously up at the vent of the hotel through which waste-food used to be thrown out at irregular intervals. He eagerly waited for that blessed moment in which fresh banana leaves with waste-food came through the vent of the hotel, like the heavenly manna for the Israelites. He was murmuring: 'I am hungry!'

Under the blazing fire-ball above his head, the black blood of the old man was transforming into sweat. It strained out through the pores of his wrinkled skin and streamed down to solidify itself into salty crystals and stuck here and there on his body. And the street bitch, without caring for its whelps that hanged onto its teats, was licking away the salt-granules stuck on to his body. And he cried, aloud: 'I am hungry!'

Suddenly, there was a flood of waste-food through the vent of the hotel. And there was the ebb and flow of joy in the heart of the old man. And a cry of cheer from the hungry crows and starving street dogs.

He threw away the plate-leaves of misers onto the face of the street dog. The food-wastes of spendthrifts provided a feast for him. Then there was the breath of satisfaction and the belch of satiety. Pressing on his full stomach and running his palm around his pot belly, he whispered: 'I am hungry!'

The old man waded along the dusty road. He walked with short paces towards his temporary shelter in the slum on which the evening sun spat a blob of yellow sputum.

As he sneaked through the cleft of his tent, there was the smell of cheap powder and fake attar. The nauseating odor of decayed hair-oil. Caressing his full stomach, the old man cried again: 'I am hungry!'

There was the daughter, trying to fix a red sari around her empty stomach. Her eyes, stained with mascara, emitted the fire of jealousy towards the old man: 'A father who fills his stomach by the day!'

In the dried eyes of the old man, there also was the jealousy towards his daughter, the jealousy unquenchable like his hunger: 'A daughter who fills her stomach by the night!'

Again and again, the old man grumbled: 'I am hungry!'

The daughter who felt sympathy towards her father opened the cupboard and took out a rusted tin-can full of coffee powder and placed it before the old man. With loving kindness, she said: 'Father, if you feel thirsty during the night, please, prepare some coffee and drink!'

Her red sari fluttered in the cold wind of the night. Feeling the call of the red street, she sneaked out through a cleft of the hut and walked away hurriedly from the slum, and disappeared somewhere within the crowds of the street. She was murmuring: 'I am also hungry!'

The rusted tin with coffee powder was inviting the old man. He could never resist temptation! He opened the tin and put his dried fingers into it. He took out a handful of coffee powder and pushed it into his mouth. Bit by bit, he swallowed all the coffee powder. Finishing the coffee powder, he even licked the last granule of it from the tin. Then he took an old, torn-out sack, spread it on the floor, smoothened by a mixture of charcoal powder and fresh cow-dung. Stretching his limbs, he lied on the torn sack and murmured: 'I am still hungry!'

While sleeping in the intoxication of the coffee powder, the dried veins of the brain began to stir up like lions shaking their mane after a deep sleep. The old man began to see dreams.

People lead him to the top of a hill. There is a heavy wooden cross on his shoulder. Flogs and whips fall consistently on his back. Spittle on his face. On his head, the crown of thorns. Once the crowd reaches the hill-top...

Somebody keeps his hands and legs close to the wooden cross and others hammer iron-nails into them. Then they raise his body on the wooden cross and fix the cross into a cleft in the rock. Lying on the cross, he cried aloud: 'I am hungry!'

Suddenly, a heavy storm arouses the huge waves of the sea, uproots the plants and trees of the earth. The earth splits apart and swallows some people; rocks break into small pieces and fall down on some others, covering them completely. A few people open their eyes to see the fundamental changes; while others close their eyes not to see such changes.

When all... all was accomplished... when all was calm and quiet, looking at the new heaven and the new earth, the old man, realizing that his mission on earth was fulfilled, cried aloud: 'It is finished!'

Did he die then? No! Son of man cannot die like that, Adam! You must undergo all the sufferings that the progeny of the First Great Adam is supposed to suffer and bear. Muslims say that Son of Man was not hanged to death on the cross. God saved him and took him away so that he could come again. The crucifixion, according to them was an illusion. Perhaps, crucifixions are mere hallucinations? And man faces them almost everyday. If so, Adam, your fate is something else. You cannot die so easily like that.

You'll be a wanderer on this earth. This is what you call hermitage, the last phase before attaining Moksha, Nirvana or Salvation!

Today, in this frightening loneliness... as I wait expecting the unknown moments in which the cold hands of death touch me... the horrifying voice of God echoes in my ears. But how long should I wander like this?

I am completely weary of toiling in this infertile soil. Even the city, built and erected by my own hands, mocks at me from a far distance. Even those who were born out of my own blood and marrow think of me with scorn and hatred. Even in the olden days, my breath was strange to my wife though I entreated for the children's sake of my own body.

How can I escape from this roll of rope that comes nearer and nearer towards my neck? Can I prevent the darts that fly in the darkness? Shall those gates of Eden which were closed forever against the face of my ancestors be opened once more for me?

And what's my sin? To live on earth itself is the sin! My sin is that I was born with a sense of guilt, a sense of sin... a sin beyond my correction. No other sin I committed consciously. But to justify yourself in and of itself is a sin, and there's no hope for you!

Whatever I did on earth, during my life span, were sins. And redemption is only by the grace of God. Perhaps, my crimes are bigger than what can be forgiven? That's why all my sins stare at me and make faces at me. If only those doors of Eden were opened, at least, for a second time.

I ran a race! I have completed the whole round successfully. And the prize is for me, I'm sure. But the pity is that I don't know whether I won the race or not! When I looked for good, then evil came unto me: and when I waited for light, there came darkness. So I am made to possess months of vanity, and wearisome nights are appointed to me.

Oh, no! I am fed up with this human life, tangled and snared in the cobweb of fear. Life is a spider web, dirty and sticky, the more you try to release yourself from it, the more you'll be trapped. It's like quicksand. The more you struggle to escape, the more you drown. Now what I wish is just death, a calm and quiet death.

But canst thou bind the sweet influences of Pleiades or

loosen the bands of Orion? When the chain of fear tangles on one's body and mind, a calm and quite death becomes a mere mirage to him. God, take away from me the horror of the fate of an unexpected death.

While the black memories of the committed or inborn sins tighten their grip over me every moment like the blood sucking arms of an octopus, what can I do but raise my heart-breaking cries to the heavens... so that the gates of paradise will be unhinged at the sharpness of my voice, and open themselves so wide... that all the generations of my ancestry and of my progeny shall be redeemed and saved forever.

In a flash... the heavenly blessing falls on him... in the form of amnesia. At last, no more memory, no more pain! All the senses, except the sense of sight, flew away from him... like tongues of fire.

The old man-who-sees-everything sat on the verandah of the self-built hut on the hill, deliciously sucking and enjoying the milk of satisfaction showered on him by solitude. Squatting like a hermit, he casually looked at the slops of that small hill where the green grass spread a soft carpet, the fruit-bearing trees spread cool shade and fragrance-stealing breeze consistently blew.

The magnificent sight of that peaceful hill... where he had been staying for a long period... of the big mountain that stood adjacent to the hill... the hill full of growing trees and thick bushes, thorny plants and python-like creepers... of the huge boulders and rocks that stood high up against the sky... of that wonderful valley that separated the mountain and hill... of the wild stream that always giggled and flowed innocently down into a silver cascade... all gave the bliss of true happiness to the tired eyes of the old man.

Then his smoky eyes were hooked for a long time on those snow-covered, heaven-touched peaks that lay meditating beyond that big mountain just opposite to his hut. There, seeing the masculinity of the snow-capped mountain piercing the pelvic depression of the cloud covered sky... the mountain that sleeps as if completely exhausted from a lengthy copulation... sleeping under the blanket of a thick, white fog that overflowed the horizon... the old man breathed a heavy, long sigh.

The old man-who-sees-everything, and who hears nothing, of course, had a bitter past. Once up on a time, while he was young and energetic, the sound-polluted cities made him deaf. When the Nature-made Man and the Man-made Nature contested each other in making excessive noise, in that extremity of the crazy, unbearable noise what he lost was his own ability to hear. He never regretted the loss of one of his senses as he had realized by this time that true happiness belonged only to those who would not hear much!

Once he had been rescued from the unbearable cruelty of noise in a natural way, he began to be afraid of the city-crowds. Many a time, he wished how better it would have been if he were incapable of seeing many of the things occurred in that much polluted city.

He could not stick to the crowds of the city that danced wildly in the drowsiness of the stench and acrid odor of it, like those worms that stick to the rotten carcass, making disgusting bubbles, swimming up and down and playing ceaseless hide and seek in their self-made foam-house. There, he lost his sense of smell too!

The adulterated food, sprinkled with pesticides, helped him in losing his sense of taste. And as the sense of touch depends mainly on the reaction of the persons whom one touches, he lost that sense too! My breath is corrupt, my days are extinct, the graves are ready for me, he thought.

And it was thus that the old man-who-sees-everything came to that beautiful hill, running away from the crazy crowds after breaking the magic spell of the city forever, and began to live in that hut made by his own hands. For, is there not an appointed time to man upon earth, he wondered.

The old man watched the fog on the snow-covered peaks amalgamating with the ash-colored clouds of the skies, and covering the pointed cliffs of the mountain. He wondered whether it was fog or cloud or the smog that hovered over the cities. He tried to console himself thinking that there was no possibility for the fog of the cities to reach these holy mountains of pure snow.

As the old man sat there deeply immersed in vague thoughts, he felt the earth trembling and grumbling under his feet. He was shocked seeing red and yellow sparks of light, swish and flash like lightning in the fog that grew thicker and thicker on the top of the mountains.

'Does it mean that it has already begun?' he murmured in fear. 'Does it mean that it has reached even this place?' Whispering in a voice of despair and agony, he tried to fix his tired eyes on those snow-headed mountains.

As the earth quaked again and again and as the sparks of lightnings flashed and disappeared in the mist, the old man saw the slates of snow breaking away from the snowy peaks, as if in a volcanic eruption and falling down on the big mountain of black rocks and thorny bushes. As the mist and fog covered the big mountain, he felt the intuition of a horrible avalanche! Suddenly he became conscious of that serene hill on which he was residing, of its charming valley where the wild stream chirped and giggled, and, also of the man-made fog that approached fast towards his hut and into his very being!

The old man-who-sees-everything felt as if the light of his eyes was gradually fading. Heedless of the drops of tears that fell drop by drop along the hairs of his beard, he lamented: 'Hey, you the city-man, with your envy and pride, are you converting this magnificent valley and its peaceful prairie into a smoking inferno of violence and death?'

The old man sat there watching the thorny bushes and wild plants which were crushed under the rolling boulders. With a strange indifference, he watched those rocks that broke into stones of various sizes and rolled down into the valley and fell into the stream with a big splash. He was shocked as he saw the body of a soldier with a ready gun in his hands stopped for a while in the air together with the stones! For a moment the soldier, though half part of his body from the waist was missing, being unaware of the fact, was pointing his gun into the vacuity of the skies. The old man stared at that horrible sight and, later, leaned onto the central pole of his hut semi-consciously, looking at the dead soldier's gun that spat fire and smoke into the air, and at his half-body, together with the gun, falling like a stone down into the valley, into the fast-flowing stream.

Suddenly, within a wink of time, the old man felt, for a moment, the whole hill on which he was living, quaking and slipping down into the valley, the plants and bushes withering and burning, the fruit-bearing trees uprooting and falling upside down, the thick smoke rising up like a gigantic rain-mushroom, and a huge rock rising up together with it, which hanged for a while in the sky, and then, coming down and down onto his hut, crushing the hut and then... he saw all these at a glimpse, in a split second... and then an eternal nothingness!

Unto dust thou return! No time for thinking! No sound! All ends within a split second! Everything is over!

Who said that death is painful? It's like a sleep... as quiet and quick as a sound sleep. You feel weightlessness. You float like a cotton flake. You hear a sort of hushed voice... like the sound of silence. You see vaguely... through a dim saffron color or the color of topaz. You feel utter indifference and the lightness of freedom. You feel as if you're experiencing a sort of pleasurable stupor.

And then the sound of the hooves is heard... as an epilogue.

As Time reached its fullness... and the Wheel of Time slowly comes to a stop!

For a moment, the earth came to a standstill. All the natural movements, even the rotation of all planets, stopped at the same time. And Nature herself stood in a stupor, as if in the extremity of a dilemma.

Only for a minute! Then... then...

The planet earth was imbalanced. It moved up and down and even upside down like a floating log in flood-waters.

At last, the exhausted earth shivered and throbbed, grumbled and rumbled, like a tired damsel after a very long classical dance.

The earth that was charred with the weight of man. The earth that stood stupefied, seeing too much injustice against man and atrocities against Nature. The earth that went crazy at the odor of human blood and poisonous gases. The earth that went deaf, hearing the horrible echoes of wailings and sobbing of all creations.

As the planet called earth stood frightened, grumbled and charred...

The human beings ran helter-skelter in a sort of madness, in a kind of crazy enthusiasm. The human beings fought tooth and nail in their excessive greed for whatever they encountered, killing each other and shouting mutual death-cries! The poor human creatures who flew away cowardly from the shocking thoughts of an indefinite future.

The knots on the legs of the vultures were untied. And the masks on the faces of the wolves were broken. All the natural laws, codified from time to time in the course of Nature, were flown away like winged-seeds flying in a storm. And anarchy moved everywhere shouting, running and dancing all over the world in utter lawlessness, like a maniac who broke free from his chains.

On this mad earth, another group of human beings, being mutually chained in blood-relationships, and being trapped in the cobweb of helplessness, stood stupefied amongst the men who had lost the equilibrium of their minds and control over their bodies. The former wept silently and shed tears standing in front of the dead bodies of their dear relatives that burned down to ashes every moment. The poor people sobbed and sighed, visualizing the inevitable sad fate of their own weak bodies!

Here... being amalgamated in the air... together with the elements of the universe... waits the spirit of Adam! The conscience of 'I' throbs everywhere. The First, the Second and the Third Persons evolve into a perfect unison.

Waiting alone, patiently, wearing the veil of indifference, for the fulfillment of the facts that went beyond all the prophecy. Waiting... being ignorant of the real state of one's own existence... waiting for the culmination, I wonder: 'Am I a man, a living creature... or... or a spirit?'

Ears lost their power to hear due to the cries and wailings of men. Eyes lost their power to see by watching the brutality of man. Noses lost their power to smell by breathing the nauseating odor of human blood.

While waiting... with the heaviness of my powerless five-senses... realizing the flood of fire that fast approaches and overwhelms all!

Tongues of fire dance around. Strangling heat and smoke seem to suffocate me. The combinations of elements are destroyed by fire, melted in the heat and disintegrated. Yet the eternal soul clutches to the thin hair of hope. Does the waiting for salvation turn futile? Do prayers become mere cries in the wilderness?

Every moment, weird and grotesque figures of demons try to frighten me. A scapegoat trapped in the tricks played alternatively by light and darkness. Utterly helpless situation! Where is that wonder-light which I have been expecting all these years? Why does the savior who has to lift me up still delay?

Are they all mere vain hopes? Are they all just waves of a mirage? Life is a bundle of disintegrating dreams and nightmares. Had they not been here, life would've become meaningless. They are angels and demons leading man to heaven and hell. Yet it's mere solidification of immaterial things. Ah vanity! Vanity! All vanity! From nothingness to nothingness! From vacuity to vacuity!

Lo! The heavens roll away like a sheet of paper. Burning meteors fall down as if raindrops in a heavy rain. The flapping fire-wings are heard from some far away place. The surface of the earth turns black and burns down to ashes. All species of flora and fauna burn to black, emitting thick bluish smoke. The earth, dancing in the intoxication of destruction, slips away from its axis. Ecology, the balance of the environment and gravitation, the equilibrium of Nature, are all turned upside down! And things fall apart!

But only for a second… all these sights, sounds and smells… and then… then…

Everything becomes pacified once again. Man, helpless in the naughtiness of Nature, stands in complete stupor for a moment. And then, a supernatural halo covers the universe.

What's that light shining from a far away place? Is it an untimely sunrise or the real wonder-light for which I have been waiting all these years? Is it the flowing mane of a white horse galloping from east to west? Together with that strange light, there echoed the rhythm and sound of horse-hooves.

In the sound of the horse-hooves, both the rhythm and the tune dissolved into a sort of nothingness. Gradually all sights and all sounds disintegrated and became part of the great emptiness. The earth, empty and void, once again wears the veil of silence.

Are these the signs to repeat a new beginning? Are the transfigured Earth and Nature preparing once again for another meditation to hear the original sound of Adam? That sound of eternal peace? That continuous sound of endless creation?

Adam... Aaa... dam... Aaaa... dammm...

THE END

ABOUT THE AUTHOR

Born on April 1st, 1952, Alexander Raju began his career as a freelance journalist as early as 1974, after completing his higher studies in the Universities of Kerala and Saugar, Madhya Pradesh. Touring almost every nook and corner of India, he acquired a firsthand knowledge of the Indian ways of life among various ethnic groups who differed totally in their culture, religion and language. When Sikkim became the twenty-second State of India, he joined the staff of *Sikkim Express* as one of its sub-editors and later became the editor of *Bullet*, a newsweekly published from Gangtok.

"A decade of my wanderings through the length and breadth of India and my not too brief sojourn in the Himalayan Valley gave me an everlasting mine of ideas and a continuous source of inspiration that would last a whole lifespan of a creative writer," says the author.

Returning to his native state of Kerala, he worked as a lawyer for a short while. In 1981, he joined the faculty of English at Baselius College, Kottayam, his own alma mater, as a lecturer. Currently he is Professor of English in Bahir Dar University, Ethiopia.

Alexander Raju, an Indian English critic, poet, novelist, short story writer and columnist, has many books to his credit. *Ripples and Pebbles* (1989), *Sprouts of Indignation* (2003) and *Magic Chasm* (2007) are collections of his poems. His first novel *The Haunted Man* came out in 1997. *Candles on the Altar* (1985), *Many Faces of Adam* (1991) and *The Sobbing Guitar and Other Stories* (2007) are collections of his short stories. *The Psycho-Social Interface in British Fiction* (2000) is a critical work.

E-mail Alexander Raju: **dr.alexanderraju@yahoo.co.in**

www.ingramcontent.com/pod-product-compliance
Lightning Source LLC
Chambersburg PA
CBHW020832260626
47169CB00003B/944